An Onerous Duty

An Onerous Duty

BERYL MATTHEWS

Allison & Busby Limited
11 Wardour Mews
London W1F 8AN
allisonandbusby.com

First published in Great Britain by Robert Hale in 2002.
This paperback edition publiished by Allison & Busby in 2023.

A CIP catalogue record for this book is available
from the British Library.

10 9 8 7 6 5 4 3 2 1

ISBN 978-0-7490-2960-9

Typeset in 11.5 on 16.5pt Sabon LT Pro by Allison and Busby Ltd

The paper used for this Allison & Busby publication
has been produced from trees that have been legally sourced
from well-managed and credibly certified forests.

FSC
www.fsc.org
MIX
Paper | Supporting
responsible forestry
FSC® C171272

Printed and bound by
CPI Group (UK) Ltd, Croydon, CR0 4YY

Prologue

London, 1802

Harry Sterling leaned against the gnarled oak tree, closed his eyes, and sighed contentedly, not giving a damn about the speculation he was causing. He listened to the birds and the sound of his horse chomping eagerly on the lush grass. Lord, but it was good to be home, after the noise of battle this was sheer paradise. Serving as an exploring officer had been dangerous and he was glad to be free of it now. His sorties behind enemy lines had often placed him in desperate situations.

But if only his homecoming could have been under happier circumstances. His father had died, and when he had finally arrived home it was to find that his brother had also died, killed in a riding accident. The pain of knowing that he had missed his brother's funeral as well, was still with him, and it had taken a while for the full import of his new responsibilities to sink in.

The sound of a musical laugh caught his attention. He opened his eyes and saw a girl running across the grass after her bonnet, which had been dislodged by a gust of wind. She was flying along, the skirt of her dress lifted to give her more freedom and her deep chestnut hair in disarray.

Harry straightened up, his interest immediately engaged, and he chuckled as she caught the bonnet with her foot, stamping on it with complete disregard for its fashionable elegance. While she was trying to punch it back into shape an elderly lady came puffing along, red in the face and clearly embarrassed.

'Isabella!' she gasped. 'What do you think you are doing? I do declare that you put a body to shame with your conduct.'

The girl kissed the flustered lady affectionately. 'I am sorry Aunt Dorothea, but how else was I going to retrieve my bonnet?'

'You should have left it.' She eyed it distastefully. 'It is beyond wearing now, anyway.'

The hat received another punch. 'I think you are right.'

Harry kept perfectly still; they had not noticed him and he eavesdropped shamelessly.

'I do wish you would pay more attention to your actions,' the lady scolded. 'How can we expect any man of quality to offer for you when you show such a disregard for proper conduct?'

The musical laugh floated on the breeze. 'Oh, you know that isn't going to happen. Not when I have two beautiful sisters – younger than me,' she said pointedly.

'Now, Bella, you must not put yourself down so. You have much to offer the right man.' She hesitated and looked at her niece thoughtfully. 'A strong man, of course.'

The girl slipped her hand through the elderly lady's arm and started to urge her back the way they had come. 'You must not take on so. You know I am past my last prayers and no man is going to offer for me, unless he is after my fortune or needs a strong wife in his old age. In either case I would rather remain a spinster.'

Their conversation faded as they walked away, and a smile of amusement tilted Harry's well-shaped mouth. He patted his horse and then swung himself up with all the grace and fluency of a man used to spending long hours in the saddle.

Then he cantered through the park, his whole attention now focused on the distasteful task ahead of him.

One

'Is that you, Harry?' a voice called as he strode into the hall.

'Yes, Grandmother,' he replied, walking into the room where the venerable lady was drumming impatient fingers on the arm of her chair.

'Where have you been? You know we are attending Lady Augusta's Ball tonight. There isn't much time to make yourself presentable.'

He turned away to mask his look of distaste, but his grandmother saw it. 'It's no good you looking so vexed.' She spoke sharply. 'I do not relish the evening any more than you, but it must be done. This family finds itself in a perilous position and it is up to you to put it right.

You have to marry and set up your nursery as quickly as possible.'

Harry sat down and stared at her, out of countenance.

'I know you never wanted the title or the responsibility that goes with it, my boy,' she said briskly. 'And I know you are distressed about losing your father and brother, but it has happened. You are now the only remaining male and it is your duty to have children.' She gave him a sympathetic smile. 'I am aware how much you hate this. To find yourself launched on to the marriage market is anathema to you, but you have an obligation to maintain the family line.'

Harry could not argue with this statement. If his elder brother had fathered children they wouldn't be in this position, but his wife had died after giving birth to a stillborn baby girl, and no amount of urging had made him marry again. Now the burden had landed on his reluctant shoulders.

'The Winslow family will be present tonight,' she continued, ignoring his silence. 'They have three strong, healthy girls. The eldest is twenty-four and, I understand, rather headstrong, which is why she has remained unwed. The second daughter would seem to be the more suitable; she has a sweet nature and has just reached the age of nineteen.' She studied him thoughtfully. 'The other one is still too young, especially for you.'

She ignored his heartfelt groan and continued. 'Being the second son, you have always had free rein, Harry, but your hedonistic days are over.'

Harry looked up astonished, and the elderly lady chuckled. 'Do not look so surprised. I have heard some tales about you…' She had to stop talking while she wiped the tears of laughter from her face.

The object of her amusement growled under his breath. 'I was not aware you indulged in mindless gossip.'

'Don't look so outraged. You are a strong man, and the future of this family now depends upon your virility.'

'Grandmother! I do not find it amusing to be likened to a prize stud.'

But all this indignant outburst achieved was to send the lady into another burst of merriment.

He waited for her to compose herself and wondered, not for the first time, how his grandfather had managed this strong-willed woman. His mind went back to the girl in the park, running along with complete disregard for convention. He studied his grandmother – had she been like that as a young lady? His lips twitched in amusement. Not much doubt about it.

He stood up. Time to get ready and face the ordeal.

'Before you go, Harry, have you a mistress set-up somewhere?'

He gave her a searching look. She never ceased to amaze him with her outspokenness. 'Well . . .'

'Come on, my boy. I am two-and-eighty and have lived long enough to know what goes on.'

'In that case,' he said dryly, 'you must realise that I haven't been home long enough to find myself a mistress.'

'Good. Do not form any loose attachments, as it will only complicate things.'

A devilish smile played across his face. 'Did grandfather . . . ?'

'No, he did not. Not after we were married, anyway.' She looked at him with a twinkle in her eyes. 'He had no reason to look elsewhere for his pleasures.'

Harry tipped his head back and laughed. Oh, he could well imagine, and what a very fortunate man his grandfather had been. But the smile on his face died as he contemplated his fate. He had always thought that he would be free to marry for love, or a deep affection, anyway. He was not sure he knew what love was, but lust he understood. However, he doubted if it would be possible to feel any of these emotions for the simpering, silly females he was about to have thrust upon him. He was unable to disguise the shudder that ran through him.

'It needn't be so bad, Harry,' she said wistfully, 'if you choose carefully.'

Harry watched his grandmother as they waited to greet their hostess. She had always been a woman

12

of great vitality and, even at this advanced age, had managed to maintain a good deal of vigour. A truly remarkable lady, he thought proudly. If only he could find someone like her, but that was most unlikely – she was unique.

'Augusta, this is my grandson.'

'Ah, yes,' the lady said, snapping her fan shut and running an all assessing glance over him. 'The new Duke of Ranliegh.'

He bowed politely.

'I was sorry to hear of your bereavements, Your Grace,' she said pointedly.

He inclined his head in acknowledgement, and wondered how long it would take him to get used to that form of address.

'It is a great shame that it took the army such a long time to find you and bring you home. However,' a calculating smile spread across Lady Augusta's face as she tapped his arm with her fan, 'got to find yourself a wife now, haven't you, and you have chosen my humble little function to look for a suitable candidate.'

Her grating laugh ran through him like a sabre.

'I do declare, I think the success of this evening has been assured.' She had a triumphant look in her eyes as she turned to the next in line, eager to pass on the exciting news.

'Wipe that thunderous expression off your face, Harry,' his grandmother told him as they walked away. Her mouth twitched as she controlled a smile. 'I admit I wasn't looking forward to this evening, but it might be fun after all.'

'Fun.' Harry snorted in disgust. 'It won't take that interfering old—'

'Harry! Watch your language; you are not with the troops now.'

He bit back the invective and started again. 'It will not take Lady Augusta long to spread the news and then we shall be besieged.'

She patted his arm. 'You ought to be pleased; you are quite a catch. We must be careful not to be knocked down in the rush.'

'Oh, God,' he muttered, looking up at the ceiling. Only the fact that he could not leave his grandmother stopped him from turning tail and running. He would rather face the wrath of Napoleon than this! 'Do we have to go through this charade? I'm sure I could find myself a wife, if given the time.'

She patted his arm again. 'Speed is of the essence and all the suitable females are gathered here, so you will be able to look them over tonight.'

'Great heavens! You do not expect me to choose one tonight, do you?'

'No, no, of course not, but perhaps you could engage Angelina Winslow in conversation and see if she would suit. She is a very sweet and obedient girl, I am assured.' She cast him an appealing glance. 'I am depending upon you, my dear. I don't want to die before I hold your son in my arms.'

He smiled down at her affectionately. 'I've got plenty of time then.'

'We don't know that.' Her sigh was dramatic and quite over the top.

But Harry knew he was trapped. The crafty old thing was playing on his love for her, and she would probably outlive them all. Still, having seen the line whittled down dramatically, she must be very worried. 'I'll see the girl, but I am not making any promises,' he added hastily.

'I know you won't let our family down.' The frail hand on his arm squeezed with surprising strength. 'Now smile.'

That was asking more than Harry was capable of, but he managed to replace the scowl with a bland, polite expression.

His grandmother gave him an affectionate look as he found her a comfortable seat where she could survey the room. 'You know, Harry, you are quite handsome when you are not at odds with the world.'

'Praise indeed,' he murmured.

'That is better,' she exclaimed. 'Now you are almost as devastating as your grandfather was.' She fanned herself elegantly. 'Get me a lemonade, will you? It's very hot in here.'

Glad of the errand he turned and strode across

the room. He would get himself a good strong drink, because he was going to need it if this evening was to be endured.

It took a while to track down the whisky, but he finally ran it to ground in the card room, where all the sensible gentlemen had retired. After downing a healthy glass full of the finest malt, he returned to his grandmother. She was surrounded by excited women, all eager to present their daughters. He bent low and handed her the drink.

'Took your time,' she said dryly and for his ears only. 'Did you find the whisky?'

He nodded.

'Ah, I see you did.' She drank half of the lemonade, pulled a face and put the glass down. 'Seeing as you are well fortified . . .'

She then set about making the introductions, and he had no choice but to dance. The first girl simpered and giggled, the next one subjected him to a constant stream of nervous chatter.

It was too much. He shot his grandmother a warning look. If this was a sample of what was on offer, he was having none of it.

She ignored his bad humour and took his arm. 'The Winslow family have arrived.'

He gritted his teeth in frustration. In his opinion this was not the way to go about finding a lifelong mate. And he didn't want a wife.

They had almost reached their destination when he heard a familiar laugh, and his step faltered. Where had he heard that delightful sound before? Something stirred in his memory, but with the crowds, noise and heat of the ballroom he could not bring it to mind.

He greeted Sir Winslow and his lady with an air of detachment. His manner was polite and could not be faulted, but his heart wasn't in it.

'Let me introduce my daughters,' Sir Winslow said, obviously trying not to show undue eagerness, and failing terribly. 'This is our second daughter – Angelina. And this is Charlotte – the youngest.'

Both girls were looking at him with some misgivings. He knew that with his exceptional height he towered over everyone else, but was he that terrifying? He tried to soften his expression – it wasn't easy. These girls were pawns in this stupid system as much as he was.

Sir Winslow turned to his wife. 'Where is Isabella, Mother?'

'She is dancing, my dear, but the set is just finishing, and she will be here directly.'

'Ah, there you are, Isabella,' Harry heard Sir Winslow say. 'Come and make your curtsy to the Duchess and her grandson – the Duke of Ranliegh.'

Harry stepped back as the young woman sank gracefully before his grandmother. She was wearing a classical gown of pale blue silk and the fitted bodice was caught high with a velvet ribbon of a slightly darker shade. It was refreshingly simple, he thought idly, comparing it with all the ugly frills and flounces of most of the other ladies, and it was not too revealing. He did not like everything to be on display, it dulled the pleasure of discovering what was underneath as he removed the clothes himself.

He was wondering if the front view was as charming as the back when she turned, and he found himself looking into a pair of the bluest eyes he had ever seen. It was the girl from the park. Of course, it was her laugh he had recognised.

She dipped low and he noticed how the overhead lights made her deep chestnut hair shine, and how it was also immaculately styled. Quite the reverse of how she had looked in the park, out of breath and her hair in disarray.

He gave her the first genuine smile he had managed to summon up that evening, and as she was the eldest of the three sisters, he led her on to the floor first. He was not disappointed – she did not simper or giggle and was certainly not frightened of him. She was intelligent, with a lively interest in the world about her, and he was tempted to tease her about the incident in the park but thought better of it. They had only just met, and he did not want to put her out of countenance. Though, as he watched her dancing eyes and smiling face, he doubted if that were possible, for he had a strong feeling that she didn't give a damn what anyone else thought of her. She was completely natural, without false airs and graces. She was a captivating creature, but not good wife material – much too strong minded; she could turn a man's life upside down. But what a mistress she would make. He fought down a surge of desire. These were not the kind of girls you took as mistresses – they would not adhere to the unwritten rules.

He then danced with Angelina, but she would not look him in the eyes, and he was sure she trembled when he touched her. There was a frown on his face when he returned her to her mother. If the families had discussed a union between them, then why was this girl obviously terrified of him?

Charlotte was more like her elder sister, bright and outgoing, but still only a child.

His grandmother was in deep conversation with Lady Winslow, and Harry couldn't help wondering why she was favouring this family.

There wasn't time to dwell on this puzzle because there was a constant stream of mothers with their offspring wanting an introduction – a title was a great attraction, he thought cynically. He danced with two more girls and tried to hide his boredom, then he turned to his grandmother in desperation. 'You must not overtire yourself we can leave as soon as you are ready.'

She kept a perfectly controlled expression. 'I am quite all right, Harry. Just relax and enjoy yourself.'

He turned away and surveyed the room. Enjoy himself! She knew he was hating this. The whole damned evening was enough to shorten anyone's temper, and the elderly lady was looking far too pleased with herself for his liking. That always meant trouble.

'Harry,' she called. 'Isn't that Dexter just arriving?'

His gaze swept in the same direction as hers. 'Good Lord, so it is, but what the devil is he doing here?'

'Do bring him over, Harry. I haven't seen him for such a long time.'

Needing no further urging, he strode across the room, eager to greet his friend.

'Dexter,' he exclaimed, slapping his friend on the back. 'You are the last person I expected to be here.'

The tall blonde man turned, a smile of pleasure lighting up his handsome face. 'Harry, it's good to see you.'

'What in heaven's name are you doing here? I thought you were still with the regiment.'

Dexter shook his head. 'No, I have resigned my commission. It was time to come home. I became weary of being shot at.' he added flippantly.

Harry hid his surprise. He knew his friend's position: he was the third son of Lord Atterton, therefore his prospect of inheriting the title was remote, and although he had an adequate income, he was by no means wealthy. He had been a fine and respected officer and Harry had assumed that he would make it his career. He was bursting with questions, but caught the warning look in his friend's eyes. Go along with this, my friend, he was urging silently.

So, he answered in the same bantering tone. 'I agree. One could get oneself killed.'

They both laughed and Dexter cast him a grateful look. Whatever the mystery was it would have to wait for a more private place to talk. Suddenly the evening had taken on a distinctly exciting air.

Dexter drew forward a young man who had been hovering eagerly at his side. 'Harry, this is my cousin – Timothy Sherfield.'

The lad stepped forward, smiling broadly. 'I say, you must be Major Sterling. Dexter has told me about you-'

'No, Tim,' Dexter interrupted, 'he is now the Duke of Ranliegh.'

'Oh, I beg your pardon, Your Grace.' The boy looked embarrassed.

'My friends call me Harry.' He took to the fresh-faced boy immediately. Then he turned to his friend again. 'Grandmother wants to meet you.'

'I noticed her sitting in state with the Winslow family. Is she steering you in their direction?' He raised an eyebrow in query.

Harry grimaced. 'She seems eager that I should marry one of the daughters.'

'That shouldn't be a hardship, Harry. They are all quite beautiful, and I have been told that they each have a sizeable fortune, left to them by a doting uncle. Is that so?'

'I really don't know, but it could be true,' he said, ushering the two men on before him. 'We must not keep grandmother waiting any longer.'

'Dexter,' she said, reaching out for his hand, 'how lovely to see you again.'

He bowed low over her hand. 'It is my pleasure to see you in such fine fettle, ma'am. I do declare that you become more beautiful with the advancing years.'

Her gracious smile was one of amusement. 'You have not changed, I see, still the master of graceful flattery. But what are you doing here?'

'Like Harry, I have resigned my commission.'

'Have you indeed. But this treaty with Napoleon cannot hold, surely? He wants to be master of Europe.'

'Yes, it is a precarious peace, I feel.'

She nodded. 'However, I am relieved to see you and Harry come out unscathed. Though how we are to do without both of you in the fray, I do not know?' Her eyes sparkled with devilment. 'I do declare that our cause is quite lost.'

They all laughed, and Timothy was brought forward to be introduced. The shrewd lady eyed him knowingly and then smiled. 'You must not let these two rapscallions lead you astray, Mr Sherfield. When they are together they like to get into mischief, and it has been so since they were children.'

'I shall be on my guard, ma'am.' He bowed low respectfully.

She looked him over with a practised eye. 'I suspect that you are cast from the same mould.'

Timothy straightened his shoulders proudly. Putting aside the difference in ages and colouring, they were remarkably similar. All dressed in the height of fashion, but soberly, the only flash of colour coming from their elegant waistcoats. They were all tall, even Timothy who had just reached the age of nineteen. They made an impressive trio and many female eyes were looking at them with longing and anticipation.

After introductions were duly made, Timothy eagerly led Charlotte on to the floor and Dexter bowed low and guided Angelina to join the dancers. Isabella was already dancing with someone and Harry watched her thoughtfully. She had a natural exuberance for life that was both stimulating and unsettling.

He endured several more dances with tiresome females, and feeling that he had done his duty, sat next to his grandmother and gave her a beseeching look.

She took the hint and stood up.

'You may take me home, Harry, I am feeling quite fatigued.' Then turning to Dexter and Timothy said, 'I shall expect you two young men to visit soon, and I should like to hear more about the war, Dexter. Harry is not very forthcoming on the subject.'

She was assured that they would call soon and as they turned to leave Dexter whispered in Harry's ear. 'Will you be at home in the morning? I need to talk to you.'

Harry nodded, his eyes alight with curiosity. 'I shall look forward to seeing you.'

As he escorted his grandmother home his mind was not on the vexing problem of finding a suitable wife, but on the mystery of his friend's sudden appearance.

Two

'Bella, Bella!' The bedroom door burst open and two excited sisters threw themselves on to Isabella's bed. 'Wasn't it the grandest ball we have ever attended?'

She pulled her legs up to make room for the exuberant girls and smiled indulgently. 'Indeed, it was very fine.'

'And what did you think of Mr Sherfield, Bella? Wasn't he the most handsome man in the room?' Charlotte sighed ecstatically.

'No, he was not,' Angelina interrupted swiftly. 'Captain Atterton was by far the most handsome. He was so kind, and he made me laugh. I was not a bit shy in his presence, Bella.'

Isabella laughed affectionately. She had heard this tale many times before and, no doubt, would hear it many times again, but she could not resist the temptation to tease. 'No, you are both wrong. Without a doubt the most handsome man there was the Duke of Ranliegh.'

The two younger girls screwed their faces up in horror and Isabella dissolved into helpless laughter at the expressions on their pretty faces.

'Quiet, girls,' their mother called, hurrying into the room. 'Such an uproar. Your father wants to see you in the library.'

The girls tumbled off the bed.

'Hurry, now,' their mother chided. 'You must not keep your papa waiting.'

Within five minutes the girls were all seated in a row, gazing at their father expectantly.

'Did you enjoy yourselves last night?' he asked.

'Yes, Papa,' they answered in unison.

He smiled. 'It was indeed a grand occasion and we were greatly honoured by the Duchess's presence.'

Isabella began to feel uneasy. Her father was looking very pleased with himself.

'They have had great tragedy in the family of late and her grandson has come home to take up the reins.' His gaze rested on Angelina. 'He has need of a wife.'

Isabella's heart seemed to bounce off her ribs. She knew it! At the same time she felt Angelina's hand seek hers and clasp it. All three girls went deathly still.

'Her Grace favours you, Angelina. Indeed, she has made her preference quite clear.'

'Oh, no, Papa,' wailed the distraught girl, suddenly finding her voice. 'He is too old for me and so harsh.'

'Nonsense, child,' Sir Winslow cut in quickly. 'He is only just thirty years of age, and moreover, he is a fine man who has fought valiantly for his country, but now he finds himself with burdens he never expected to have to shoulder.'

'But I am sure he does not even like me. He hardly spoke as we danced.' She made a sound which was a cross between a gulp and a sob.

'Of course he likes you,' her father added quickly, his voice softening as he looked at her. 'Who could fail to like such a beautiful, gentle girl?'

The compliment did nothing to soothe Angelina's fears and her grip tightened painfully on Isabella's hand.

Sir Winslow's expression and tone changed to that of a stern father who would brook no argument. 'It is a very great honour that one of my daughters should be considered by the Ranliegh family. No offer as yet, has been made, because it is only natural that His Grace should want to make your acquaintance before coming to a decision. So, if he should call upon you, you will receive him graciously, and Isabella will act as chaperone.' His gaze rested on the two girls with unwavering determination. 'You will obey me in this. Do you understand?'

Angelina's head dropped as she murmured, 'Yes, Papa.'

'Good. Now, we have an invitation to dine with Her Grace on Wednesday evening.'

The discussion was obviously over, so Isabella stood up and started to lead her sisters from the room. It was clear that their father was very set on an alliance with this exalted family, and she knew from experience how difficult it would be to change his mind. She remembered the tussles she had had with him. She had always won, but Angelina was not strong-willed enough to face him down.

Once back in the bedroom, Angelina began to sob uncontrollably, holding on to her sister fiercely. 'W-What am I to do, Bella? He is so big and fierce. Wh-when he looked at me with those strange orange eyes, I was sure he could see right into my soul.'

'Shush,' Isabella soothed. 'Papa has the right of it. He is a fine man and I am sure there is nothing to fear. No doubt his war experiences have made him appear withdrawn.'

'But Captain Atterton served with him and he is not a bit harsh,' Angelina wailed.

So that was it. Her affection had been engaged by the handsome soldier with the gentle grey eyes. Isabella sighed. That might have been a more suitable match for her timid sister, but that was not to be if her father had anything to do with it. She could see how delighted he was with the prospect of marrying one of his daughters to a Duke, and that was a prize beyond his expectations.

'Nothing has been settled, Angel. We can only wait and see what happens.' She began to mop up the distressed girl's tears.

'Quite right, Isabella.' Their mother swept into the room. 'I am disappointed in you Angelina, making all this fuss when you should be excited at the prospect.'

'I'm sorry, Mama.' She fought back another flow of tears. 'You know how frightened I get.'

'I know, my dear, but you must be sensible. Your father has only your best interests at heart, and this would be a prestigious alliance.' She paused. 'When I married your father, it was an arranged match. I hardly knew him, and I also was frightened, but we have dealt well together. My fears were unfounded – as yours will be.' She smiled encouragingly.

'Yes, I am sure you are right.' Angelina gave her a wavering smile.

'Good girl. Now wash your face and we shall go shopping this afternoon.' She turned and left the room.

'Isabella? You will not leave me alone with him, will you?'

'Not until you are wed,' she answered teasingly.

'Oh, that will not be for a long time, I think.'

'No, no,' Charlotte said, joining in the conversation for the first time. 'I was told he must marry quickly. The family have need of an heir.'

Isabella groaned inwardly at her young sister's impetuosity. They were just getting Angelina to pull herself together, but now she was shaking badly.

'But that means I would have to . . .' a look of horror crossed her face, 'let him touch me,' she whispered.

'Of course, Angel,' Isabella said gently. 'Has not Mama been very clear on what will be expected of us when we wed?'

Angelina nodded. 'If only he wasn't so tall and dark and stern.'

'Now, now, Angel, you must not let your fears overset you. You heard what papa said – nothing has been decided, and the Duke of Ranliegh might have other ideas, regardless of what his grandmother wishes. He does not look like the kind of man who would be swayed by anyone's opinion. If he does not believe that this would be a suitable match, then nought will come of it, you will see.'

Her sister gave a tremulous smile. 'Do you think so?'

'Of course.' Then she hustled the girls out of her room in order to get ready for their promised shopping trip.

As she tidied herself she tried to dislodge the feeling of hurt inside her. Why had her father cast her in the role of chaperone? Aunt Dorothea usually had that task, so had her father given up on the prospect of her ever marrying? She was quite happy and had not given her unwed state much thought, until her father had assigned this duty to her. She would like to marry, but she wanted love. What most people did not realise was, that underneath her lively, unconventional self, was a romantic – a passionate woman who could only surrender to a man out of deep love and respect. She sighed sadly. Was she looking for the impossible? Did that special man exist for her, and by her intransigence, was she condemning herself to a life without a family of her own?

But the thought of marrying a man she had no affection for was abhorrent to her, so she must wait and hope that such a paragon of a man would appear one day.

Harry frowned at the papers in his hand. Why had Robert purchased someone's gambling notes? It was a very odd thing to do. He emptied out the contents of the private box and went through each item carefully, but there was nothing to throw light on the mystery.

An hour later he was frowning again. 'Jenson,' he called.

His steward came hurrying into the room.

'What the devil is this?' He spread a document out on the desk and they both peered at it. 'Do you know anything about it?'

'No, Your Grace. It appears to be the deed for a parcel of land your brother bought just before he died, but he never told me anything about it.'

Harry ran a hand through his thick, dark hair. What the blazes had Robert been up to? First the gambling notes and now this. He had been a very astute businessman, so there must be a sound reason behind these purchases, but Harry could not fathom it.

'Does it make any sense to you, Jenson?'

The steward shook his head. 'No, sir. If it joined Ranliegh's boundary, I could understand it.'

Harry sat down, deep in thought. After a while he looked up. 'Perhaps a visit to the property will throw some light on this unusual purchase?'

His steward nodded his agreement. 'It's the only thing to do.'

'Good. We will go first thing tomorrow.' He smiled at the middle-aged man standing beside him. Jenson was efficient, trustworthy, and had been with the family for more than twenty years.

'Everything else seems to be in fine order. I'll call you if I need you.'

As Jenson went out, Carter – Harry's batman and now personal manservant – entered.

'Captain Atterton to see you, sir.'

Harry got to his feet eagerly. 'Send him in, please.'

They greeted each other enthusiastically. They had been friends from their youth and were close enough to be brothers.

When they were comfortably seated, Harry looked at Dexter quizzically and raised a dark eyebrow. 'Are you going to tell me what this is all about, or are you going to make me wait until I explode with curiosity?'

Dexter took a deep breath. 'Do you remember the man you found just as you were returning home?'

'Yes. He had been beaten and robbed. I brought him back to camp to see if he could be saved.'

'Unfortunately, we were unable to keep him alive, although we did everything we could for him he died before we could question him.'

'Question him?'

'Yes. When his clothing was removed some papers were found concealed in the lining of his coat.'

Harry sat forward eagerly. 'What were they?'

'Plans which could have been very useful to Napoleon.'

'So, the old devil is making use of this time and gathering all the information he can.'

'Yes, and we need to find the person who is betraying us. From the content of the information we are fairly certain that the informant is someone in the higher echelons of society.'

Harry stood up and prowled over to the window, his movements fluid and silent. 'Perhaps we can work together on this?'

'I would welcome your involvement.' He stood beside his friend and grinned boyishly. 'It will be quite like old times.'

Harry chuckled. 'Some of those sorties we went on were dangerous, weren't they? How we escaped with our lives, I will never know.'

The two men fell silent, each one lost in his own thoughts, but it was a companionable silence. Their friendship was deep and the experiences they had shared made the bond between them stronger.

Harry gazed out at the immaculate garden. His life had been turned upside down, and he was plagued with restlessness, but this assignment of Dexter's might help to take his mind off the wretched business of finding a wife. However, there wasn't a hope in hell of his grandmother letting him drag his heels, but the thought of wedding and bedding a woman he had no regard for, just to fulfil his duty to beget an heir, made his insides heave. Of course, it was done all the time, but he suspected that he did not have the stomach for it. He had only ever taken a woman for enjoyment – mutual enjoyment, and he had to have some feeling for her. He had always treated his mistresses with kindness – and there hadn't been that many of them. Well, not as many as rumour would have it.

He turned away from the window, walked over to the drinks table, picked up a glass and filled it with brandy, then he held it out to Dexter. 'I know it's early in the day, but I could do with a drink. Would you like one?'

'An excellent idea.'

'So, you haven't resigned your commission?' Harry said when they were seated once again.

'Yes I have, that is quite genuine. It had to be,' he explained, 'in case anyone checked up on me, but when this assignment is completed, I shall have the option of returning to my former rank.' He surveyed the liquid in his glass thoughtfully. 'That's if I want to.'

'Hmm. You don't sound too sure.'

'I would like a more settled life.' Dexter looked up and grimaced. 'Lord knows what I'm going to do, but I'm tired of the army – always on the move.'

Harry nodded understandingly. 'Don't worry about your future, Dexter, that can be sorted out later, but first we must find this traitor. Do you have any idea where to start?'

'With anyone who has a connection with the War Department, and I am meeting someone in about an hour who will give me a list of names. They will all have to be investigated.'

'We must be discreet,' Harry leant forward, 'mustn't let anyone get wind of what we are about.'

At that moment the door opened, and his grandmother glided in. He smothered a grin – she could still make an impressive entrance.

'Drinking this early in the day? I hope you haven't picked up too many bad habits in the army.' Her expression was forbidding, but there was a saucy glint in her eyes, which neither man missed. They put their glasses down and leapt to their feet, caught like wayward children.

'I know, I know,' she said, turning her cheek to Harry for a kiss. 'You would not tell me if you had, and I'm sure I don't want to know. You might put me to the blush,' she added coyly.

That remark caused much hilarity.

She smiled and turned to Dexter. 'What are you doing about at this hour?'

'I needed to see Harry, so I came early in case he was going out.'

She eyed them suspiciously. 'Why do I get the impression that you are both up to no good? I have seen you closeted together like this many times and it always heralded mischief of some kind.'

They presented her with expressions of pure innocence.

She threw her hands in the air. 'I am not fooled, but whatever it is, please be careful.'

'Do not concern yourself, Grandmother. We only need to find someone, that is all. Nothing dangerous.'

She sighed. 'I have been given those assurances before, but danger seems to stalk you two.'

'Not anymore,' Dexter hastened to assure her. 'We are not in the army now.'

'I don't think that will make any difference, for if there is trouble around, you two will find it . . . or it will find you. How you have survived thus far is a mystery.'

'We have always watched each other's backs,' Harry said seriously.

'Well, I sincerely hope that you will continue to do so.' She turned to Dexter. 'I have a strong premonition that your sudden homecoming is not what it appears, otherwise Harry would not have been unaware of your return. However, I will not quiz you. You are, no doubt, aware of the desperate position in which this family finds itself, so do not go leading Harry into any danger.'

'I would not dream of it,' he assured her with an earnest expression on his face.

Harry bit his lip and looked down, intent on removing an imaginary piece of fluff from his jacket, but the wise lady was not fooled by their bland expressions.

She gave a wave of resignation. 'You were always in trouble, right from the moment you met as boys.' Her face softened in remembrance and she gave a quiet laugh.

Harry reached across and took her hands in his. 'There isn't anything to worry about, Grandmother. We are just going to do a little investigating, and the authorities will deal with anything that might be dangerous. However, you must not mention this to anyone.'

'Of course.' She patted his hand. 'Although you have a wild streak in you, I do not consider you reckless. If that had been so, you would have met your Maker long ago. If there is ever anything amiss you will let me know. My mind is as it ever was.' She gave them an endearing smile. 'It is only my body that has aged, and that can be a damned nuisance at times.'

'You will never be old to me,' Harry told her with heartfelt sincerity.

She turned to Dexter with a smile. 'He is almost as good at flattery as you are. Now, I am giving a select dinner party on Wednesday evening. I hope you will be able to attend?'

'I would be honoured.'

'Good, good. And bring that young man with you – Mr Sherfield, wasn't it? Such a personable boy,' she said, rising to her feet and not waiting for an answer.

After she had left, Dexter grinned at his friend. 'She doesn't change much, does she?'

Harry threw back his head and laughed. 'No. She is still a force to be reckoned with.'

'Who will be attending this dinner party?'

'The Winslow family.'

Dexter regarded his friend seriously. 'You have a lot of pressure on you, and you don't have to become involved in this investigation.'

'Oh, but I want to. It is just what I need at the moment and I have a little mystery of my own to solve. You can help me with that, if you would?'

'Gladly.' Dexter's response was immediate. 'What is it?'

He spread out the map. 'Before my brother died, he bought this land.' He pointed to the place. 'I cannot understand what he was about – it doesn't join

Ranliegh, and it seems a strange purchase to make.'

His friend studied the map carefully. 'I agree, but Robert must have had a good reason. He always had a sound business head on his shoulders.'

'Yes. That was my first thought and I'm taking Jenson with me tomorrow to have a look at the place. Would you like to come?'

Dexter nodded. 'Are you going on horseback or carriage?'

'Oh, horses.' He stretched and flexed his broad shoulders. 'I could do with a good ride. Did you bring your animal home with you?'

'Yes. I couldn't leave Dancer behind, but he's getting mighty restless, and a hard gallop will calm him down a touch, I think.'

'Lucifer is causing quite a rumpus as well. They are not used to being confined.'

Dexter grinned. 'They will relish riding side by side once again.'

'Bring Tim with you as well. We leave at first light.'

Three

The pale light of dawn was creeping across the sky when they assembled. The two great war horses were so excited that it took firm hands and considerable skill to hold them back.

'I swear that I could not manage such strong beasts.' Tim exclaimed.

Harry laughed. 'They are excited because they haven't seen each other for some time, and they think they are going into battle.'

The two animals tossed their heads impatiently as they were led out, but once in open country they pranced and snorted with pleasure as they felt the grass under their feet. Some of the tension left Harry as he galloped through the countryside. This was just what he needed.

It was the middle of the afternoon before they reached their destination. The house was of a fine, solid construction and had a pleasing appearance. To the left was a stable block and on the right were three small cottages. It was obvious that everything had been neglected of late. As they dismounted an elderly couple emerged looking hesitant and worried.

Harry introduced himself and they bowed, unsmiling.

'I'm Baxter and this is my wife, Harriet, Your Grace. We've been looking after the place.'

'Are you on your own here?' he asked, noting the absence of any workers.

'Yes, Your Grace, the rest of the staff were dismissed when the property was sold.'

'We will have to do something about that. Show my steward around while we attend to the horses.'

'I'll see to them, Your Grace.' He stepped forward and Lucifer watched him with a look of murder in his eyes.

Harry stopped him just in time. 'No! Baxter. He will not allow anyone near him but me; he is a mean tempered old devil. You go with Jenson; the Captain and I will deal with the animals.'

Once that was done, they strolled into the house. It was obvious that it had once been a charming residence, but now it was in desperate need of attention. He wished he knew why his brother had bought this place. There was enough to do without this added burden. But he could not let it go to ruin.

He was startled out of deep thought by Timothy who had thrown open the large garden doors and was running towards some trees. When his gaze swept the countryside for the first time he exclaimed, 'What the . . . ?'

'Yes, it is quite a sight, is it not?' Dexter laughed.

'Trees, as far as they eye can see,' Harry murmured then he joined in the laughter. 'Just look at that boy! Why is he so excited?'

'Fruit trees,' his friend explained. 'They are the love of his life, and I doubt if there is anyone who knows more on the subject.'

'Does his family have orchards, then?'

'Yes, but unfortunately he is the fifth son and is not needed at home. Finding an heiress is his only chance of obtaining land of his own.'

'Five sons,' Harry murmured. 'And here I am in desperate need of one. Perhaps I should adopt him.'

His friend shook his head. 'That would solve your problem, but I fear that your grandmother would not have it. For your estates to be secure you must have a direct heir. There is no way out of it, Harry.'

'I know it,' he sighed.

Timothy burst back into the room, cheeks flushed and eyes sparkling. 'This is a fine property, but it has been sadly neglected. There are apples, pears and plums,' he rattled on excitedly. 'Clear the ground and prune the trees and you will double the yield next year, Your Grace.'

'Harry.'

'H . . . H . . .' the boy shook his head. 'Dash it, I cannot call you that.'

'Well that's a pity, Tim, because I need to ask a favour and I can't do that unless you treat me as a friend.' Harry cast the boy a suitably crestfallen look.

'I would be honoured to be your friend, Ha . . . Harry,' he stuttered. 'What can I do for you?'

'Well, I find myself in some difficulty. Much needs doing here, and I would deem it a very great favour if you felt you could oversee the work.'

Timothy started to hop from foot to foot. 'I would be delighted to get this place into shape, and you would be doing me the favour.'

'Good. That's settled then.' He turned to Jenson who had just come into the room with Baxter. 'Can you spare some men from Ranliegh to clear this ground of brambles and weeds?'

The estate manager nodded. 'Yes, Your Grace.'

Harry put his mind to the necessities. 'Tim, I will pay you a fair wage, and you will have complete control here. Just report to me from time to time on the progress. The house will be refurbished, and you can use it as your own.'

Timothy appeared too overcome to speak.

He turned and looked around the room. 'Where is Mrs Baxter?'

'I am here, Your Grace,' she said coming into the room carrying a tray of refreshments. 'Will you be staying the night? I have kept some rooms in good order.'

'No. Ranliegh is less than two hours away. However, this is Mr Sherfield.' He pulled the boy forward. 'He will be taking over here, and I'm sure you will take good care of him.'

She bobbed a curtsy and smiled for the first time. 'That I will, Your Grace.'

Harry took a purse out of his jacket and handed it to Mrs Baxter. 'You will have a lot of men to feed for a while. That should take care of it, but if you need more, send word to Ranliegh. Oh, and would you see that this house is brought back to its former glory?'

The housekeeper smiled again. 'It would be a pleasure.'

Well satisfied with the day's work, Harry strode from the house, mounted and turned his horse towards Ranliegh, eager to be home again.

As they left the Orchards behind, Dexter leant across to his friend. 'That was kindly done, Harry. The Baxter's were fearful that you were going to dismiss them, and Timothy is so excited he can hardly stay in his saddle.'

'He is doing me the favour. Dashed if I'd know what to do with the place otherwise.' He leant forward, whispered into Lucifer's ear and the huge animal lengthened his stride.

'We will stay at Ranliegh for two nights,' Harry informed then when they eased the horses into a walk a while later, 'then make our way back to London.'

'Just in time for your grandmother's little gathering,' Dexter said, his face wearing an amused smirk.

'Hell, yes, we must not be late for that.' He gave a dramatic shudder, and galloped away, leaving the other men laughing.

'No, no, my friend,' chuckled Dexter, 'even faithful Lucifer cannot distance you from this danger.'

Sir George surveyed the three girls standing in front of him awaiting his inspection and smiled. What a beautiful sight they were. Isabella with her deep chestnut hair and sparkling blue eyes; Angelina's colouring was lighter giving her a delicate look; Charlotte was a mixture of the two with eyes more grey than blue.

He sighed quietly. He would not be able to relax until they were all betrothed to decent men, for they were prey to fortune hunters. Isabella was not such a concern, for she had an abundance of good sense, and was not taken in by fancy airs and flattering speeches. Angelina was the most vulnerable – she was easily frightened and needed protecting, and he was praying that the Duke of Ranliegh would offer for her. She would be safe with him; he came from an honourable family and was wealthy enough not to be swayed by her fortune. Then there was Charlotte, the youngest at sixteen, and she was already showing signs of her elder sister's strength and determination.

Suddenly his expression turned into a scowl. That scoundrel Garston had had the nerve to approach him for Charlotte's hand. He was a womaniser, drunkard and gambler. How dare he cast his lustful eyes on his lovely, innocent daughter.

'Papa, do we not please you?' Angelina asked hesitantly.

The fury was wiped from his face and replaced with a smile. 'Indeed, you do. You are all so beautiful, it is enough to take a man's breath away.'

They laughed at his flattery. He could be a stern father, but he always showed his affection for them. Indeed, Isabella was very conscious that she would not have been given such freedom of choice had she been born into another family.

'They are a credit to us, my dear,' Sir George said, holding his arm out to his wife. 'Now we must be on our way; it should be a very pleasant evening.'

Isabella took Angelina's hand and squeezed it. 'Try to enjoy yourself, Angel. There's nothing to be concerned about, I am sure.'

'I shall endeavour to do that, Bella, but I do declare that I am exceedingly nervous. The Duke only has to look at me with those strange eyes and I become quite speechless.'

Isabella patted her sister's hand reassuringly.

Angelina smiled tremulously, then straightened her shoulders in a rare gesture of determination. 'I shall try to be brave.'

The Duchess was waiting to greet them when they entered the large salon. It was decorated tastefully with an eye to comfort rather than being ostentatious. Isabella found it very pleasing and smiled as she dipped into a graceful curtsy before their hostess.

As her sisters made their curtsies, Isabella glanced around the room and was relieved to see Captain Atterton and Mr Sherfield were in the party. That should help the conversation, she thought with amusement, for His Grace looked as stern as ever. It was obvious that he did not want to be here – it was written on every line of his handsome face. She dropped her gaze in an effort to hide her amusement. With his formidable grandmother insisting he marry he did not have a choice. However, he was clearly a man who did not respond well to pressure, and she suspected that it was only his love for his grandmother which gave her the upper hand. If it had been anyone but her gentle sister being offered to him, she might have felt sorry him. However, her sympathies were all with Angelina, and if he made her sister unhappy, he would have her to contend with.

When she looked up again, she was staring straight into his eyes. Why did Angelina think they were frightening, she thought breathlessly. They were stunning; not orange, as her sister had said, but amber and they appeared to have a fire burning behind them. At that instant she recognised that underneath the impressive self-control, was a volatile and passionate man. A strange feeling ran down her spine, and it was exciting. No man had ever elicited such a response from her before.

She curtsied, keeping her eyes lowered, for she was momentarily disconcerted by these strange feelings, and when he turned away to greet someone else, she sighed. Why did she find him so unsettling. She gave a mental shrug; she was just being silly. He was meant for her sister, and that was making her look at him too deeply, trying to grasp his character, which was elusive.

'Miss Isabella?' a soft voice at her elbow queried, 'May I escort you to dinner?'

She looked up to find Captain Atterton smiling at her and she placed her hand on his arm. 'Thank you, Captain.'

The food was excellent, and Isabella was finding the company diverting. She was laughing with amusement at a tale the captain was telling when she felt a pull on her attention. Glancing down the table her eyes clashed with the Duke's and they were cold with disapproval, but she could not fathom the reason for his censure. Her conduct had been exemplary, and she was sure she had not done anything to warrant such a glaring look. Her chin came up and she held his gaze unwaveringly. If he was going to be her brother-in-law then he would have to accept her as she was, for she had no intention of changing to suit his particular likes and dislikes. He raised an eyebrow and she dropped her gaze, realising that she was staring at him with defiance, and that was not something well-brought-up females did. They should appear to be a little shy and subservient, but, darn it, she was not anything like that. Unconventional, society called her, and that was to her face. What they said behind her back was quite another thing, she suspected, but the tittle-tattle had never worried her.

A rich chocolate pudding was placed in front of her and she attacked it with gusto. She enjoyed her food whereas most young ladies picked delicately at it. A smile of amusement flitted across her face as she swallowed the last tasty morsel – it was too late to try and change her ways now.

'Would you like another helping of pudding, Miss Isabella?' the captain asked.

Her grin spread and she leant towards him, speaking

softly, for his ears only. 'I must decline, Captain. I do declare that I could easily eat more, but it might appear a trifle greedy, do you not think?'

His laughter echoed around the table. 'You are a relaxing dinner companion, Miss Isabella. Indeed, I don't feel as if I have to choose my words carefully before speaking.' He grinned boyishly.

'You mean I'm too outspoken to be a lady?' she replied, pulling a face.

'The thought never entered my head,' he denied, but his gentle grey eyes were sparkling with merriment.

'Now, why is it that I do not believe you, Captain?'

He turned to face her with such an absurdly false expression of hurt that she could not contain her mirth. A slight hush fell upon the room and she did not dare cast a glance to the other end of the table. He was glowering again – she could feel it, and she didn't care.

When the ladies had adjourned to the other room, Harry poured himself a stiff drink, sat back and took some reviving deep breaths. The meal had been interminable. Try as he might he had not been able to get more than a few words out of Angelina, and if it hadn't been for Timothy and Charlotte, there would have been silence at his end of the table. Which was certainly not the case with the other end, as Dexter and the other sister had been having a high old time and their laughter had irritated him beyond reason. There he'd been, struggling with an unresponsive female and . . . He tossed the drink back and emptied the glass in one swallow. Good grief, what was the matter with him? The emotion gnawing at him felt like jealousy, which was ridiculous. He sighed again and refilled his glass. This task of finding a wife was scrambling his wits.

'Isn't that so, Harry?'

His head jerked up. 'Sorry, what did you say, Timothy?'

'I was telling Sir George about the Orchards.'

Harry nodded. 'Indeed. There's a good deal of work to be done, but it appears to be a good property.'

'I know it well,' Sir George informed them. 'The last owner was a recluse and in the latter part of his life he let the property run wild. It joins my land and I considered buying it myself, but I really didn't want it as I don't have a son to pass the estate on to. Your brother bought it because he was determined to stop that odious creature Garston from obtaining it.'

Harry sat up, suddenly alert. The name sounded familiar, but he could not immediately place it. 'You obviously don't like the man, Sir George. Who is he?'

'He inherited the property adjoining the Orchards from Lord Langton. A distant relative, I believe. He is a scoundrel.' Sir George's face coloured with rage.

'He had the effrontery to offer for Charlotte, and he is more than three times her age.'

Garston. Harry puzzled over the name. Where had he come across it before? 'Robert knew this man?'

'It seems so. Your brother hated him, but I don't know any more than that.'

Harry stood up and paced over to the window. He would not have thought his brother capable of hating anyone.

He turned abruptly and headed for the door. 'It is time we joined the ladies.'

After their guests had departed Harry looked at his grandmother's tired face. 'Would you like a nightcap to help you sleep?'

'A small brandy would be most acceptable, thank you, but I don't think I will need anything to make me sleep, for I feel quite fatigued.'

'You should not take on so much, Grandmother.' Harry handed her the glass.

'When I see you settled then I will relax more.' She paused. 'How did you get on with Angelina?'

'Not very well, I fear. She is uneasy in my company, and it was hard work to get her to say more than three words at a time.'

'She is rather shy.' She looked at her grandson and smiled. 'Nevertheless, you can be very persuasive when you set your mind to it, and if you treat her gently she will come around, I am certain. Are you calling on her soon?'

He nodded. 'I have arranged to take her for a ride tomorrow.'

'Good, good. That is the very thing.'

Harry changed the subject. 'Grandmother, do you know anything about this man Garston?'

She sipped her brandy and nodded. 'He is a thoroughly disreputable character.'

'What did Robert have against him?'

'You remember his friend, James?'

'Yes, I only met him once, but I recall hearing Robert talk about him. He died in a shooting accident, didn't he?'

'Well that was what his family said, but Robert believed that he had killed himself. He was too much of an expert with guns to have made such an error. He would never have tried to clean a gun while it was still loaded.'

'Do you know the story?'

'Robert did talk to me about it. James was being blackmailed, but I don't know the details. He came to Robert a week before he died – he was distraught and begged for a loan. Your brother gave it to him, of course, but the next we heard he had died.'

'And Garston was the blackmailer?'

'We never knew for sure, but Robert was convinced of it. However, nothing was proved, and Garston disappeared after that.'

'But he's back now. Have you heard anything about him since he inherited the estate from Lord Langton?'

'He's not well liked. He drinks too much and according to the gossip has been losing heavily at the tables for some time.'

'Gambling!' Harry shot out of his seat and hurried from the room. In the study he tipped out the contents of the box he had been looking at the other day. Ah, there they were. That was where he'd seen the name before, on the gambling notes Robert had purchased.

He went back to the other room and handed them to his grandmother. 'It appears Robert was set on revenge.'

'Oh dear.' Her hands started to tremble. 'I did not know he had these. If I had I might have paid more heed to my suspicions.'

Harry bent down in front of her and stilled her shaking hands. 'What do you mean, Grandmother? What suspicions?'

She gazed past his shoulder as if looking at something in the distance.

'You and Robert were riding before you could walk, and you were expert horsemen before you were ten.'

Harry nodded, wondering where this conversation was leading, but he left her to speak in her own time.

She looked at him and gave a slight smile. 'But Robert was the better, I think.'

'No doubt about it. When he was seated on a horse

he became a part of the animal, and I could never hope to match him.'

'Exactly.' She paused. 'Did you not think it strange that he should have died in such a way?'

'I did think it was a damned silly way for him to . . .' His brow gathered into a fierce frown. 'You don't think it was an accident?'

She gave a weary sigh. 'I am just being fanciful. Everyone was adamant that it had been an accident.'

'I'll start looking into it, Grandmother.'

'Thank you. I must admit that I would rest easier if I knew the truth. It might have been an accident . . . a moment of carelessness.' She shrugged.

'I'll get to the bottom of it.'

She framed his face with her hands and looked at him earnestly. 'Be vigilant and walk with care, Harry, for I fear this man could be dangerous.'

Four

'Ah good, you're ready.' Isabella hurried into her sister's room. 'You do look beautiful in that shade of green.'

Angelina started to fidget with the fasteners on her jacket.

'Come, Angel, we must not keep the gentleman waiting and the horses will be getting restive.' She hustled her sister along, not giving her a chance to voice her fears.

Harry was impatiently slapping his gloves against his leg when they entered the room.

'I hope we have not kept you waiting too long, Your Grace?' Isabella enquired.

He bowed. 'I have been here only a few minutes

and it is no hardship to wait for such charming companions.'

Isabella fought back an impish grin. Liar, she thought. You would rather be with your regiment then here.

Just as they were turning to leave, the door burst open and Charlotte ran in. 'Oh, Bella, what colour ribbon did you say you wanted? I'm going shopping . . .' She skidded to a halt when she saw that her sisters were not alone and sketched a hasty curtsy. 'I beg your pardon, Your Grace.'

Isabella was relieved to see his mouth twitch at the corners. 'I would like a pale lemon, if you can get it, Lotte.'

Charlotte nodded and went to leave the room.

'A moment.' Isabella stopped her. 'Who is to accompany you?'

'Agnes.'

'And you are just going to the haberdashery.'

Charlotte looked down at the carpet and ran the toe of her shoe along one of the designs.

When she would not meet her eyes, she knew the girl was planning something, and she had a good idea what it was. 'You are not to go to the fair without proper protection, Charlotte.'

'Oh, Bella, how is it that you always seem to know what I am going to do? I wanted to see the gypsies and—'

'Your sister is quite right, young lady,' said the voice of authority. 'If you can curb your enthusiasm for one more day, I shall escort you all to the fair, and I'm sure Captain Atterton and Mr Sherfield will join us. You shall bring your maid and my man Carter will come with us. We should all be safe then.'

'Oh, sir.' Charlotte danced up and down. 'That is kind of you.'

A gentle smile softened his harsh expression, but it was quickly gone. 'Your sister has not yet agreed to the outing.' He looked at Isabella enquiringly.

'Oh, Bella . . . please!'

Isabella saw her sister's animated face and couldn't refuse. 'We would like that very much.'

'Tomorrow then,' he said briskly. 'Now we mustn't waste any more of this beautiful weather.'

It was a perfect afternoon and the park was crowded. Isabella dropped back so that His Grace could give her sister his whole attention. Angelina was still far too timid in his presence and cast anxious glances back from time to time. She smiled encouragingly at her, but it was an effort, for she felt unusually out of sorts and would have loved to leave the bridle path for a good hard gallop across the park, but it was not allowed. And anyway, she was here to chaperone her sister. That thought made her grip the reins tightly and her horse started to prance nervously. Before she had him under control again, strong hands released her grip and the animal was quickly soothed.

'Gently, Miss Winslow. He has a soft mouth, I think.' He glared at her accusingly.

'I'm well aware of that,' she snapped angrily. Whether her bad humour was because of him or her own thoughtless actions, she was not too sure. She dropped her gaze and started to stroke the horse's neck, asking forgiveness in a soft voice, then she looked at the glowering man beside her. 'I was momentarily distracted.'

He took hold of the reins and urged her forward. 'I would prefer you to ride with us, and not so far back that we cannot see you.'

She bristled at his tone. 'I am only the chaperone. That is my place!'

'Your place,' he leant forward until he was only inches from her face, 'is where I tell you to be.'

'I am not one of your soldiers that you can order around, Major Sterling.'

There was a slight pause as she clenched her teeth and awaited the outburst, but it didn't come. Instead he tipped back his head and laughed. She was sure her heart stopped beating for a moment. The transformation was astonishing: gone was the serious, harsh-looking expression, and in its place was the most captivating man she had ever come across. She was looking at him in awe when realisation hit her – he was probably going to be her brother-in-law!

She urged her horse into a trot. She must not let herself be attracted to him. It would be extremely foolish and would cause the utmost pain – not only to her sister, but to herself.

'Stop champing at the bit, Miss Winslow.' He spoke softly and was still obviously amused.

She gave him a glare that would have withered a lesser man. How she endured the rest of the ride she didn't know, for her thoughts were in turmoil. However, she couldn't help noticing that he was trying very hard to put Angelina at her ease. He was charming, amusing and polite, and for some strange reason, she fumed all the more.

It was a relief to get back home, but Angelina was very subdued and went straight to her room. There was a glint of tears in her sister's eyes and Isabella sighed – things were not going well.

'Did you enjoy the ride?' her mother asked, a gentle smile on her still-beautiful face.

'I fear that Angel is not at ease in his company, but he made a great effort today and was the perfect gentleman towards her. If he has decided to make her his wife, he will spare no effort to make her like him, I'm sure.'

'Yes, you are right, my dear, as usual. He is a very imposing man with a strong character, but once she gets to know him . . .'

Isabella nodded. 'Mother? Why was I asked to act

as chaperone? Aunt Dorothea usually takes on that task.'

'Your aunt has gone to stay with her son and his wife in Yorkshire. Her daughter-in-law is with child and not in the best of health. It was not our idea, Bella. We would not have cast you in such a demeaning role, but the Duchess particularly asked that you chaperone your sister.'

'But why?' She couldn't hide her astonishment.

'We are not sure, but Her Grace is aware that Angelina is of a timid nature, and she probably believed that she would be more at ease if you were with her. You are such a sensible girl,' she added fondly. Now, I must go and see about arrangements for dinner.'

As Isabella watched her mother leave the room, she was open mouthed in amazement. A sensible girl. Great heavens, was that how people, even her own family, were beginning to view her? When had she changed from being unconventional, outspoken – a hoyden in fact? Sensible. She never thought to hear herself described in that manner.

She turned and looked out of the window, not seeing the well-manicured lawns and gardens. It was time she took stock of her life, she ought to get married. The thought of remaining unwed had suddenly lost its appeal, but who could fill the role of husband to her. She chewed her bottom lip thoughtfully. Captain Atterton – he was handsome and fun to be with. She didn't love him, of course, but they might deal well together. She raced up the stairs in a most unladylike fashion. She was not going to sink into the dismals – life was too much fun and this strange attraction she felt for the Duke would soon fade. Perhaps it was time to try out this new image. She laughed out loud. It might be amusing trying to be sensible.

When Harry arrived home Dexter and Timothy were there drinking tea with his grandmother.

'Did you enjoy your ride?' his grandmother asked, looking at him speculatively.

He sighed wearily. 'It was pleasant enough. The weather was good.'

'Have you made arrangements to see the girl again?'

'As a matter of fact, I have.' He turned to his friends. 'I have committed you both to an outing tomorrow. I hope you will be agreeable?'

They nodded. 'Where are we going?' Timothy asked eagerly.

'I have promised the Winslow girls that we will take them to the fair. Charlotte was about to sneak off there with only her maid in attendance.'

'She is young and will learn prudence, I'm sure.' The Duchess looked pointedly at the three men. 'You will keep a sharp eye on her, won't you?'

Harry snorted. 'It's the eldest one who needs watching.'

'And why is that?' his grandmother asked, her expression one of bland interest.

'She is wilful, opinionated and has a sharp tongue.'

'So, you were rude to her.'

'I was not!' Harry exclaimed indignantly. 'I called her to order and she flew into the boughs.'

His grandmother could not contain her amusement. 'If you called her to order then I'm sure she had good reason to be overset. You are not in the army now, Harry.'

'That is what she said.'

His companions burst into laughter and Harry shook his head, a wry smile on his face. 'She is too outspoken, and any man who thinks to take her on will have to be brave indeed.'

His grandmother rose to her feet. 'I must get ready for dinner. You will all be staying?' She walked out of the room, taking their acceptance for granted.

'I don't know why she bothers to phrase that as a question when all the time she's giving an order,' Dexter remarked.

Later that evening Harry and Dexter found themselves alone. 'Now we can talk,' Harry said, swirling the brandy around the glass. 'What have you managed to find out about this traitor?'

'Not much at the moment. I have been making discreet enquiries about some of those on the list my contact gave me, but so far . . .' Dexter shrugged.

'Is Garston mentioned?'

His friend took the paper from his pocket and looked at it. 'No. Does he have some connection with the War Office?'

'Don't think so, but I know Robert hated him, and bought the Orchards to stop him from obtaining them. It also appears that Garston has been losing heavily at the tables.' Harry handed his friend the notes. 'Robert also bought these and if I called them in, he would be in dire straits.'

Dexter whistled through his teeth. 'It's time we tried our hand at the gambling clubs ourselves, Harry. It could be interesting to see who's in need of money.'

'I was going to suggest the same thing. Shall we start tomorrow night?'

'After we've seen the ladies safely home, eh?'

'That should be an interesting outing.'

'What time tomorrow, Harry?'

'Come early and we can hold a strategy meeting to decide how to deal with the Winslow girls.'

It was a perfect day. The sky was clear, except for a few wispy clouds, and there was enough breeze to temper the heat. The girls were in high spirits and even Angelina seemed to have lost some of her reserve in the excitement. They all looked delightful in their simple dresses of sprigged muslin. The men had dressed down somewhat, forsaking their fashionable clothes for the day, hoping they would be able to mingle with the crowds without bringing undue attention to their little party.

They had brought two carriages with them and these were to be left in a field nearby with the grooms in attendance. Before they started to walk towards the fair, Harry gathered everyone around him.

'Just for today we will drop all titles.' He glanced at the girls. 'We will call you by your given names and you will address us as – Harry, Dexter and Tim.'

Charlotte giggled and Harry shot her a stern look.

'This is a serious matter, young lady. We don't wish to become the target for pickpockets. It is prudent that we appear to be ordinary people enjoying a day out.'

'Yes, Harry,' Charlotte said seriously. Then she ruined her submissive attitude by looking down at her feet and giggling again.

Isabella groaned inwardly. His Grace was not blessed with an abundance of patience.

'Would you like to tell us what is amusing you?' he asked.

Charlotte looked around the group, a smile quivering on her lips. 'Well, even if you were in rags I don't think it possible for any of you to blend into the crowd.'

Isabella examined the men critically. 'She's quite right, Harry. Although you gentlemen are not dressed as usual, your breeding cannot be disguised.'

He gave a wry smile. 'Then we shall have to be extra vigilant, don't you think? Carter will follow behind with Agnes and they will keep a sharp lookout for trouble. Now, shall we go?' he said, holding his arm out for Angelina and looking in quite good humour.

The fair was busy and noisy. The crowds jostled and pushed their way around and Isabella was grateful for the strong presence of their escorts. However, they soon became oblivious to the crush as the excitement of the occasion took over.

'Don't wander off,' Harry called as Charlotte headed for an interesting stall.

'I wanted to see what that man is doing.' She pointed to her left.

'Ah,' Dexter said. 'Find the lady, but don't bet on it for you will not win.'

'Why did you say it was impossible to win?' Charlotte asked. 'See, that man has just won something and I'm sure I could. If you watch the thimbles carefully it's easy to remember which one the pea is under.'

'No, Charlotte,' Timothy explained patiently, 'that man was an accomplice. He is working with the gypsy and every so often he comes along and seems to win, and that encourages others to try.'

'Oh, I see. At least, I think I do. But why is it that no one else can win?'

'Because the man palms the pea so that all the

thimbles are empty, then he places it back under one you haven't chosen.'

'Ooh, he must be very clever. I have been watching with great care and have not noticed. But is it not dishonest?' she asked, edging closer to the gypsy.

The men led her away before she could reprimand him for cheating.

'Oh, look,' Angelina cried. 'May we roll pennies?'

Isabella joined her sisters at the stall and they became absorbed with the game, laughing and clapping their hands as they tried to win something, when Isabella felt strong hands grip her cruelly, then she heard Charlotte and Angelina cry out in fear.

Before she could see what was happening, the grip on her loosened and someone grunted, then she was swept into a firm embrace. She fought like a wild cat. 'My sisters!' she cried desperately.

The man holding her was far too strong, but that didn't stop her from kicking, biting and using any means available to free herself. She ground her heel into his toe and had the satisfaction of hearing him grunt with pain.

'Hell fire, woman, stop that, will you?'

Her struggles ceased as she recognised the voice, and she looked up cautiously. Harry had her locked in his arms, protecting and shielding her from the crowd. An anxious glance at her sisters and she was assured that they were safe. Dexter had Angelina and Timothy was comforting Charlotte.

'What happened?' She asked breathlessly, but Harry wasn't looking at her. His gaze was sweeping the area and came to rest on something in the distance.

'Carter!' he snapped.

His man nodded and took off, moving swiftly through the crowds. Harry was still holding her, cradling her head with one of his hands in a protective gesture, and to be truthful, she found this very pleasurable, but she needed to be free – needed to find out what was going on. When further struggle did not bring about her release, she gave him a sharp thump on the chest to gain his attention.

He looked down at her, a thoughtful expression on his face, then he stood back, releasing her and rubbing his chest. 'Have you had instruction in the noble art, Miss Winslow?'

'Will you please tell me what has happened?' she asked.

'Oh, just some ruffians who got too close,' he said with a disinterested air. 'Nothing to worry about.'

'If it was such a trifling thing then why has your man gone after someone?' She held her hand up. 'And don't try to tell me otherwise, I am not a fool.'

'He has gone to see they leave the area,' he said smoothly.

She didn't believe him. Although details of the incident were hazy, there was a lingering impression in her mind that it had not been a chance encounter. There had been three or four men and robbery was not what they had been about. For some unaccountable reason, Isabella had the impression that she and her sisters had been in danger. But why?

'I say,' Timothy said, rolling his eyes in relief, 'what a good thing you girls didn't have anything of value on you. Those men came out of nowhere.'

That was just the thing, Isabella thought. Their father had admonished them not to wear jewellery, so what had those men been after. She looked at Harry's impassive expression and sighed in exasperation.

'Look, Bella,' Charlotte said indignantly, as she pointed to red marks on her arm. 'I swear that two of those ruffians were trying to pull me into the crowd.'

'And I was pushed up against the stall,' Angelina said, her voice quivering slightly. 'I don't think I want to stay here longer.'

Harry gave her a gentle smile, took her arm and looked around. 'Agnes, take Miss Angelina's other arm, will you? There is a sumptuous picnic awaiting us, so we shall return to the carriages.'

'What a good idea,' Isabella said brightly, taking hold of Dexter's arm. 'I'm quite famished after all the excitement.'

There was a ripple of laughter and Isabella was relieved to see the anxious looks disappear from her sisters' faces. 'We are not going to let this silly incident spoil our day, are we?'

'Indeed not,' Charlotte answered, skipping over to Timothy and placing her hand on his arm. 'It's time for luncheon, anyway.'

'Ah, the resilience of youth,' Dexter said softly.

'Do you have any idea what happened? I would dearly like to know.' She looked up at Dexter, but his face had assumed the same expression as Harry's. They were two of a kind, she realised; no wonder they were such good friends.

He shook his head. 'Saw the ruffians jostle you and we moved in.'

'What happened to the men?'

'They ran off, after a little persuasion,' he said looking down at his bruised knuckle. 'Just a gang of pickpockets, I think.'

She sighed again. What was the use, if they thought there was something sinister going on, they were not going to say.

The grooms had seen them coming and had the blankets already laid out under the tree. The girls were unpacking the hampers when Carter arrived back. The men walked a short distance away and were talking earnestly. Isabella was unable to hear what they were saying, so she picked up the empty basket and walked towards the carriages. The fact that it brought her closer to the men had not entered her head – had it?

70

All this secrecy was infuriating.

She got as close as she dared but could only catch a few words as they floated towards her on the breeze.

'. . . think the carriage had a coat of arms on the side, but it took off before I could get a proper . . .'

Isabella put her head on to one side and listened even harder. 'Darn it, wind,' she muttered, 'keep blowing in this direction.'

'. . . sure the men were with him?'

'Yes, Major. Saw them talking to . . .'

She pursed her lips in irritation. If only she could get closer; they were discussing the incident.

'. . . get a good look, Harry? Would you recognise him again?'

Good, the wind had changed direction again.

'Oh, yes. I would know him again.'

Isabella shivered. Those few words held a lot of menace. Whoever they were talking about would do well to run for his life.

Five

Dexter sat back, looked around the elegant room and smiled. 'That was an excellent meal, Harry.'

His friend nodded. 'I inherited this club with the title. I must frequent it more often; the food is first class.'

'And the clientele.'

Harry laughed softly at his friend's wry expression and signalled for more coffee. 'It's a good place to start our search, don't you think?'

'Yes, and we have someone else to look for now. That was a rum do today, Harry. What did you make of it?'

'Not sure. The first impression was that a gang of ruffians were trying to rob the girls, but my instinct tells me otherwise. The crowd around us had stopped, their whole attention focussed on the rumpus, but when I looked up there was one man moving away very quickly. His action was out of place, and you know how we've been trained to spot the unusual. I only saw the back view of him, but I will know him again – his right shoulder was higher than the other and he held his head at a slight angle.'

'Whoever it was didn't enlist the best of help – those scoundrels ran as soon as we stepped in. There were at least four, I think?'

'Yes. Perhaps someone had recruited them in haste, taking advantage of an unexpected opportunity. After all, I don't think many people knew we would be there.'

'And Carter believes the man got into a carriage bearing a coat of arms.'

'Yes, it's a great shame he was not able to get a closer look; but I don't doubt him, he has a good eye for detail.'

'Indeed. We both have reason to be thankful for his skills.'

'Whoever instigated that attack was someone of substance.' Harry looked thoughtful.

'Who was the target? It was hard to tell in the struggle of the moment.'

Harry shook his head. 'It could have been us they were interested in.'

Dexter looked sceptical. 'Why attack the girls – they were not wearing anything of value or carrying reticules?'

'Ah, it is a mystery. We seem to be surrounded by them – it is almost as if we were still in the army. We might need to watch the Winslow girls, Dexter, in case it was more than a chance attack. Wouldn't like to see them hurt.'

'Especially as you're going to wed the charming Angelina,' Dexter teased.

'Oh, it's decided, is it?'

'Of course it is, Harry, everyone is buzzing with speculation. She would be a fine choice, but she is a tender girl and will need to be handled gently.'

He gave his friend a quizzical look. 'You doubt I am capable of that?'

'No, no,' Dexter hastened to assure him. 'But she is easily spooked, and you are a touch rough around the edges. That is why you made such an outstanding soldier.'

'I will endeavour to act with restraint.' The tone of his voice suggested he would find that exceedingly difficult. 'And what about you? You seem to be getting along famously with the eldest sister. Thinking of taking her on?'

'You know that is not possible. I have nothing to offer and I will not be branded a fortune hunter.'

Harry shook his head sadly. 'It is crazy when a man's suitability is judged by a title and wealth, and a woman by the size of her dowry. Character and affection should be the prime consideration, surely?'

'Unfortunately, it is not so.'

'Let us hope that one day society will change.'

'I doubt that it will, and that leaves people like Tim and myself in an untenable position.'

Harry stood up and rested his hand on his friend's shoulder in an understanding gesture. 'Best be on our way, Dexter. We have a long night ahead of us.'

Harry stifled a yawn. This was the third club they had visited and nothing unusual had caught their attention. Dexter, who had been walking languidly around the room with a disinterested expression on his face, came back to his side. One brow rose and his gaze swept over a table in the far corner of the room. Harry glanced across and took in the scene with a swift look.

Anyone watching the two men would have assumed they were idling away their time, rather bored. It was only their eyes that gave any indication of interest, and these they kept hooded. They had been used to working behind enemy lines and knew how to school their expressions. Their lives had often depended upon it, and they were experts.

'I say, Ranliegh.' A tall, thin man came and stood beside them. 'Don't expect to see you in a place like this. Didn't think you were a gambling man.'

Harry stirred himself. 'I am not, Pearson, but we find ourselves looking for amusement tonight.' He introduced Dexter. 'Lord Pearson, this is my friend, Captain Atterton.'

He bowed. 'Ah, I understand. You are both missing the excitement of the army, are you not?'

'You could say that. Are you playing the tables tonight?' Harry asked, changing the subject.

His lordship scowled. 'I'm looking for someone. I was foolish enough to get involved in a game three weeks ago and took someone's marker, but now he won't pay up. I didn't know at the time, but the man is not quite the thing. Got a bad reputation, don't you know?'

Harry and Dexter made suitable noises of disgust.

'You must tell us who this man is, Lord Pearson, so we can avoid sitting down with him.' Dexter's tone was casual.

'Of course, of course. Wouldn't want you to suffer the same fate. Distinguished soldiers, and all that. Not right, not right at all. His name is Garston – Lord Garston.'

Harry didn't even blink. 'Thank you, Pearson. Good of you to tell us.'

There was a pause as the men secured themselves a drink, then Harry nodded towards the table in the corner.

'Who is that in the bright green coat. He appears to be losing heavily.'

'Oh, that's young Viscount Percivale. The damned fool. Good thing his father has deep pockets. He is in the clubs most nights, and never seems to win much.'

'Don't think I know his father.'

'Yes, you do, Ranliegh. It's Stanton – an acquaintance of your father's.'

'Good Lord.' Harry took a closer look. 'The last time I saw Percy he was but a boy.'

Lord Pearson snorted. 'Still is. Never grew up. Too spoilt, you see?'

'Indeed, that does seem to be the case.' Harry took a sip of his drink and looked casually around the room. 'You have not been able to track down your quarry, then?'

'No. Could do with finding him,' Lord Pearson muttered.

'He owes you a sizeable amount then, Pearson?'

'Enough, enough. Can't afford to wait too long for the money.'

'A bet must be honoured. A man could lose his reputation if he doesn't.' Dexter's expression was suitably outraged.

'Humph. His reputation is already sullied. A few of the more select clubs are already refusing him entrance. Word soon gets around, don't you know?'

Harry nodded and said casually, 'I'll buy Garston's gambling slip from you if you are in needs of funds, Pearson?'

The man turned and looked at him in amazement. 'I say, Ranliegh, would you? That's damned decent of you. I must admit I have a pressing need at the moment.'

'Call on me in the morning. I'm sure we can come to some agreement.'

They watched Lord Pearson walk away and he was almost rubbing his hands in glee.

'Stanton has connections with the War Office, Dexter.'

'I know. He's on our list.'

'Might mean nothing, of course. From what I can remember, Stanton is a mild-mannered man, but with a son addicted to gambling . . . ?' He shrugged. 'Worth looking into.'

'I agree.'

Harry stifled another yawn. 'Let's call it a night.'

They walked out of the club and took a deep breath of fresh air. It wasn't often you could do that in London, but it was a warm, clear night and the chimneys were not belching out smoke. They were also in a less crowded part of town, not far from the exclusive houses of the nobility.

A handsome cab clattered up beside them, but they waved it away and set off at a steady pace, glad of the exercise.

'Why are you interested in buying Garston's note, Harry?'

'Two reasons. Lord Pearson could be a useful source of information – there's no harm in doing him a favour, and I thought I would add it to the others my brother bought. I would like to find out what Robert was up to, and the more I have Garston in my debt, the better.'

'Hmm. Dangerous game.'

'I know.' Harry's mouth lifted in a grin and both men laughed.

They bid each other good night at Dexter's residence and Harry continued his walk. His grandmother's establishment was only fifteen minutes away and he lengthened his stride. He had great reserves of energy, and during his years in the army, had become accustomed to always being on the move.

He was deep in thought when he saw a movement out of the corner of his eye. He acted with speed, but not quickly enough, and caught a glancing blow to the side of his head. Although he was dazed, he reacted instinctively and caught hold of his assailant, then pushed the man against the wall and leaned his weight on him, thus giving himself a breathing space in which to clear his head.

'What the devil are you about, man?' he growled, using his considerable height to render the man helpless.

'Oh, my Gawd. Major Sterling.' The attacker was gasping for breath. 'Sorry sir. I didn't know it was you.'

Harry moved back a little. 'You know me?'

'Yes, Major. I was in your regiment. Dobson's the name. Corporal Dobson, as was.'

'What the hell are you doing assaulting innocent people?'

'I was desperate, Major.'

There was a warm trickle of blood running down Harry's face and he was finding it difficult to focus on the man in front of him. Although he had avoided the full force of the blow, it had still been severe enough to cause him considerable pain and he felt as if his wits had been scrambled. He swayed slightly and Dobson caught hold of him.

'Show me where you live, sir. I'll see you gets 'ome safely. If I'd known it was you I'd never have done it.'

The man sounded genuinely contrite, so Harry nodded, wincing with pain at the unwelcome movement. 'What did you hit me with?' he groaned.

'Wiv a piece of wood, Major. Oh, Gawd, I 'opes I ain't done you no 'arm.'

When they reached the house, Dobson propped him up against a pillar and pounded on the door.

'Not so loud. I swear the noise is tearing my head apart.'

'Beggin' your pardon, sir. I just want to see you safely indoors. That head needs looking at.'

Harry held on to the pillar for support. He was well aware of that!

The door was wrenched open by a furious Carter. 'What's all this confounded row about? You'll wake—'

Then he caught sight of his master and grabbed hold of him. 'Inside with you, sir. That's a nasty gash you have there.'

As he was being helped through the door, Harry caught hold of Dobson's arm and pulled him along with them.

'You've got some explaining to do,' he muttered through clenched teeth.

He slumped into the nearest chair and Carter hurried off, returning quickly with a bowl of water containing a repulsive-smelling something, and some clean cloths. He tolerated Carter's ministrations for a while, but as he began to feel less dazed, he pushed him away. 'Enough!'

'I've managed to stop the bleeding,' Carter informed him, 'but you're going to have a sore head and a black eye by morning.'

'Won't be the first time,' he remarked, turning to a cowering Dobson standing in the middle of the room. 'Sit down, man. I don't want to keep looking up at you,' he remarked, testily.

The man perched on the edge of an elegant chair and started to crumple his hat in his hands.

'Tell me what this is all about.'

The man recognised the authoritative voice of his major and sat to attention. 'It's like this, sir. I've not been able to get work and I've got a wife and little one.' A wistful smile touched his face. 'It's a girl – not yet three. Well she needs proper food and—'

'So, you thought you would rob to get the money?'

'I never would have done it, sir, but,' he dropped his head in shame, 'this cove comes up to me and says he'll give me a guinea if I attacks some gentleman. Don't 'ave to kill him, he says, just 'urt him a bit. Well, as I said, Major, I was at my wits end. Should 'ave known it was you,' he moaned. 'Didn't look too close.'

Harry held up his hand to stop him. 'How did you know who to assault?'

'He showed me the club you was in and told me what you was wearing.'

'Did he now?' He raised a brow at Carter who was listening intently. 'And what were you instructed to do after you had carried out your commission?'

'I was to take something from you and give it to this man. Proof, you see.'

Harry eased himself out of the chair and took an invitation card off the mantelpiece. 'Tell them you found this in my pocket.'

Dobson frowned in puzzlement. 'I don't understand, Major. Ain't you gonna hand me over to the law?'

'No. You can do something for me.' He started to sit down again.

'Anything, sir.' Dobson leapt to his feet to give Harry a helping hand. 'I'll try to find out who's after you, Major.'

'No, I don't want you to get involved. This could be dangerous. And you have your family to think about.'

'That's true, sir. Don't know how they would go on without me, though I'm not much of a provider.' His shoulders slumped in misery.

82

'I might be able to do something about that. Leave me your address.'

'You'd help me, even after what I've done to you?'

'Oh, I'll soon recover. This isn't the first time I've taken a beating.'

'No, Major, it ain't. I've seen you coming back to camp in a sorry state after some of your sorties. We all admired you and the captain. So brave . . .'

Harry waved away the man's fulsome praise, feeling embarrassed. There were many he considered much braver than him, like the poor wretches who had lost limbs or had them removed by the surgeon. He shuddered, remembering the carnage.

'When this man contacts you again,' he continued, changing the subject quickly, 'give him that card and tell him you left me in an alley – alive, but badly beaten. I will confirm the story by retiring from society for a couple of days. Word will soon get out to the perpetrator of this deed.'

'I'll do that, sir.'

'Get back to your family now. They will be worrying, I'm sure.' He reached into his pocket and handed over some coins. 'This will keep you going for a while.'

'Blimey, Major! This is a ruddy fortune and I don't deserve it.' He went to hand the money back.

'You may not, but your wife and child do.' He studied the man in front of him, angry at the position many faithful ex-soldiers found themselves in when they returned home. Where was the country's sense of gratitude, for God's sake!

'If you can find me work, Major, you won't be sorry. I'm still strong,' he added earnestly.

'I'll see what I can do. Now, go home and don't forget to spin this villain a good tale – and take his guinea.' He touched his head and grimaced. 'You carried out the instructions.'

Carter ushered the still-apologising ex-soldier from the room, then helped his master up to his chamber, undressed him and pulled back the covers.

Harry fell into bed with a groan of relief and watched as his man settled in a chair by the bed.

'No need for that, Carter. I'll be better after a good night's sleep.'

'I'm sure you will, sir, but that's a nasty knock you've taken, and I don't want you sinking into a fever while I'm not here.'

Harry closed his eyes, knowing it would be useless to argue.

'Someone means you harm, sir. Who have you upset?'

Harry opened one eye. 'No one, yet.'

'Oh, I think you have, sir.'

Six

Isabella tapped her foot in irritation. What was taking him so long?

'Perhaps we should not have come so early, Miss?' Agnes remarked nervously.

'Nonsense! It is past ten o'clock. Soldiers are accustomed to rising early and I cannot imagine His Grace has got out of the habit, just yet.'

At that moment a door opened and Carter walked towards her. 'His Grace will see you now, Miss Winslow. If you would like to follow me?'

'At last!'

He showed her into a room which was obviously a study. It was the kind of room she would normally have explored with excitement, but not today – today she was determined to get some answers.

At first she didn't see him – he was standing by the window, and the light streaming through obscured all but his outline. He looked even larger and she could almost feel his amber eyes drilling into her. She lifted her head defiantly – she would not allow him to intimidate her.

'I'm afraid you are too early for a visit with my grandmother. She does not appear until noon.' He moved away from the window as he spoke.

'I have come to see you, Your Grace.'

'In that case you had better sit down, Miss Winslow.'

'I prefer to stand. I _am_ here because you would not talk to me yesterday, and I wish to know what happened at the fair.'

'You know as much as I do.'

'Oh, come.' She bristled. 'I will not be put off with a few placating words. Your man discovered something, and I demand to know what it was.'

'Demand!' His voice was harsh and he stepped towards her. 'I think not.'

'I want an explan . . .' Her words tailed off as he moved to hold on to the back of a chair and the other side of his head came into view. She gasped.

'You have been injured. Sit down, for heaven's sake!'

'I cannot sit unless you do, Miss Winslow,' he ground out.

'Oh, do stop trying to be a gentleman.' She pushed him into a chair. 'Let me have a look at your head.' She examined the wound very carefully. 'It appears to be clean. Have you had a physician examine it?'

'No. Carter is quite capable of looking after me. Now,' he brushed her hand away impatiently, 'please be good enough to sit down.'

She did as ordered. His tone indicated that he would brook no nonsense. 'What happened?'

'I was attacked on my way home, last night.'

The door opened and Carter looked in. 'The captain to see you, sir.'

'What's this all about, Harry?' Dexter strode into the room, looked at his friend and frowned. 'Hell, that is quite a knock. Do you know who did it?'

'Only a suspicion at the moment. I'll tell you about it later.' He looked across at Isabella. 'Miss Winslow was just leaving.'

'No, I'm not!'

Dexter spun round to face her. 'Oh, Miss Winslow, I was not aware you were here. I do beg your pardon for not greeting you when I entered.'

'You don't need to apologise, Captain Atterton. I understand that your attention was focused on His Grace.' She settled back in the chair. 'I shall not leave until I hear the whole story.'

'This is none of your business, Miss Winslow.' Harry started to stand up, grimaced and sat down again.

'Of course it is. First, we had that disagreeable incident at the fair, and then you are attacked on the same day. Something is going on and I want to know what it is, so the sooner you talk to me, the sooner you shall be rid of me.' She settled back in the chair and folded her arms.

Harry muttered something very uncomplimentary.

'I fear nothing will move her, Harry. You might as well tell us the story.'

Recognising the stubborn tilt of her head, he started to relate the events of the night before. There was silence when he came to a halt.

Isabella was by then sitting on the edge of her chair, eyes gleaming with interest. 'Someone wishes you harm. Do you know who it is?'

Harry shook his head and wished he hadn't. 'I do not, Miss Winslow.'

'Oh, do stop calling me that. My name is Isabella or Bella, I answer to either.' This was too exciting to bother with the social niceties. 'Perhaps I can help. We meet a great many people in the social round—'

'You will do no such thing!' He did stand up this time and towered over her, feet planted apart, his stance threatening.

She didn't flinch. 'If you are trying to frighten me then you are wasting your time. I have to listen to a great deal of mindless chatter, but the ladies often know what is going on. Some of the gossip can be very enlightening.' She looked up imploringly.

'Miss Winslow—'

'Bella.'

He sighed wearily and sat down again. 'Isabella—'

'If anyone has anything against you,' she interrupted, 'I might be able to find out who it is. Nothing much gets past the ladies.'

'Harry.' Dexter intervened for the first time. 'It might be useful.'

He shook his head again. Damn, he must stop doing that. It felt as if a whole cavalry regiment was charging through his skull.

'You should get a physician to examine you,' she remarked as the colour washed out of his face. Then she stood up and poured him a large brandy. 'I know it is early in the day for strong drink, but I feel you have need of this.'

He took it without a murmur and downed the liquid in one gulp. She was right, he did need it; he was not up to dealing with this troublesome woman today. Why was he arguing with her? She would do whatever she wanted to.

'Very well. You may listen to the gossip, but that is all. If you involve yourself in any other way, you will have me to deal with.' He glared at her fiercely. 'Is that understood?'

'Perfectly.' She sketched a quick curtsy, and with a look of eager anticipation on her face, she left the room.

'Determined little thing, isn't she?' But she's right, Harry. She is in a position to hear things that would never be said in our presence.'

'I know, Dexter, but I don't trust her – she has a reckless nature. Did you see her face? A mystery excites her.'

'Let us see how she gets on. She might well forget all about it after a while.'

Harry snorted in disgust. 'We can only hope so. We have enough problems without that young lady getting in our way.'

'At least she is only going to see if she can glean anything about your attacker. She knows nothing about our other investigation.'

'And heaven be praised for that!'

'Lord Pearson to see you, sir,' Carter announced.

His lordship bustled into the room. 'Came as you said, Ranliegh, but this is a dashed unearthly hour to be about. Don't usually open my eyes until mid-afternoon, you know.'

'I apologize if I have inconvenienced you, Pearson. Can't seem to lose the habit of waking with the birds.'

'Of course not. Quite understand. Wasn't complaining, you know.'

Harry managed to stretch his lips into a smile. 'Did you bring the gambling note with you?'

'I have it here.' He held it out and stopped suddenly. 'I say, Ranliegh, what has happened to your head?'

'An overzealous thief. Nothing to be concerned about.'

'Did you catch him?'

'I'm afraid not,' Harry lied.

'Pity, pity. Not safe to walk around these days. Ought to round up the ruffians and put them in the army. That would cure them, eh?'

'Indeed.' Harry turned away to hide his anger. People like Pearson did not have any idea what it was like. They were cocooned in their own privileged world, without a thought for the masses. For many people it was a constant struggle to put food on the table and keep a roof over their heads, and most of the poor beggars were ex-soldiers.

He schooled his features into a bland expression and turned back, taking the paper from Pearson's hand. 'The usual terms?'

Pearson nodded eagerly. 'This is damned decent of you, Ranliegh.'

'Not at all, Pearson.' He waved the man's thanks away. 'Pleased to be able to help. Now the business is settled would you like a drink?'

'Bit early in the day, don't you think?'

'Some tea, then?' Harry persisted.

'No, no . . . er, perhaps a small brandy.'

Dexter hid a smile. Lord Pearson was obviously anxious to get away now he had his money, but he was too polite to refuse Harry's offer of hospitality.

'You'll join us, Dexter?' his friend asked.

He nodded and the three of them settled down.

'We have been out of society for some time, Pearson. Lost touch with things, you know.' He mimicked Pearson's way of talking, but the man in question did not detect the note of derision in Harry's voice.

Dexter nearly choked on a sip of the fiery liquid.

'Don't doubt it. Been away fighting that dreadful man, Napoleon, isn't it? Brave of you both. Very brave.'

'Just doing our duty, you know, Lord Pearson.' Dexter joined in the game.

'Indeed, indeed. Damned fortunate to have people like you. Couldn't do it myself, you know.' He gave a dramatic shudder and downed his drink.

'Would appreciate it if you'd give us all the news, Pearson. Wouldn't want to make any faux pas when we meet people.'

'Ah, yes, indeed. That would be most unfortunate. See your point.'

The next hour was one of the most entertaining the friends had experienced for some time. Once Lord Pearson was in full flow, they never had to say a word – a small gesture or shocked expression was quite sufficient to keep the man talking. Most of the information was useless to them but, now and again, there was something of interest.

His lordship finally stopped, looked at the clock

and stood up. 'Must be on my way, Ranliegh. Most pleasant morning, most pleasant.'

When their visitor had left, Harry walked over to the desk and spread the gambling notes across the table. Dexter whistled softly through his teeth. 'That's a tidy sum. What do you intend to do?'

'Nothing, at the moment. First, I want to find out what Robert was about.'

'You take care, my friend. This man Garston could be desperate.'

Harry's hand hovered near the injury again.

'Do you think he was responsible for the attack on you?'

'It is a possibility. Perhaps he was trying to give me a message: think twice about calling in those debts? Trying to frighten me, perhaps?'

'Humph. Then he is wasting his time.'

They grinned at each other, knowing that any threat to either of them would have the opposite effect.

At that moment, Carter came into the room again. 'Dodson is at the rear door, sir.'

'Send him in. He might have something to report.'

Dobson hurried in his face clouded with concern. 'Sorry to bother you so soon, Major, but I've been that worried I couldn't sleep. A man gets desperate when he can't feed his own, but I should never 'ave done this terrible thing.'

Harry held up his hand to stop his outpouring of

remorse. 'Please do not concern yourself. As you can see I am alive and the injury will soon heal. Now, do you have any news?'

'Yes, sir. The man who hired me came this morning – before dawn. Couldn't wait to find out if I'd hurt you.' He shuffled uncomfortably and looked at his boots, giving one a quick polish on the leg of his breeches. 'Told 'im I'd hurt you bad, sir. Which was only the truth.'

'Did you find out his name?'

He nodded eagerly. 'Weston, sir. He became quite talkative after I'd told him the story and given 'im the invitation card, and I also had some blood on my clothes, so that got him quite excited. Said I'd done a good job, but he wouldn't tell me who he was working for.'

'Pity. But it was most unlikely he would divulge the name of his employer.'

'I did try, sir, but I didn't want to put my wife and little girl in danger 'cos they mean the world to me.'

'You did right not to press him, Dobson. Did you get paid?'

He held some coins out. 'Gave me more than we agreed, he was that pleased. Can't keep it, though, Major. Not after what I've done to you.'

'Nonsense, man, you need that money.'

The man shuffled the coins through his fingers, then slipped them back into his pocket. 'Thank you, Major. You're a real gentleman.'

Harry ignored the compliment. 'Keep in touch, but don't take any chances. The captain and I will take care of everything.'

'I won't never do nothing like this again, sir, I promise.'

'I know you won't.' Harry patted the man on the back in a friendly fashion and saw him out of the room.

When they were alone again, the two men sat quietly for a while, lost in thought.

'Would you like me to go, Harry? You look exhausted.'

'No. Please stay a while longer. Grandmother will be appearing soon. She will be disappointed to have missed you, and,' he gave a wry grin, 'I have yet to explain about last night's incident. She is, quite naturally, worrying about my safety. If anything happens to me before I produce a male heir then the family line comes to an end. I am no longer in the army, but my life is becoming fraught with danger, and that will not please her.'

'And you think my being here will temper her tirade?'

Harry looked at his friend quizzically. 'We both know her better than that!'

The door opened and the Duchess sailed in. 'Harry, I hear you have been injured. Why did you not inform me immediately?'

'There was no need, Grandmother, it is but a bump.'

'Good morning, Dexter. Are you involved in these unsavoury goings-on?'

She didn't give him a chance to speak. 'Of course you are. Don't know why I ask these silly questions. Must be due to my great age.'

Harry choked back a shout of laughter. She might be two-and-eighty, but her mental faculties were sharper than any twenty-year-old.

'Let me have a look at you,' she demanded. 'Sit down, Harry. How can I see when you are towering above me like that? You are a monster, just like your grandfather.'

Harry watched the wistful look creep into her eyes, as it always did when she spoke about her late husband. He had been dead for ten years, but her love for him had not diminished.

She pushed him into a chair. 'It's a good thing you have a hard head – someone was serious when they hit you.'

Her manner was brisk, but he wasn't fooled. 'I'm quite all right.'

'That's as may be, but I am convinced that it is not safe to let you out of the house, or you Dexter.' She turned her gaze accusingly on to the other man who was trying hard to merge into the background. 'You are as bad as each other. And where were you, might I ask? Or are you injured as well?'

'I wasn't with Harry, ma'am. It happened after we parted company.'

'You had better tell me all about it.' She settled comfortably in her favourite chair. 'And do not leave anything out, I want the whole story. You don't have to protect my sensibilities; I am too old to be shocked.'

She listened intently as Harry and Dexter ran through the events of last evening. When they had finished, she sat in silence for several minutes. Then she lifted her head. 'It's that blasted man, Garston, is it not?'

'It appears the likely answer, Grandmother.'

'And you say you have bought another of his gambling notes?'

Harry nodded.

'I'm not sure that was wise. He must know you could take his estate from him if you had a mind to.'

'Yes, I could. However, at the moment I don't intend to take any action. If he did have anything to do with Robert's death, then I want some evidence before I confront him.'

She reached out and took hold of his hand. 'If you do unearth anything suspicious, I want your promise that you will let the authorities take care of it.'

'I promise.'

'And you, Dexter, I want your word as well. You have always been like one of the family and I do not

97

want you taking chances, either.'

'We will not do anything foolhardy – we are too well trained for that,' he added, smiling at her affectionately.'

'Well, let us hope so. Although you are no longer in the army, I fear that you are still behind enemy lines. Do not become careless.'

Her lecture finished, she started to get out of the chair. Both men jumped up to help her, but she shook them off.'

'There is no need to treat me like an invalid. I am still able to get myself in and out of a chair.'

When she left the room, they sank back with a sigh of relief.

'What a morning, Dexter! Thank goodness it is over.'

But it wasn't.

She quickly returned. 'I have decided to visit Ranliegh for a few weeks. I feel the need to get out of town for a while. You will make all the arrangements, Harry.' It was an order.

'When do you want to leave?' he asked mildly, not at all surprised by the sudden announcement. Once she made a decision, she expected it to be acted upon immediately, and without question.

'Tomorrow.' Then she looked at him and hesitated. 'No, the day after. You do not look in a fit state to make the journey.'

'Thank you. I will appreciate a day to get my strength back.'

'I will never see the day when you are weak. You are built like that massive war horse of yours.'

Harry controlled a grin. She really was outrageous.

'You will come too, Dexter, and that nice cousin of yours.'

'He is already in Kent, Grandmother.'

'Oh, good, how convenient.' She started to leave and then stopped again. 'I shall invite the Winslow family to stay with us and we will give a ball.'

'A ball,' he croaked.

'Yes. Haven't had one of those for years. It will be quite diverting.'

After the door had closed, there was silence for a moment. Dexter took one look at his friend's dark scowl and roared with laughter.

'What's so damned funny?' he wanted to know.

Dexter tried to compose himself. 'You are not going to be able to get away from the Winslow girls now.'

Harry's expression changed from a scowl to outright fury. 'Dammit, I am not ready for marriage, and especially to a girl who has a fit of the vapours whenever she sees me!'

'You don't have a choice. You are dragging your heels; your grandmother knows it and is afraid you will slip your leash. By putting you in the same house as Angelina you will have to stay and court her.' He collapsed into another fit of laughter. 'Oh Lord, but she is priceless.'

'I know.' A reluctant smile touched Harry's face, his anger disappearing as quickly as it had erupted, 'and it is a good thing I love her so much, because her constant matchmaking is enough to drive me back into the army. But she is right, I must marry, there is no avoiding it.'

'Well what is stopping you? Angelina is beautiful and you already have her father's blessing.'

'As I have already pointed out, the girl is terrified of me.' He massaged to back of his neck, trying to ease the tension. 'Can you imagine what a wedding night we would have. Miss Angelina cowering in the bed, clutching the bedclothes to her and me trying to have my wicked way with her.'

Dexter started to laugh.

'I fail to see the amusement in the situation.' He looked stern, except for a slight twitch at the corner of his mouth. 'I have never forced myself on a woman in my life, it does not appeal. And when I do wed I would like it to be with someone who will not flinch every time I touch her. How else am I to beget an heir?'

'I do understand the difficult position you are in, Harry, but give her time.'

'She is too timid. I feel grandmother has made an unwise choice.'

She would not wish you to be unhappy, so I am

sure she has taken great care with her choice of wife for you.'

Harry sighed gustily. 'I know, I know.'

'The ball at Ranliegh will give you a chance to get to know her better.'

He looked at his fried suspiciously. 'You are very eager to see me leg-shackled.'

'It is your duty, my friend.'

'A very onerous duty.' Harry scowled and walked out of the room, muttering, 'I'm going back to bed, I must get rid of this bloody headache.'

Seven

'Good morning, Mama.' Isabella bounced into the breakfast room. 'You are about early today.'

'Yes, dear. I am making some calls this morning.'

'Who are you going to see?' she asked casually, helping herself to a plateful of kidneys, bacon and scrambled egg.

Her mother shuddered delicately. 'I don't know how you can eat like that first thing in the morning.'

'But it is almost half past ten and I am starving. I have been riding in the park, there are so few people around before breakfast.'

Lady Winslow looked horrified. 'I cannot understand this habit you have of rising with the sun.

Most ladies would be ashamed to admit to such a thing.'

'I have constantly been told that I am not like most ladies,' she said with amusement.

'That is true, my dear. One does wonder where you get all this energy from.'

Isabella smiled affectionately at her mother who could never understand her vitality and restlessness. 'Who did you say you were visiting?'

'The Greenwood sisters and Lady Sutherland.'

'May I come with you?'

'But . . . but,' her mother stuttered in astonishment, 'they are the biggest gossips in town, and you have always refused to set foot in their establishments.'

'I have decided to try and be more sociable and mend my ways.' How she kept a straight face after that announcement, she did not know.

Her mother's expression said that she doubted her daughter could reform. However, she smiled. 'I shall be delighted to have you accompany me.'

Isabella emptied her plate and went back for more. She was going to need extra strength to survive these visits, but however distasteful she found them, she was determined to help His Grace. A ripple of anticipation ran through her – this was all very exciting.

She was just debating whether she could manage another piece of toast when her sisters arrived at the breakfast table.

'Good morning, my dears. I trust you slept well?'

'Yes, thank you, Mama,' they answered in unison.

'Angelina, your father has had a message from the Duke of Ranliegh, informing him that he is incapacitated and will not call for a day or two.'

'I'm sorry to hear that, Mama,' she remarked politely, but did not successfully hide the look of relief that swept across her face.

'What is the matter with him?' Charlotte wanted to know.

Their mother shook her head sadly. 'A most regrettable incident. I understand he was attacked by a thief and sustained a head injury.'

Angelina's expression immediately changed to one of concern. She might not want to marry him, but her gentle heart would not wish to see him harmed. 'I hope he is not badly hurt?'

'No, my dear.' She looked at her daughter fondly. 'You must not worry. He is a strong man and will soon be well again.'

Isabella kept quiet. No one knew she had visited his home, except Agnes, and she could be trusted to keep a secret. It was not the thing for a single lady to call on a gentleman, but then, when had she ever shown a proper regard for convention? It was only when she realised that she had been so enthralled by accounts of the attack upon him, that she had quite forgotten the purpose of her visit – to find out who those ruffians were at the fair.

'What an eventful time we are having!' exclaimed Charlotte. 'First we are assaulted and then someone attacks the Duke. Do you think he was the one those men were after?'

'I think that might have been the case,' their mother agreed. 'Perhaps they were just making sure that you all stayed out of the way. After all, I cannot conceive of anyone wanting to harm any of you.'

Isabella was about to protest that that did not make sense but held her peace. If her mother felt relieved by believing that her daughters had not been the targets, then it was best to let her think that way. However, Isabella was not convinced. There was something decidedly odd going on, and she was determined to get to the bottom of it.

'Do you have any plans for today?' Lady Winslow asked Angelina and Charlotte. 'I'm paying some visits this morning. You may accompany me, if you wish.'

Both girls shook their heads.

'We are going for a walk in the park,' Charlotte told her mother. 'It is such a pleasant day. Do you want to come with us, Bella?'

'No, thank you, Angel. I'm going visiting with Mama.'

Her sisters regarded her in silent astonishment.

Isabella slowed her pace in an effort to match her mother's sedate steps. Thank heavens that was over!

She had listened to a great deal of idle gossip and had, somehow, managed to hold her tongue. It was beyond her comprehension how the ladies could spend their time in such a way, but they loved it. She had watched their faces as they had related each new piece of scandal, which, no doubt, grew in proportion with each telling.

'You behaved with great decorum this morning, Isabella.'

'Thank you, but it was most difficult to remain silent at times.'

'I know, my dear. I saw you struggling, but you managed very well. I also find some of the gossip distasteful, but I try to be sociable for your father's sake.' She smiled at her daughter. 'One has to make an effort at times. Unfortunately, we cannot always do the things that please us.'

'I do understand that.'

'You are a good girl.' Her mother sighed. 'I do wish we could find you a suitable husband. I am not happy about Angelina becoming betrothed before you, but your father appears set on the alliance. The Duke of Ranliegh is a fine man and I would be honoured to have him as my son-in-law, but Angelina's reaction to him is of concern to me.'

'I don't think you should worry. He is treating her with gentleness, and I am sure he will bring her around.'

'I expect you have the right of it, and I am being silly, but I do so want all my children to be happy. I have been blessed with a congenial marriage and want the same for all of you.'

When they reached home, Sir George was waiting for them. 'Ah, there you are. Come into the drawing room, I have some news.'

Angelina and Charlotte were already there, and Sir George took his customary position by the fireplace.

'The Duchess is retiring to Ranliegh for a few weeks and we have been invited to join her there.' He looked at his daughters, an indulgent expression on his face. 'I understand there is to be a Grand Ball, so I expect you will need new dresses.'

'How exciting!' Charlotte was on her feet, bubbling with excitement. 'When do we leave, Papa?'

'In four days.'

'Come girls, there is much to do.' Their mother urged them from the room. 'We must summon the dressmaker at once.'

Harry was writing a long list of instructions to his lawyer when his grandmother entered the study.

'Good morning, Harry. How is your head?'

He stood up and kissed the proffered cheek. 'Much better, thank heavens.'

'I am relieved to hear it. You will be well enough to travel tomorrow?'

'I shall.'

'Dexter will accompany us, I hope?'

He gave her a wry smile. 'Are you still concerned for my safety?'

'Of course I am, and I'm hoping to keep you out of danger at Ranliegh.'

'Ah. I guessed that was behind this sudden need to go to the country. However, I am not going to be attacked again, I have taken certain steps—'

'Good, good.' She did not wait for him to finish. 'Knew you would come up with a solution. I wish to make an early start in the morning. Are all the arrangements in hand?'

'Everything is ready.'

'I am quite looking forward to this, Harry. It will be a pleasure to have the Winslow family staying with us. They are a charming family, don't you agree?'

He was not fooled by the innocent expression on her face.

'They are most agreeable,' he told her. He felt like adding all but one. However, he bit the words back.

She gave him a satisfied smile and walked away.

His sigh was heartfelt as he watched her leave the room. It was useless dragging his heels; it was time he faced the inevitable. A lot of men wouldn't hesitate if they had such a docile and charming woman offered to them as a wife. He couldn't understand his reluctance – after all it was saving him from the distasteful duty of doing the rounds. If only he felt some stirring of emotion for her, but she left him quite unmoved. Still, perhaps things would change as they became better acquainted.

'The captain to see you, sir.' Carter held the door open for Dexter.

'You look very industrious this morning, Harry.'

'I'm laying out a plan of action to see if I can stop Garston's evil deeds.'

Dexter sat in a chair by the desk. 'So, what are your plans?'

'I have set up a rear-guard action, and when that is firmly in place I intend to approach Garston and let him know that if any harm befalls me, he will be in dire trouble. If I stay healthy, he will keep his land.'

'Capital idea, Harry. That should leave us free to find this traitor.'

'Yes, this is a distraction we can do without. Let's run through the list of suspects again.'

Dexter pulled a paper out of his pocket. 'We can discount the first two. One is too sick to leave his room and the other one died last week. The next one is Lord Stanton, but we can also forget him because he has married again. The lady is young and, it is said, he will not leave her for she is breeding already. He has had a blazing row with his son and threatened to disinherit him if he does not stop gambling.'

Harry sat back his expression thoughtful. 'Where is

Percy getting his funds from then?'

He shook his head. 'Percy might have connections we know nothing about.'

'Quite likely. It is evident that he is gambling heavily and losing most of the time, so someone is keeping him supplied with money.'

'Sir.' Carter came into the room. 'Lord Garston has returned to his estate in Kent. Left yesterday at first light.'

'That is most obliging of him.' Harry's grin spread. 'I will be able to call on him and pay my respects.'

They were all enjoying the joke when the door opened and Timothy strode in. He gave the occupants of the room a cheery greeting and turned to Harry. 'Good morning. I have come to report progress.'

'Tim!' Harry was on his feet and greeted the boy with pleasure. 'I was not expecting you to return so soon.'

'The work at the Orchards is going ahead with great speed. The workers from your own estate have almost cleared the ground, and I have employed local craftsmen for the building work. One cottage is fit for habitation and the stable block is close to completion.'

'Good Lord, Tim, you have made remarkable progress.' Harry watched Tim's animated face and was glad he had been able to do something for him. His whole demeanour had changed – he now had a purpose in life and the joy of the challenge radiated from him.

110

'Thank you, Harry. I would like to employ someone to help. As I've said, one cottage is ready, and I thought it would be a good idea if we could engage a family man.'

'Dobson?' Dexter looked at his friend expectantly.

'I was thinking the same thing. Carter!' he called.

The door opened immediately. 'Sir?'

'Go and see if you can find Dobson and bring him here. Use the back entrance and be careful, we don't want anyone to see him.'

'Have no fear, sir, I know how to blend into the surroundings. I have had the best of instructors.' He favoured Dexter and Harry with a jaunty wink and left the room.

They laughed, remembering some of the dangerous situations they had been in, and extricated from, because of Carter's talent for disguise and subterfuge.

'I think we have the very man for you.' Harry turned to Timothy. 'He's an ex-soldier and has fallen on hard times.'

Harry then proceeded to relate the whole story to Timothy. 'So, you see, he has a wife and little girl to support and he was driven by desperation.'

Timothy nodded. 'The poor man obviously needs help, but do you feel you can trust him?'

'Yes, I do, but if you are not in agreement, you only have to say.'

'I'm sure that will not be necessary. It will be good

to have a child running around the place, and Mrs Baxter would like that.'

'Good. And they are looking after you well?'

Timothy grinned. 'They could not treat royalty with more respect. She is a splendid cook and they are both hard workers. They have a great attachment to the Orchards and are relieved to be staying on.'

'We can't keep calling the place the "Orchards". I think we should rename it.' He gazed into space for a moment. 'I know! Timothy is doing all the work, so we will call it Sherfield House.'

'But, Harry!' Timothy exclaimed. 'You cannot do that, for it is your property, not mine.'

'My mind is made up. From now on it shall be known as the Sherfield estate.'

'Oh, Your Grace, I am overwhelmed.' Timothy's voice was just a whisper.

'The name is Harry.'

'Of course. I do forget when I'm excited or . . . shocked,' he added.

'Dobson, sir.' Carter had returned in less than half an hour and ushered the hesitant man into the room.

'I hope your 'ead is getting better, sir.'

'It is already well on the way to healing. Do sit down Dobson.'

He brushed the seat of his breeches before sitting on the edge of the chair.

Harry talked to him for a while and then looked

across at Timothy who nodded emphatically. When he then offered him the position at Sherfields, the man was so overwhelmed that he nearly slipped from his precarious position.

'You won't regret it, sir,' he exclaimed, looking as if all his dreams had come true. 'Oh, to take my little girl to live in the country, and after what I've done to you, it's more than I deserve, sir.'

Harry waved away his thanks. 'Just work well for Mr Sherfield. That will be reparation enough.'

So, it was arranged. The little family would travel with them on the morrow.

When the three men were alone at last, Harry massaged the back of his neck and sighed. Then hearing a carriage drawing up outside he stood and walked over to the window.

He cursed roundly. 'Miss Winslow has arrived.'

'Which one? Timothy wanted to know.

'Hah! Do you need to ask that? There is only one Miss Winslow who would call at a gentleman's home without an invitation.'

'Miss Isabella,' Dexter chuckled.

She seemed to glide into the room and Harry couldn't help noticing her graceful deportment.

'Have I come at an inopportune moment, Your Grace?' she asked, noticing the other occupants of the room.

'It has been a busy morning, Miss Winslow, but as

you are here . . .' He indicated to a chair, inviting her to sit.

She ignored the seat and walked over to him, standing on tiptoe to examine his head. 'That is much improved, but you must still take care. I hope your man is still putting a soothing balm on it?'

Her hand reached up to part his hair in order to get a better look at the injury. He brushed her away.

'Please sit down, Miss Winslow.'

She obeyed but said nothing.

'Well? You can speak freely.' Harry's patience was near to exhaustion. This young lady had the ability to annoy him, and just being in her presence made him edgy.

She leaned forward eagerly. 'I said I would try to help you and I have made a note of all the gossip being aired in the drawing rooms.'

She pulled out a small notebook and started reading from it. Certain gentlemen who have taken mistresses; ladies who were not keeping to their marriage vows; a list of those in debt; those looking for husbands or wives – his own name included – and who they were paying court to.

Isabella finally came to a halt, looked around expectantly and handed the book to Harry.

'I don't see that any of this is of much help in finding my attacker.' He tossed the book on to a small table, as if it held little interest.

She was clearly overcome with indignation. 'I will have you know that I had to endure a whole morning if mindless chatter to obtain that information.'

He couldn't hide his amusement. 'You found all that out in one morning!'

'Yes, and I don't like to spend my time in such a way. The least you can do is show a proper respect for my efforts. I am, after all, trying to help you.'

'How many visits did you make?'

'Two.'

'Two! Great heavens, in a week you would be able to fill a dozen books with useless women's chatter.' He didn't hide the derision in his voice.

Isabella stood up. 'If you are going to ridicule my efforts than I shall not stay. You are most ungracious.'

Harry was immediately sorry for his thoughtless remarks. She was upset, her cheeks were flushed and her eyes over-bright. He took hold of her hands: they were trembling – with anger, he suspected.

'I apologise. I did not intend to belittle your efforts. You have gathered much information, and I am sure some of it will prove useful when we have had time to examine it properly. Please sit down again.'

He spoke gently, earnestly. She obviously disliked indulging in gossip, which was commendable of her, but she had done it believing she was helping him. He was, indeed, being ungracious.

Her hands moved and he realised he was still

holding on to her, but she wasn't pulling away. In fact, her long delicate fingers had curled around his hands and it had a strange effect upon him. Perhaps it was because her sister always shied like a frightened filly if he so much as touched her, but this lovely, spirited girl was not afraid of him. It was a strangely arousing thought.

She slipped her hands from his and sat down. He gazed at her for a few seconds, as if puzzled, and then returned to his chair. 'Am I forgiven?' he asked softly.

She nodded and gave a little smile. 'Of course. I should have realised you would find gossip distasteful, but a great many ladies indulge in this pastime. Other people's business is considered amusement by them.'

'But you do not find it so?'

'Indeed not!' Then her face lit up with amusement. 'Some of mama's acquaintances have been taken aback by my presence in their homes.'

'But that did not stop them talking.' Harry looked at the book, filled with copious notes.

'Only momentarily, but I sat quietly, and they soon forgot I was there.'

Dexter laughed. 'That must have been quite a feat, Miss Winslow.'

'Oh, it was. I remained quiet with great difficulty as I found most of their remarks offensive and cruel.'

'I noticed I have been included in the tittle-tattle, but you noted down very little.' Harry raised a brow in query. 'Are you trying to protect me?'

'Oh, no, Your Grace.' She dismissed the suggestion. 'It is common knowledge that you are showing an interest in my sister, so you would not be discussed in a derogatory manner in our presence. Mamma would have given them a severe set-down had they tried to do so.'

He inclined his head, acknowledging the compliment. 'Then there was little chance of hearing who might be out to harm me.'

'That may be so, but I don't know anything of your . . .' she hesitated and looked at him boldly, 'private life, so I did not discount any item of gossip.'

Harry kept his features perfectly schooled, but he didn't miss the gleam in Dexter's eyes. The saucy baggage was suggesting he had a mistress.

'What about Dexter and myself?' Timothy picked up the book and started to turn the pages.

'The captain, like His Grace, has been absent from society for some time and very little is known about them. They are acknowledged as heroes and, therefore, command respect. As for you, Mr Sherfield,' Isabella continued, giving the boy a sympathetic look, 'I fear you are rather young and have not yet caught their interest, but no doubt that will change in the near future?'

'A certainty,' Dexter remarked dryly. 'From the amount of gossip you have recorded, Miss Winslow, these . . . er . . . ladies must be on a constant search for new victims.'

'I am sure they are, Captain.' She turned to Timothy her eyes alive with mischief. 'So, you take care, Mr Sherfield or you will soon be included.'

'Thank you for the warning.' A wide grin spread across his face. 'I shall take great care not to cause a scandal.'

Isabella stood and curtsied gracefully. 'Now, if you will excuse me, I must return home before I am missed. I slipped out during a deep discussion about the contents of our wardrobes.'

'You did not wish to do the same?' Harry had been under the impression that all ladies were concerned about fashion.

'It is not of prime importance to me.'

He watched her walk – no, glide – out of the room. What a puzzle she was. When he was in her presence he felt a wide range of emotions: dislike, irritation, respect. For a moment, when he had been holding her hands, he had experienced a fierce surge of desire, and he had wanted to find out if the rest of her was as warm and soft as her hands. He pushed the memory away. It was evident that he had been too long without a woman. That was all it was!

Eight

Harry let Lucifer have his head, leaning forward in the saddle as the powerful horse took off with a snort of pleasure. The pounding of the massive hooves on the ground and the wind in his face was exhilarating. It was wonderful to be at Ranliegh again, but he felt a heightened sense of loss for his brother. How often had they raced across these very fields, each one trying to beat the other to the top of the rise? Of course, he had never managed to win. Robert had been by far the better horseman, and that was why the manner of his death was so hard to accept. His grandmother felt the same way.

She had been like a mother to them from the time they could walk. After giving birth to him, their mother had been in poor health, confined to her room, and they saw her only occasionally. She had died when he was three and he could hardly remember her. From then on their grandmother had taken over and brought them up as if they were her own children, and she knew everything about them: their likes and dislikes, their strengths and weaknesses. If she harboured grave misgivings about Robert's death, then her doubts should be heeded.

He stopped at the top of the rise. Ranliegh was spread out before him, and on the horizon the sea shimmered in the morning sunlight. France was only a short boat-ride away.

'What do you think old Bonaparte is doing, Lucifer? Is he looking across the sea and planning his next move? The Amiens Peace Treaty is only a temporary cease-fire, I think, and we have not heard the last from him.'

The horse nodded his head vigorously.

'I see you agree with me. However, if war comes again we shall not be joining in, old boy, for we have responsibilities here now, and being the last remaining heir, I must put family first.'

Lucifer whinnied in sympathy.

Harry's gaze swept over the Kent countryside again. It was a glorious place and he loved it, but it should have been Robert's, not his. He had never expected, or wanted, to inherit the land and title. His brother had been a fine man and would have made a much better Duke of Ranliegh than himself. The anger he felt was powerful, and if he did discover there had been foul play, he hoped he would have enough self-restraint to hand the perpetrator over to the law. The temptation to mete out justice himself would be great indeed.

'Come on, old boy.' He slapped the horse affectionately on the neck. 'Enough of this speculation, time we were getting back. I think I shall pay Lord Garston a social call this afternoon.

By the time he reached the stables his horse was blowing, and his sides heaving with the effort. He tossed his head, pawing the ground, and Harry knew he was expressing his pleasure at the gallop they had just enjoyed.

A groom came forward and reached out to catch hold of the harness. Lucifer gave him a malicious look, dropped his head and pushed the man away with such force that he almost toppled over. Harry reprimanded the animal, his voice stern as he dismounted in one smooth movement and reached to steady the man.

'My apologies. You must be new here.'

'Yes, Your Grace.' He took a step back as the huge war horse eyed him with malevolence.

'Lucifer is not very friendly,' he informed the groom, stating the obvious, 'he will only let me attend him. You go about your duties and I will see to him.'

The groom bowed and scuttled away. Harry caught

hold of Lucifer's head, pulled it down and whispered in his ear. 'You are a nasty tempered old devil and I am convinced that you enjoy yourself immensely, for you nearly frightened that poor man to death.' The horse showed his teeth in a parody of a smile.

As Harry rubbed Lucifer down, he remembered the first time he had seen this magnificent horse. He had not long returned to camp after spending five perilous days behind enemy lines. He had been exhausted and trying to get some rest when a rumpus had awoken him. He'd stormed out of the tent and headed for the crowd of men gathered nearby. A new shipment of horses had arrived, and Lucifer was standing in the middle of a circle of men. There was an evil gleam in his eyes and anyone who dared to approach was soon made to retreat. He had already injured several men and looked big and mean enough to take them all on.

Harry had shouldered his way through the crowd and roared, 'What the devil is going on here?'

The animal's head had shot up and his ears pricked forward. Man and beast eyed each other belligerently, but Harry had been in no mood for insubordination from anyone, and that included this animal. He had placed his feet firmly apart, hands on hips, and glared at the cause of all the trouble. 'Come on, you nasty-tempered old devil. Take me on, I dare you,' he had taunted.

The big horse had snorted, taken one step forward and then another until he was within two feet of his opponent. Harry had remained unflinchingly in his path. Then, much to the surprise of everyone, the animal had done an unexpected thing – he had dropped his head in submission.

Harry smiled as he recalled the incident, and from that moment on they had become inseparable.

'You are an evil old devil,' he told him as he finished rubbing him down. 'I don't know why I ever took you on.'

The horse gave him a playful push and then set about his feed.

'Where is Dexter?' the Duchess inquired at luncheon.

'He's gone to meet with Sergeant Drake. He has some information.'

'How is the investigation going?'

'Slowly, Grandmother, slowly.

'Humph. Like everything else you are involved in.'

Harry concentrated on the succulent beef on his plate and said nothing. He didn't have to be a genius to know what she was referring to.

'I have never seen a man so reluctant to bed a beautiful woman.'

He looked up then. 'I am not, Grandmother. It is only the matrimonial state which dulls my ardour.'

'Rubbish! I have never heard such nonsense. Your grandfather could hardly wait for the ceremony to be completed.'

'Ah, but you are a most remarkable lady. I doubt it would be possible to find the like today.'

'Do not try to charm me, Harry. Remember, I know you too well, and I am beginning to lose all patience. You have had long enough to come to a decision. It is not fair to keep the girl waiting.'

Harry dropped his knife and fork with a clatter. 'The girl is afraid of me, damn it! What am I to do? Disregard her feelings and force myself upon her?'

She looked affronted. 'I am not suggesting you act in such a manner. I did not realise things were that difficult.'

He stared moodily into his glass of wine. 'I appreciate the trouble you have taken to find me a suitable wife, but I have grave doubts about your choice.'

'Do you, Harry? Well, the answer is in front of you. All you have to do is open your eyes.'

That was a very mild reply, not like her at all. And he knew only too well that when she started to act out of character that was the time to be suspicious. What the devil was she up to now?

'Lord Garston will see you now, Your Grace.'

About bloody time, Harry fumed as he followed the butler. He had been kept waiting for twenty minutes, and it was a bad mistake for Garston to make.

The man who rose to greet him was unimpressive – he was below average height, and Harry towered over him. Signs of overindulgence were clearly visible in his red-rimmed eyes and expanding waistline. His disagreeable disposition was etched on his face, and he was clearly not a man one could trust.

'Good of you to call, sir.'

Garston extended a hand, but Harry ignored it and gave a perfunctory bow. 'I thought it was time we met.'

'Won't you sit down, Your Grace.' This time he addressed Harry in the proper manner, obviously uneasy about the powerful presence of the man in front of him. Harry was not averse to using his height and superb physical condition to intimidate if the occasion called for it, and he wanted Garston at a disadvantage.

'Thank you, but no. This will not take long.' He wasted no time in getting to the reason for his visit. 'As you are aware, my brother met with an untimely death and among his personal papers were some gambling notes, signed by you. They are for a considerable sum.'

He waited for this declaration to sink in and had the satisfaction of seeing all the colour drain from Garston's florid face.

'I am surprised that you have not redeemed them as yet. After all, settling a gambling debt is a matter of honour.'

'I have every intention of settling my debts,' he blustered, 'but I am not in a position to do so at this time. Your brother understood that and was prepared to wait.'

Harry knew that was an outright lie; Robert had

hated this man and would never have made such a promise. He changed tactics, lowered himself into a chair and even managed a smile. He had played this game many times.

'Of course you intend to pay.' He sounded as if he believed it. 'It was merely an oversight – is that not so, Lord Garston?'

'Indeed, that is the truth of the matter.' Perspiration was forming on his upper lip.

'As you appear to be short of funds at the moment shall we say three months for settlement?'

'That would be acceptable. My financial embarrassment is only temporary.'

'That is settled then.' Harry stood up and started to leave, then he stopped. 'Oh, you should know that I was attacked a few days ago.'

'How . . . how regrettable. Do you know who it was?'

'Unfortunately, I do not. I was stunned and the villain got away.'

Harry watched carefully from beneath lowered lids and saw relief spread across Garston's face. The man did not know how to dissemble. He moved in for the kill.

'As I was saying, you ought to be aware that if anything untoward should happen to me, all money owing to the Ranliegh estate, and that includes your markers, will be called in, immediately. I have issued my lawyer with the necessary instructions.'

Lord Garston had turned a nasty colour now and he couldn't hide his dismay. If Harry had harboured any doubts about his involvement in the assault upon him, they had now been swept aside.

It wasn't until he was well away from the house that he allowed himself a grim smile of satisfaction.

'That should shackle him for a while, old boy.' He slapped Lucifer on his powerful neck and the horse pranced as if enjoying the joke. He had often been his sole companion as he had weaved about trying to avoid capture by Napoleon's forces, and he had fallen into the habit of talking to him. He was damned sure the cantankerous old devil understood him.

The groom stood well out of range this time as they thundered into the yard. After taking care of the horse, Harry went into his study and found Dexter waiting for him.

'Have you enjoyed your ride?' his friend asked.

'A reasonably successful afternoon. I have just paid a visit to Lord Garston.'

He then related the story of the visit and had Dexter chuckling with mirth.

'I wish I could have been there with you.'

'If we had both confronted him, I am sure he would have fallen into a fit. He is not a healthy man.' Harry gazed into space, obviously searching his mind for some information. 'It is strange – I have never met the man before, and yet . . . something about him seemed familiar.' He shrugged. 'It will come to me. Now, tell me about your trip.'

'Sergeant Drake has become friendly with a maid from young Percy's household, and he says she is very talkative. The boy gambles continually and loses most of the time, but never seems short of cash.'

'Wonder where he is getting it, then? It's certain that his father is not dubbing up?'

'Rumour has it that Stanton is exasperated with his son's lifestyle, and if his new wife produces a son in two months, then the boy could find himself disinherited. That maid also told Drake that about once a month, Percy disappears for several days, and when he returns he is back at the tables, flush with money.'

'He is up to no good, then.'

'Undoubtedly. But I doubt Lord Stanton is divulging state secrets to a wayward son.'

Harry shook his head. 'Unlikely, but we must follow this up. Does the girl have any notion where Percy goes?'

Dexter sat forward in excitement. 'That is the interesting thing, Harry. She has heard Kent mentioned.'

Harry started to pace the room. 'Did Drake manage to find out when the boy is likely to come here again?'

'Well, if he keeps to his usual visits, then it should

be in about a week's time. A message will be sent to us when Percy makes a move.'

'Good. In the meantime we will scout the coastline – there are some secluded coves quite near here. If Carter can become friendly with the local residents then we should be able to find out if anything unusual is going on.'

'Perhaps we should send Miss Isabella visiting when she arrives,' Dexter joked.

Harry raised his hands in horror. 'Let us leave her out of this, my friend. The last thing we need is that meddling girl putting her dainty feet into our affairs.'

'You are too cynical, Harry. She was only trying to help. It's not like you to have such a closed mind.'

Harry scooped the small notebook from the table and tossed it to his friend. 'Stop analysing my character and read what the gossips are saying about the boy.'

'Ah, here he is . . .' He fell silent, reading the pages over to himself. 'There isn't much. They are speculating about his constant supply of money and his regular disappearances from the gaming tables. They think he might have a mistress, someone not from the first circles, and he wishes to keep her a secret.'

'I doubt that. A penniless woman would be of no use to him. If he has a mistress, he would undoubtedly choose one who is independently wealthy, but we must find out what he is up to.' Harry pulled a bell rope next to his chair and waited. Carter entered the room within seconds.

'I want you to go to the local inn tonight and get friendly with the customers. We need to know if there is anything going on along the coast that is unusual or illegal. Also, see if you can find out some news about Lord Stanton's son – there is a rumour that he visits this area regularly and we would like to know why.'

'Yes, sir.' Carter had never lost the habit of standing to attention when Harry was giving him instructions.

'Do you think you can gain the confidence of the locals?'

'Easily, sir. If I have enough money to supply them with ale.'

Harry handed him some coins. 'Will that suffice?'

'Very generous, sir.'

'Good. We shall await your return.'

'No, no, Madam. That will not do.' Isabella caught hold of the material and pulled the bodice up. 'I do not wish to have every gentleman at the ball taking bets on whether I shall remain in my dress for the entire evening.'

'Bella is right, Madam,' Angelina told her. 'She is far too well endowed to wear such a low-cut dress.'

'But it is the fashion,' the dressmaker wailed. 'What will everyone think if I turn you out in a dress that is not in the latest mode?'

'I care little for fashion or people's opinions; my

only concern is that I remain suitably clothed. My bosom is far too large to be so scantily covered.'

'If your waist were not so tiny, then this would not present a problem.' The dressmaker sounded highly offended at being told how to do her job.

'I cannot help my shape, but I am sure you can still make me look fashionable.' Isabella had moderated her tone and managed a smile. 'After all, you are renowned for dressing some of the most difficult figures, are you not? The style and cut of your gowns is much talked about.'

'That is true, Miss Winslow.' Modesty was not one of her virtues. 'Let us address the problem. The neckline should be about here, I think.'

Isabella eased it up another inch. The dressmaker sighed and pinned it in place, a pained expression on her face.

'Thank heavens that is over,' Isabella exploded as soon as the lady had gone. 'I cannot abide these sessions. Why do dressmakers not learn to cater for the lady, and not the latest fashion?'

Charlotte started to giggle. 'Did you see that gown Lady Savage was wearing at the last ball? Bright purple and almost transparent. Her bosom must be three times the size of yours, Bella.'

'Oh, Charlotte.' Angelina tried to keep a stern expression and failed. 'You are unkind. It is because she is so very overweight. Bella is slender, it is only her . . .'

'You see what I mean!' Bella declared.

The younger sisters collapsed on to the bed with shrieks of laughter and Isabella joined in with the merriment. It was lovely to see Angelina so relaxed and happy, but shortly they would be at Ranliegh. Was the Duke going to make an offer in time for the betrothal to be announced at the Grand Ball? It was highly likely.

She felt unaccountably low in spirit at the thought, which was silly, for she should be rejoicing that her sister was going to make such a prestigious match, and with a man of honour. The memory of her hands clasped in his came to mind. His hands were large and strong, yet gentle. Her sister had nothing to fear from him, she was sure of it. She was not afraid of him – she would trust him with her life. It was such a clear realisation that it made her feel uncomfortable, and slightly ashamed of herself for entertaining such thoughts about Angelina's prospective husband. It was not at all proper!

It was very late when Carter returned from the village.

'Did you have any success?' Harry asked.

'The locals were a bit doubtful about me at first and held their tongues. It took quite a lot of ale before they started to talk freely.'

Dexter grinned. Carter had obviously downed a fair amount himself.

'Sit down, man, before you fall down,' Harry ordered.

'Thank you, sir, but I'm not drunk.' He looked offended, but nevertheless, sat in the offered seat. 'I had to drink as much as them or they would have become suspicious, but when they saw I could sup the ale as good as them, then they accepted me.'

Harry sighed and sat back. It was no use pushing Carter while he was in this state. He could hold his liquor with the best of them, but when he was in his cups, as he clearly was now, then it took time for him to get to the point.

'It's a nice little inn, sirs. You should pay a visit sometime. They don't only serve food and drink, you know.' He tried very hard to give them a knowing wink, but all he managed to do was screw his face up in the effort.

'And you sampled the wares, of course?' Harry enquired.

'Had to, sir. Would've looked strange if I hadn't. Ex-soldier, and all that. Have a reputation to maintain.'

Harry kept a straight face with difficulty, and Dexter was chuckling quietly.

'So, you've enjoyed the services of the local hostelry?'

'I've had less pleasurable assignments, Major.' He gave him a lopsided grin.

'Would you like to tell us what you found out?' Harry coaxed.

'Yes, sir.' He tried to sit to attention. 'It seems your

suspicions were correct. There is something going on at night along the coast. There is a small bay, quite near here, and some nights a boat comes ashore.'

'Did they know how often and when the next boat is due?'

Carter shook his head sadly. 'Couldn't find that out. I will need to visit the place regularly before they trust me with details like that, but I did find something else out. About once a month they have a visitor – a young man, and they said he doesn't drink or anything, just goes straight upstairs with one of the girls. Always the same one.'

Harry sat forward. 'Did you get a chance to talk to her?'

'Oh, I did more than that, sir.' He tried to wink again. 'She said she didn't know his name, but he was a gentleman and always paid her well. Don't talk though, just takes his pleasure and leaves.'

Dexter nodded. 'That could be Percy, don't you think, Harry?'

'Quite likely. That destroys the theory that he has a mistress down here. So, he must be visiting for another reason.'

He turned to Carter who was beginning to sway in his seat. 'I want you to go back there again tomorrow and see if you can find out when the next boat is expected.'

'Yes, sir.'

'Go to bed, Carter. You have done well tonight.'

'Thank you, sir.' It took him a while, but he managed to stand upright.

They watched him lurch out of the room.

'Hope he's in a fit state to go through that again tomorrow night,' Dexter remarked dryly.

'He will be. He recovers very quickly.'

'Something is going on, Harry, and we are in the perfect spot to find out.'

'Agreed. However, we must not get too excited. This might have nothing to do with our investigation.'

'I know, but the traitor is getting information across to France, and this is the most likely place for a courier to obtain passage.'

Harry nodded and stood up. 'We can do no more until we have further information. Let us get some rest. The Winslow girls will be arriving soon, and I shall need all my strength to cope with them.'

Nine

The carriage lurched along and Isabella looked at her sister with concern. As the journey progressed, Angelina became more and more withdrawn.

'Angel, will you not tell me why you dislike the Duke so much?'

'Oh, I do not dislike him, Bella. He is a very fine man,' she hastened to assure her sister.

'Then what is it that troubles you?'

She took a deep breath. 'You know how it is when he walks into a room, everyone is aware of him.'

'He is very tall, and would be hard to ignore,' Isabella remarked with amusement.

'No, no. You do not understand. It is not his stature

that makes everyone turn and look at him. It is more than that. Oh, I cannot explain!'

'I think I know what you mean, Angel,' Charlotte said, thoughtfully. 'It is as if he has some kind of power inside him and it seems to fill the room.'

'Oh, Lotte, how perceptive of you.'

'But surely you cannot dismiss his build? Underneath the fashionable clothes he is obviously a very strong man.' Isabella had been very conscious of that fact when he had been holding on to her at the fair.

'Of course you cannot dismiss it, for it is all too evident, but when you add that to a sharp, penetrating mind and an iron will, you have a very formidable man.'

Isabella listened carefully, trying to understand. Power and strength did describe him perfectly, but she could not see that as a reason to fear him. 'I still cannot understand why that should make you view him with trepidation.'

'When he comes near me, he seems to rob me of my wits and swamps me with his presence. I am not right for him,' Angelina wailed.

'But the Duchess has chosen you,' Charlotte reminded her.

'I don't care! She has made a mistake and he will not be happy with me. He is a good man and a brave soldier, and he deserves to have someone who will please him. He needs a strong woman, someone with more vitality.' She looked hopefully at her eldest sister. 'Someone like you, Bella.'

'No, Angel, he finds me irritating. In fact, I would go as far as saying that he cannot stand to be in my presence.'

The small gleam of hope died in Angelina's eyes. 'But you are the eldest and he should be considering you for his wife, not the younger sister. It is not proper, Bella.'

'But you are aware that I am considered unsuitable,' she told her sister gently.

'Society has no right to condemn you like that!' she declared with great force. 'You would make any man a wife he could be proud of.'

Isabella was touched by her sister's love for her, but she knew only too well that they were bound by what 'society' believed.

'You must tell papa,' Charlotte suggested helpfully.

'I cannot do that,' she squeaked. 'He is set upon this marriage and he would not understand my silly fears. I can just hear him now – "What nonsense have you been filling the girls head with, Mother?"'

It was such a perfect imitation of their father at his most imperious, that they all started to laugh.

Angelina fiddled with the ribbon on her gown and then gave an over-bright smile. 'Do you know I am considered the luckiest of girls, for he is the catch of the season.'

* * *

Harry watched the carriages rumbling up the long driveway. He was going to make a big effort to win Miss Angelina over, for he had to marry, and she was of good breeding, well brought up and beautiful, and she was also quiet. Not one to make a noise or present a man with unreasonable demands, and he would hardly know she was around, for she did not chatter endlessly like so many young ladies. He could appreciate why his grandmother had suggested her. Life with Angelina Wilson would be peaceful – and dull.

His grandmother came up beside him and slipped her hand through his arm. 'Ah, they have arrived. Remember, Harry, the answer to your problems is in front of you.'

'Hmm?' He gave her a suspicious glance. 'I don't have the faintest idea what you are talking about.'

'You will.' She patted his arm. 'I have every faith in your powers of deduction. You will solve the puzzle.'

What the deuce was she on about? Was old age catching up with her and addling her brain? He looked down into a pair of bright eyes, full of intelligence and mischief and gave a wry smile. No! There was nothing wrong with her; he was the one losing his wits.

Dinner that evening had gone well. With Timothy and Dexter present the conversation had flowed smoothly and Angelina had appeared more relaxed, even uttering a sentence or two. She really was quite lovely, he mused.

He walked across the well-tended lawns and

propped himself against an old oak tree, remembering that he had been standing like this in the park the first time he had seen Isabella. She had been flying along in pursuit of her bonnet and he had been amused at her antics – but not anymore. She was the most opinionated, irritating female he had ever met. Thank heavens his grandmother had not suggested her as his wife. She was most unsuitable, life with her would be a constant battle and he had been in enough skirmishes.

His gaze swept over the house. It was a magnificent building especially like this – bathed in moonlight. He sighed with pleasure; everyone had retired for the night and he could enjoy a few precious moments of solitude.

A movement caught his attention – someone had come out of the house and was gliding towards him. He knew who it was, because light from the moon was catching her hair, making it look as if she had a halo of fire around her face. Damn the woman! Could she not leave him alone?

'How did you know I was here?' he snapped, thoroughly annoyed at her intrusion.

'I saw you from my window.'

She appeared quite unperturbed by his foul mood. He could make a regiment quell before his gaze, but not this woman. His eyes swept over her, and he couldn't believe what he was seeing. 'What the blazes are you wearing?'

'I was ready for bed when I saw you, but you

needn't look so scandalised,' she retorted sharply, 'my wrap is adequate covering.'

He caught hold of her and pulled her round to the other side of the tree, away from the house. 'Do you care nothing for your reputation?'

'What others think of me is of little matter.' She tipped her head to one side and gave a mischievous smile. 'Is it my reputation that concerns you, or your own?'

He pulled her robe together until it covered her right up to the neck. In doing so, he caught a brief wave of delicate perfume and felt the softness of her skin against his fingers. The rush of desire he felt was like a cavalry charge at the start of a battle. He moved in, his lips only inches from hers, when a picture of her sister's gentle face brought him back to his senses.

His hands dropped, and he stepped back a pace and went on to the defensive. 'It matters not whose reputation is at stake, Miss Winslow. The fact is that you should be more circumspect in your conduct,' he snapped.

'There is no need for you to be irritated, for I shall not keep you long. I have not had the opportunity to speak to you since our arrival.' She gave him a look of pure mischief. 'You are avoiding me.'

She was impossible! 'Get to the reason for this clandestine visit.'

'I wanted to ask you if you have discovered who your attacker was?'

'I believe I have found the culprit.'

'Oh, that is well done.' She gave a little clap of excitement. 'Who was it?'

'That need not concern you.'

'Come, do not use that tone with me. Of course it concerns me. Have I not tried to help you track down the villain?'

'Miss Winslow!' The words rasped out; all patience now flown. 'The man is dangerous, and if you knew his identity it might put you in peril.'

'I am quite able to look after myself,' she told him haughtily.

'That may be so, but your sisters do not have your disposition.'

That silenced her for a moment – but only a moment. 'Do you believe he would harm anyone you are acquainted with?'

'Yes, I think it is a possibility.'

'I see. And it is common knowledge that you are on the point of offering for my sister, and you would not wish to see her hurt?'

'Your sister has a gentle nature and I would not like to see her frightened.'

'I understand, and that is very commendable of you, but could you not tell me? I will not utter a word to anyone – you have my promise.'

Harry groaned quietly. She was completely unconcerned about his brusque manner, and in the light of the moon he could see that her eyes were sparkling with excitement. Did she ever give up? 'Return to the house before you are missed. This is my problem and I will deal with it!'

'There is no need to raise your voice. You have made it quite plain that you find my interest a great nuisance, but I do love a mystery, and it is frustrating to be kept out of any exciting goings-on just because one is a female. Why do men consider woman to be lacking in brains?'

'Perhaps because they are?' He could not resist the derisive remark.

'Oh, there is no reasoning with you! I do declare that you are the most infuriating man, and your manners could do with a polish.'

'Ah, sadly, I am a rough soldier.' He was beginning to enjoy himself.

'Nonsense! You may have lived in unsavoury conditions for some time, but you were brought up a gentleman. You have merely forgotten some of the social graces.'

'And what is your excuse,' he taunted softly.

He saw her generous mouth curve into a smile that was almost a grimace. 'I am considered strong-willed and unconventional. Polite society shakes its head, but I am tolerated because I am my father's daughter and an heiress.'

Was there a note of sadness in her voice? For some unaccountable reason he wanted to hold her in his arms and offer comfort, but before he could act upon the urge, she turned from him.

He watched her walk away, and the moment of compassion he had melted as if it had never existed. It was no wonder she was still unwed. No man in his right mind would take her on – fortune or not.

Timothy came into the breakfast room and bowed to the ladies, then he turned to Harry. 'Do I have your permission to leave today? There is still much to do,' he added, smiling with eagerness.

'Good heavens, Tim, you don't have to ask my permission. If you need to go to Sherfields, then do so.'

'What is this?' Charlotte asked. 'Do you have property near here, Mr Sherfield?'

'No, it is the Orchards and Harry has honoured me by calling it Sherfields.'

'That was exceedingly kind of you, Your Grace,' Angelina remarked softly.

Harry was startled. That was the first time she had addressed him without being forced into it. Perhaps there was hope of a union between them after all. She would make a charming wife and he could not understand why he did not feel any stirrings of desire for her.

There was that tentative smile again, and he returned it. 'Mr Sherfield is doing me the great favour of getting the place into shape, for it has been sadly neglected. He is an expert on fruit trees, and I am relieved to leave the management in his hands. I felt it was fitting to name it so.'

She flushed prettily and smiled again. 'Indeed, it would appear to be very fitting.'

Good Lord. That was the most encouragement he had ever received from her. However, his reaction was most odd – he couldn't decide if he was pleased or worried by her change of attitude.

'Could we go and see it?' Charlotte asked.

'What does everyone think?' He looked around enquiringly and was greeted with nods of agreement from everyone.

'That is settled then. We shall take a carriage for the ladies' comfort. Dexter, Timothy and myself will take our horses. We shall leave in an hour. Does that suit everyone?'

It did, and the girls left to make themselves ready for the journey.

When they arrived at Sherfields, the place was all activity; men were repairing roofs, clearing ground, building walls, and Timothy was in his element, striding around, inspecting the progress that had been made during his absence.

Mrs Baxter came hurrying out of the house, a worried expression on her face. 'Oh, we are in no fit state to receive guests, Your Grace.'

'Please do not concern yourself, Mrs Baxter, we will not get in the way.'

'But, food, Your Grace? I have nothing prepared.' She rung her hands in distress and looked at the girls who were being helped out of the carriage by Dexter. 'The men are working in the kitchens today.'

'Mr Sherfield informed me of the position. We have brought everything with us, and we have so much food that I think we could feed everyone here.'

She relaxed then. 'We have some ale, and lemonade for the ladies.'

'Thank you, that would be most acceptable.'

'What a transformation, Harry.' Dexter came up beside him. 'Look at the stable block. Why, it was almost a ruin the last time we saw it.'

'It's quite remarkable. A lot of hard work has been going on here.'

Mr Baxter and another worker led the horses away to unhitch them and settle them down in the newly refurbished stables. In deference to the ladies, the war horses had been left behind, much to Lucifer's obvious fury.

The girls were naturally interested in the house, and the housekeeper took them off to have a closer look.

Harry started to walk towards the cottages to see if Dobson and his family were settling in all right, when a small girl came running out as fast as her little legs would carry her. He had seen her on the way down, but then she had been pale and fretful, and it was hard to believe she was the same child, for she was laughing and had colour in her cheeks. She had fair hair, blue eyes and was wearing a pink dress, which was obviously new.

She stopped in front of him and looked up, and up, until she nearly toppled over backwards. 'Big,' she said quite distinctly.

He hunkered down and steadied her. She had an apple in her hand and held it out to him.

'Nice,' she told him.

He shook his head. The apple was badly bruised – the brown juice was running over her hand and the sticky mess was in danger of spoiling her new dress. He took it away from her, pulled a pristine handkerchief out of his pocket and wiped her fingers.

'Would you like to pick a nice apple?'

She nodded vigorously.

He scooped her up and she squealed with delight making all heads turn in their direction. One of the nearby trees had a good crop on it and he held her high so she could reach one of the choice fruits. Her tiny hands worked furiously until the chosen apple came free.

'Nice?' she asked, holding it out for his inspection.

He nodded in agreement, giving it a good polish on his sleeve and placing it back into her little hands. Then he carried her back to the cottage where her mother was waiting, looking very anxious.

She curtsied. 'I'm so sorry, Your Grace, I didn't

mean for her to be a nuisance, but she slipped out without me knowing.'

'She has not been a nuisance,' he assured the agitated mother. 'You have a beautiful daughter and I am delighted to see her in better health already.' He put the wriggling bundle carefully on the ground and stood up again. 'You are quite comfortable here, I hope?'

'Oh, it's like paradise! We are so grateful to you.'

He felt a tug on his leg and stooped down again. The child had taken a bite out of the apple and was holding it out to him. 'Don't you like it?' he asked.

'It isn't that,' her mother interrupted. 'We've never had much, but we've told her that a lot of people are worse off than us and that she mustn't be selfish. You gave it to her, and she won't eat any more until you've had some – but you don't have to,' she added hastily. 'I'll explain to her that you are a great gentleman and do not need the apple.'

He smiled at the girl, took a small bite out of the apple and handed it back to her. 'Thank you,' he said seriously. 'Now you eat the rest.'

She looked at her mother enquiringly, and when she smiled and nodded, the girl sat on the ground and bit into the fruit.

'You are bringing her up to be a generous child.'

'We've lived in awful conditions, and there seemed no way out to escape the dirt, thievery and violence, but we didn't want our daughter to grow up like those around us. We may have lived in the dirt, but we didn't have to sink down to their level.'

'You are a very special woman, Mrs Dobson. Your husband is a lucky man.'

'I am, sir. Right proud of them, I am.'

'And rightly so.' Harry turned to the man who had just joined them. 'I have been asking your lady if everything is to your liking here?'

'Perfect, sir. We love it here and with the new baby on the way . . .'

'Your wife is with child?'

'Yes, sir. We've only just discovered it.'

Harry looked at the small cottage thoughtfully. 'May I have a look inside?'

'Certainly, sir.'

The inside was small and sparsely furnished, but spotlessly clean. There were two rooms and an outhouse downstairs, and two bedrooms upstairs. After giving the modest dwelling thoughtful consideration, he went outside again and called Timothy.

'Could we extend the cottage, Tim?'

'I'll get the builder and he will be able to tell us.'

The man hurried over and doffed his cap.

'Can you add two rooms to the end of the cottage?'

'Easily, Your Grace. They are sturdy buildings.'

'Good. I'll leave you to work out the details with Mr Sherfield.'

Dexter joined him as he strode across the yard. 'A

sweet little girl, isn't she?' There was a teasing note in his voice.

'Quite delightful,' Harry replied, not slackening his stride.

'Does the marriage grow in appeal? Were you getting in some practice for the future?'

He stopped so suddenly that Dexter found himself several steps ahead and had to turn back.

'What are you on about? I do happen to like children, Dexter, especially well-brought-up ones, and I don't see the reason for your amusement.'

'It is not so much amusement as astonishment. When I saw you holding her up, I couldn't help remembering you as the war hardened soldier. The two images do not blend, Harry.'

'I don't suppose they do.' He gave his friend a wry smile. 'She was not afraid of me, did you see?'

'Indeed. I think she fell in love with you.'

Harry tipped his head back and roared with laughter. 'That is a thought. However, I cannot wait for her to grow up. There is a pressing need for an heir, and by the time she is old enough, I will be past my prime.'

Isabella watched the Duke's broad back as he guided the horses skilfully along a narrow path and mused about the scene she had witnessed.

She had been looking out of the bedroom window of the house with Angelina beside her, and they had seen him playing with the little girl. She had almost been able to feel the tenderness as he had wiped the child's fingers with his handkerchief, and it had given her pause for thought. Could that be the same man who had snapped and snarled at her last night in the garden?

Angelina had not uttered a word, but she had watched very carefully. His gentle concern for the child had not been the action of a man without sensibilities.

She cast a glance at her sister's thoughtful expression. Was she beginning to realise that he was not the monster she had imagined? Surely, she would fall in love with him now. It would be so easy.

Isabella did not know why the thought should cause her pain.

Ten

The next day the house was thrown into chaos as the Duchess began the arrangements for the ball, which was to be held in ten days.

'But, Grandmother,' Harry protested, 'that is not enough time. Invitations have to be sent out, rooms prepared, musicians engaged, food to be ordered, and guests have to make travelling arrangements.'

She cast aside his protests. 'There has not been a ball at Ranliegh for a long time, and everyone will be overcome with excitement at being invited. Now, stop fussing, Harry. Cast your eyes over the guest list and tell me if I have overlooked anyone.'

'Good Lord,' he exclaimed as he saw the multitude

of names. 'Where the devil can we put them all?'

'We shall manage. When I was a young girl we had more guests than this, and anyway, they will not all be able to attend.'

He hoped that at least half of those invited were otherwise engaged. 'Why have you invited Lord Stanton? He will not come.'

'I know, but he was a friend of your father's, and it is only proper that I should include him.'

'From what I hear, he will not leave his young wife, even to carry out his duties at the War Department.'

'That is so. The girl is half his age and he is so enamoured with her that he will not leave her side. She is with child and he wants another son, quite desperately. He is most displeased with Percy.'

'That I can understand. I saw him in London, and if he inherits the estate, it will be gambled away in short order.' He cast a glance over the list again. 'You have invited all our neighbours except Lord Garston. He will feel slighted.' He gave a smile full of devilment. 'It would be interesting to see if he dared accept the invitation.'

'No, Harry, I will not have that odious man in the house. If we discover he had no hand in Robert's accident, then I shall apologise. Until then he is not welcome here.'

'Your Grace.' The door burst open and a flustered groom tumbled into the room. 'One of the young ladies has entered Lucifer's stable.'

The chair Harry had been sitting on crashed to the floor as he leapt to his feet and ran out of the house towards the stables. He was swearing, using language that would have shocked the roughest soldier. Damn the woman! He didn't have to ask which sister it was. He bloody well knew.

He halted at the stall door, ready to wrench it open and do battle with Lucifer, but he stopped, his heart thumping alarmingly, when he saw the horse was standing right across the doorway, making exit or entrance impossible. Where was she? He could not see into the stall with Lucifer's bulk in the way, but the animal was standing quietly.

Harry took a couple of deep breaths. 'What are you up to, old boy?' He spoke softly. 'Let me in.'

Much to his relief the horse looked at him and moved just enough to allow him to slip into the stall. The sight that met his eyes nearly made him roar with rage. This was impossible.

'Oh, hello. What a magnificent beast he is.' Isabella ran her delicate hands over his nose and leant forward to kiss the animal.

Harry was rendered speechless and pulled her away quickly.

'He is a war horse, is he not?'

'Yes.' He finally got his voice back. 'And a very dangerous one.'

She gave a tinkling laugh. 'He is not. I think he is quite sweet.'

Sweet? He was fighting the urge to shake some sense into her, but the immediate need was to get her out of the stall. The animal was quiet for the moment, but Harry could not guarantee he would stay that way, and it would be the highest folly to take chances with Lucifer.

'I suggest, Miss Winslow, that you walk carefully out of here.' He spoke through gritted teeth. She was much too fragile and could be crushed.

Lucifer had other ideas about letting his prize leave. He eyed Harry belligerently and blocked the doorway again. Harry caught hold of Isabella and pushed her behind him, but the animal lowered his head and tried to shove him out of the way.

'Don't fight me, old boy,' he growled, 'you know you will not win.'

Isabella laughed and eased her way out from behind him. 'He wants the other apple I have for him.'

'Another apple?' he exploded. 'You have been feeding him?'

'Only a small apple, and there is no need to shout, you will frighten the poor animal.' She pulled the other piece of fruit out of her pocket. 'Perhaps if I give him this one as well, he will let you leave.'

Let him leave? She was the one who needed to leave, not him.

He watched in disbelief as Lucifer took the proffered gift gently out of her hand and munched contentedly, letting her pat his neck as if he did not have an evil bone in his body. Having finished the piece of fruit he turned his lip back and showed all his teeth.

'Oh, see, he enjoyed that and he is laughing.'

This was too much for Harry and his temper snapped. 'But I . . .' he gripped her around the waist and lifted her off the floor '. . . am not laughing. Move, Lucifer,' he ordered in a voice that no one dared disobey.

The horse shifted away from the door. Without putting Isabella down he strode out, and a groom hastily closed the door.

Harry set her on her feet but kept a firm grip on her arm and pointed to a notice on the door. 'What does that say?' he thundered. 'You can read, I take it?'

'Of course I can. I have had a good education,' she informed him haughtily.

'Then read it – out loud.'

'Do not enter – this animal is dangerous.'

'Beautifully done,' he said sarcastically. 'Do you understand the notice?'

She nodded and started to stroke Lucifer's nose, who was looking over the door with great interest.

Harry pulled her away. 'Leave the damned animal alone!'

'Stop shouting at the poor girl, Harry. I could hear you right back at the house,' his grandmother reprimanded sternly. 'You have picked up some rough habits in the army.'

'I also picked up a malicious, bad-tempered horse, as you well know, but this termagant ignores the notice and goes into the stall to pet him.' He tried to moderate his tone, without success. He was in a red rage.

'Do not be rude to your guest, Harry.'

'Your guest, Grandmother. I did not invite her.'

He turned on Isabella, his amber eyes the colour of a fire out of control. 'Two more things you should know. He bites . . . and so do I.'

He stormed out of the stables, his booted heels ringing on the stone floor. Of all the stupid, irresponsible things to do. She could have been injured, or even killed. He did not know why Lucifer had allowed her near him, for it was the first time he had permitted anyone, except himself, to touch him. If the animal had reacted in his usual manner . . . he shuddered to think what might have happened. The woman was a menace to herself and everyone around her. The horse was not to be trusted, and neither was he. Good Lord! Even in his fury, he had wanted to possess the infuriating woman with a passion that was a revelation to him. His self-control had always been talked about with awe, but just look at him now. He had never been so angry.

Harry walked for nearly an hour and did not turn for home until he had calmed down.

Isabella was waiting for him as he strode through the door, and she curtsied gracefully. 'I apologise for my behaviour, Your Grace. I acted without proper thought and have offended you, so I feel it wise not to burden you with my presence any longer.' She curtsied again, walked out of the door, got into a waiting carriage and was driven away.

He watched in astonishment. 'Where is she going?'

'My husband has had to return to our estate on business,' Lady Winslow told him. 'Isabella has clearly overstepped the bounds this time and has gone to join him. It is but a two-hour drive from here.'

As the carriage rumbled along, Isabella gazed at the passing scenery. What a dreadful incident. She had never seen such powerful rage, although she understood the reason now. Captain Atterton had explained about the horse and told her how it had injured many men before Harry had taken him in hand. Man and animal had great respect for each other, but he was always very careful not to let anyone get too near Lucifer.

She had not known this, of course, but the notice had been very clear. However, she was not completely without sense. When she had approached, he had appeared to be quite docile, and spying such a magnificent animal she had wanted to have a closer look, that was all. She sighed and rubbed her temple wearily. Why did she act so thoughtlessly? She had always been like this, right from a young child. What a trial she must be to her parents.

She'd had to leave; he had made his opinion of her very clear – he could not tolerate her. Her sisters had begged her not to go, but her mother had agreed with her decision.

The carriage started to slow down. She was home, but now she had to face her father.

'What are you doing here, my dear?' he asked as he helped her from the carriage. 'Is anything amiss?'

'Yes, Father. I fear you are going to be angry with me . . . again.'

He guided her into his study and took up his customary position by the fireplace. 'You had better explain.'

He listened to the whole story without interrupting. There was silence as he considered the importance of what had happened, then he sighed wearily.

'Isabella, you have always got yourself into scrapes, but this last one is the most serious. Have you considered how His Grace would have felt if you had been injured? He is a man of honour, and would have felt obliged to shoot the horse, and that would have been a cause of great sadness to him. The animal is fierce, but I understand that it has saved his life on more than one occasion.'

'I did not know that.'

'I am most displeased with you, Isabella. We are hopeful that he will offer for Angelina, but if your thoughtless actions have made him consider this family in a bad light, then I shall find it hard to forgive you.'

'I am sorry that I acted so, Father, but I was never in any danger. The animal was very friendly.'

'And thank heavens he was! But he could have turned on you at any moment. Why do you think His Grace was worried? He knows the horse, Isabella – you do not.'

'I do not think he would have hurt me'

'I am not interested in what you think,' he interrupted sharply. 'You have had your own way for too long. I shall find you a husband and you will not be allowed to refuse this time. Now, go to your room.'

Isabella gazed moodily out of the window. She had really done the most unforgivable thing today and placed herself in an impossible position. Her father was going to pick a husband for her, but it was her own fault of course. His patience was exhausted.

He would not have much difficulty, she feared. The fact that she had a strong will was well known, but many men would marry her for the inheritance alone, and she could not contain a shudder of revulsion. They would wed her, take control of her fortune and then find themselves a mistress. She could not live like that – she would not live like that.

She undressed and got into bed, closed her eyes and tried to sleep, but it was impossible. The picture of that impressive man in a thunderous rage would not fade. What was he doing now?

Harry made his way to the stables and Lucifer greeted him with a whinny of recognition. 'I must thank you for not harming the lady, old boy. Why you did not attack her I will never know, but I am grateful you didn't.' He grimaced. 'You showed more restraint than I did.'

The animal was moving around restlessly, so he picked up the saddle. 'I think we would both benefit from a hard gallop.'

It was dark by the time they returned, and Harry spent a long time rubbing Lucifer down, trying to use up some of his energy before he retired. He winced when he remembered the insults he had thrown at the girl, but it was only because he had been so concerned for her safety. However, there had been no need for her to leave; he would have calmed down, eventually.

When he entered the house, he was surprised to find his grandmother had not retired.

'Are you feeling more the thing now, Harry?'

He nodded and poured himself a brandy.

'You missed dinner. Cook has left you a tray.'

'Thank you, Grandmother.'

'The girl is headstrong.'

'She is.' He sat down and stared into his drink.

'She was not harmed.' His grandmother persisted, although she was getting little response from him.

'No, thank God.'

'Surprising, knowing the temperament of the animal.'

'Miraculous.'

'Do you want to talk about it?'

He looked up and frowned. 'Is that why you have not retired at this late hour?'

'Yes, dear boy. I have never seen you so upset, and I was concerned.'

'There's no need to be. You go to bed.' He helped her out of the chair and kissed her cheek.

'It would break your heart if anything happened to that fractious animal, would it not?'

He nodded. 'If he had harmed her I would have had to shoot him. I could not have done otherwise, and I would also have had the knowledge of her injuries or death on my conscience for the rest of my life.'

'Your anger was understandable, but she meant no harm. I'm sure of it.'

'She was not even aware that she had done anything wrong.'

'I don't suppose she was . . .' She paused. 'Are you going to fetch her back?'

'No.'

She sighed. 'I thought not. Good night, Harry.'

During the long, sleepless night he had come to a decision; he would offer for Angelina. He was tired of the whole damned business.

The fact that he had settled on a wife gave him no pleasure. He was heavy of heart, but he could not understand why, for he should be feeling pleased to have the matter settled. The choice had been made, and that foolish girl had removed her irritating presence from his home, so why wasn't he jubilant?

Dexter entered the breakfast room and the sisters followed him. Harry rose to his feet and bowed. 'Miss Angelina, would you like to ride this morning? The weather is still holding fair.'

'That would be pleasant.' She wasn't looking at him.

'Good. I shall have the horses ready in an hour. What are your plans for today, Dexter?'

'I'm taking Miss Charlotte and her maid into the village. They have expressed the desire to see the old church and do some shopping.'

'Are you not coming riding with us?' Angelina looked at her sister in alarm.

'No, Angel. The Duchess has asked us to collect a book for her.'

Harry frowned at Angelina. She appeared quite pale and would not look him in the eyes. Damn! Just when he had made his mind up, she was showing signs of being frightened of him again – though after yesterday's fracas it was hardly surprising.

He chose gentle mounts for them both, but it did not turn out to be an enjoyable outing. She had been quiet and withdrawn, and when he'd helped her off the horse for a rest she had trembled under his hands, appearing near to tears. He was relieved to return her to her mother.

He made for his study. There was always a lot to occupy his time, for Ranliegh was a large estate.

About an hour later, Dexter joined him. 'Did you have a pleasant ride?'

'No, the girl started to tremble in my presence. It will not do, Dexter.'

'She is very upset about her sister leaving. I heard her begging Isabella to stay, but she would not be swayed.'

'Do you think the absence of her sister is all that is worrying her?'

'No. Your temper may have something to do with her nervousness. She is very gentle, and raised voices appear to frighten her.'

'Damn it, Dexter, I had every right to be furious. How would you have reacted?'

'Much like you, I fear, but without the violence.'

'I was not violent!' He started to pace the room.

'Harry, I would have trusted Lucifer more than you in that mood. It was an awesome sight.'

'I didn't know you were there?'

'Of course not. Your whole attention was focused

on Miss Isabella and the horse; you were unaware of anything else.'

He stopped pacing. 'Did Miss Angelina see?'

'No, but she heard you, and I saw her retreat back into the house.'

'Oh, God, no wonder she was frightened today.' Harry shrugged disconsolately. 'I didn't expect Isabella to leave.'

'Why not ride over and bring her back? That will please her sister.'

'I will think about it. Now,' he changed to subject, 'did you find anything out while you were in the village?'

'The owner of the bookshop was very talkative. I asked him if there was a secluded beach where one could bathe in private.'

'There are quite a few. Did he mention one in particular?'

'Yes. In fact, it is only about two miles from here.'

Harry was immediately on his feet, relieved to have something positive to do. 'Come, let us have a look at this place.'

They galloped along the water's edge, spray flying from the horses' hoofs, and drew to a halt as they rounded a corner. In front of them was a small bay, and no one would know it was there unless they approached it from the sea.

'That looks like a cave over there, doesn't it, Dexter?'

They dismounted and walked towards the spot Harry had pointed out. It was indeed a cave – deep, and very dark.

'Wish we had a lantern with us,' Harry remarked as he went inside, feeling his way carefully along the rough walls. 'It appears to be empty,' he called out.

He emerged after a short time and blinked in the bright sunlight. 'It is very cold in there and the floor is covered with pools of water.'

'I can see that from the condition of your boots. One could not leave anything in there – when the tide comes in it floods the cave.' Dexter pointed to a watermark along the outside.

'Yes. But it is quite likely this is the place we are looking for. Let us examine it thoroughly because it will be dark when we come again, and we will need to know every twist and turn of the terrain.'

Harry took a marker and paper from his saddlebag, then they started to make a creditable map of the area. They had done this many times in the past and it presented no problems for them. When they were satisfied that they had not missed one tiny detail, they rode back up the beach and along the cliff top.

'This will be an excellent vantage point. See,' Harry pointed to a small copse of trees, 'the horses could be hidden there.' He stretched out on his front and moved towards to cliff edge. 'Good, this is just the thing, we will not be seen if we keep low.'

Dexter started to examine the area. 'Look at this, Harry,' he exclaimed. 'There is a path leading down. It has been covered with brambles, on purpose I suspect, but they can be moved aside.'

'I'll see where it leads.' Harry was immediately scrambling down the narrow, uneven path.

A few minutes later Dexter saw him stride towards the water's edge, turn and wave, a broad grin on his face. The climb up took a little longer.

'That is excellent, Dexter. There had to be another way out of the cove. One could easily get trapped down there when the tide starts to come in.'

Harry carefully marked the winding path on their map. 'I think we have all the information we need for the time being. All we can do now is wait.'

Eleven

'Where have you been, Isabella?' her father demanded.

'I have been to see Mr Sherfield, Papa. I had a doll for the little girl who travelled down with us and I also took some small clothes for her. She has very little and Mrs Baxter is going to alter them to fit her.'

'That is very commendable of you.' He started to say something else and then stopped. 'What the devil have you been up to?'

She brushed her hand down the skirt of her riding habit. 'I went into the attic to find the clothes and doll. It is rather dusty.'

'Did you not think to clean yourself up before you

168

went out?' he asked, in exasperation.

'No, I would only have gathered more dust on the journey.'

He sighed at her logic. 'You have a visitor. He has been waiting this past hour to talk to you.'

Isabella spun round and came face to face with the Duke. She curtsied hurriedly. 'I beg your pardon, Your Grace, I was not aware of your presence.'

He accepted her apology with a curt nod of his head and she endured his contemptuous gaze as he surveyed her dishevelled condition. She lifted her head in a defiant gesture; he had arrived unexpectedly and she could not help it if she was dusty.

'Why did you leave Ranliegh?' he demanded.

'Because I had greatly displeased you, and it was the only thing I could do.'

'It is true that you made me angry. However, I should not have reacted in such a . . . a . . .'

'Violent way?' she suggested helpfully as he stumbled over the word.

'I was not violent!'

'Furious, then?'

'Well, yes, that cannot be denied. I apologise for frightening you.'

'Oh, you did not frighten me.'

Her father gave an audible groan. 'Isabella!' he murmured.

She continued without heeding her father's

exasperated rebuke. 'I was distressed to have caused you concern.'

He nodded abruptly. 'I would like you to come back to Ranliegh.'

Her face lit up. 'You would?'

'Yes, your mother and sisters miss you.'

'Oh, I see.' Why was she disappointed? Did she think he had come all this way because he wanted her back? If that had been her hope, then she was indeed a very foolish female. Nevertheless, she wanted to return to Ranliegh.

'Papa?' She turned to her father. 'May I?'

Her father nodded. 'You may go back, Isabella, but I must have your promise that you will try to behave. You must not do anything or go anywhere without the permission of His Grace.'

'That will be rather restricting . . .'

'Isabella! Your word, or you will stay here.'

'I promise to try very hard not to misbehave, Papa.'

He rubbed his brow wearily. 'I suppose I will have to be content with that.' He looked at Harry. 'What about you – will that tenuous promise suffice?'

'I will accept it.'

'Very well, Isabella, you may go, but do clean yourself up first.'

She smiled happily and left the room.

* * *

'It is good of you to take her back,' Sir George remarked. 'From the moment she was born she has been a trial. She started to walk well before her time and when she could talk,' he threw his hands in the air in a gesture of despair, 'questions, questions, they never stopped. She has grown into a beautiful, loving and generous young woman, but we have never quite been able to tame her. She has a reckless and inquisitive nature, I'm afraid.'

'She must be a constant worry to you.'

Sir George nodded in agreement. 'I am determined to find her a husband; I have let her have her own way for too long. Now, Angelina is quite different. She has a sweet, biddable disposition and would never cause a man a moment's concern.' He looked at Harry, hopefully.

It was the most opportune moment to ask for Angelina's hand in marriage, but for some strange reason the words would not come. 'I am surprised Miss Isabella is not already wed?'

'She has had several offers, but she would have none of it. They were fortune hunters, she had declared, and she would not hand her inheritance over to a man who would squander it. No doubt she was right, but this time, however, I shall do the choosing.'

Harry smiled politely and said nothing. He did not envy Sir George his task.

'I will take the opportunity to cast my eye over

the guests at the ball. There will be many eligible gentlemen there, will there not?'

'Without a doubt. Grandmother has invited the cream of society.'

'Good. All I have to do is persuade some gentleman to take her on.'

The object of their discussion bounced back into the room, scrubbed clean and in a fresh outfit.

'There, I have not kept you waiting long, have I?'

Her father looked at the clock. 'You have hardly had time to pack, Isabella.'

'I left most of my things at Ranliegh.'

'You expected me to come after you?' Harry wanted to know.

'Oh, no. I did not think you would ever forgive me, but I left in a hurry and mother would have fetched my clothes back with her.' She gave him a beguiling smile. 'But I am exceedingly grateful you have asked me to return. I would have been very sad to have missed the excitement of the ball, for I have been helping with the arrangements. It is to be such a grand affair.'

'Damn the ball!' Harry muttered. It was but a week away and everyone would be expecting an announcement about the betrothal, especially his grandmother and Sir George. He seriously doubted if Angelina was ever going to accept him, but she would marry him, of course – her father would demand it – and hadn't he just pointed out that she was obedient.

He cursed fiercely under his breath. He would rather face Napoleon's army unarmed than to bed an unwilling woman.

Isabella's arrival back at Ranliegh was greeted with cries of delight from her family, and Harry disappeared into his study as soon as was polite, but he had hardly settled down to work when the sound of a horse coming up the driveway brought him out of his chair. It was Dexter and he was in a devil of a hurry.

'Harry!' He came into the room and closed the door behind him. 'I have just received word that Percy is making plans for a journey. The maid told Drake that he leaves around this time each month and she is sure he goes to the same place. If that is the case, then he should arrive sometime tomorrow.'

Without being summoned, Carter entered the room. 'Saw the captain, sir. Thought something might be afoot.'

'We have received word that young Percy might be here by tomorrow,' Harry informed him.

'I'll go to the inn tonight, sir. I have been accepted by the locals now, and if anything is about to happen, I should be able to find out.'

'If you can discover the exact date it will save us spending every night on top of the cliff.'

'You can rely on me, sir.' He marched smartly out of the room.

'He is enjoying himself,' Dexter remarked. 'I believe he is missing the excitement of the army.'

'He is a good man. Do you remember when we were hiding in that barn, surrounded by enemy troops?'

'Oh, I do. We had been taken by surprise, because according to our information they should have been ten miles away.'

'Someone made a mistake there,' Harry remarked. 'And we couldn't understand why they hadn't found our horses. Luckily for us, Carter found them first and hid them.'

'That was a damned uncomfortable night. Those sacks we were hiding under were verminous and stank – and so did we.'

Harry laughed. 'What a relief when they all moved out at dawn. One of them had been sleeping right next to me, and how I kept still all night, I will never know. It was agony trying to get my legs to work again.'

Dexter grimaced as he remembered. 'I was so pleased to see Carter waiting for us a mile down the road with our horses. He had the cheek to ask us if we had had a pleasant night and suggested we jump into the first river we came across.'

'Which we did, much to his approval.'

'Good Lord, Harry,' Dexter said, shaking his head, 'we did find ourselves in some perilous situations.'

'That is true.' He looked at the clock. 'And if we

are late for dinner, we will have to face grandmother's wrath.'

'Oh, no. That is too terrible to contemplate,' his friend joked.

'Bella! I am so pleased you are back. I felt sure His Grace would never want to see you again, you made him so angry,' Angelina whimpered. 'I was very frightened for you. Did he hurt you?'

Isabella looked surprised. 'Of course he did not hurt me. His anger was fierce, but he would never strike a woman.'

'How do you know? He is a strong man.'

'It is precisely because he is a strong man that he does not need to use violence against someone weaker than himself. He has been brought up a gentleman, Angelina, and even in the throes of a black rage he would not have harmed me.'

Her sister looked unconvinced. 'You will not do anything else to enrage him, will you, Bella?'

'I will try. Now you must not let this unfortunate incident make you nervous again.' She looked at Angelina enquiringly. 'I thought you were beginning to like him a little?'

'I do like him, Bella, but I cannot be easy in his company.'

'Well, do try, Angel. He was thinking of you when he asked me to come back. I am a constant irritation to him, but he was concerned because you were unhappy about my absence.'

'Was he?'

'Yes. Does that not show he has your happiness at heart?'

'I suppose it does.' She examined her fingers thoughtfully.

Charlotte came in, dressed for dinner. 'You will be late if you do not hurry.'

'Oh, Lotte, His Grace brought Isabella back because I was unhappy. Is that not surprising?'

'No. If he intends to offer for you, then he will not wish to risk you refusing him. It would be a severe put-down for a man in his position.'

'Lotte,' Angelina wailed. 'You are so unromantic.'

'And you, Angel, read too many of those novels.'

'I know the stories are not true, but they are so beautiful.' She sighed wistfully.

Harry received a tentative smile from Angelina and relaxed. Bringing her sister back seemed to have eased the girl's fears, but he would not press his presence on her for a day or so. Perhaps a gentle ride with her sisters in attendance, and if all went well . . . He smothered a sigh. If only the girl would show some liking for him then he could get this vexing matter settled.

When the evening came to an end, Harry and

Dexter took their leave and went into the study to await news from Carter.

It was almost midnight when they heard someone arriving, but were surprised to see Timothy enter the room, looking angry and distressed.

He greeted them briefly. 'I am pleased to see you have not retired.'

'What brings you here at this time of night, Tim? Nothing is amiss, I hope?' Harry asked, a frown furrowing his brow.

'I have grave news. Someone has tried to burn down the stable block.'

Both men leapt to their feet.

'Was anyone hurt?' Harry questioned.

'No. A stable lad was attending one of the horses when he smelt smoke and raised the alarm. As we ran towards the stables, Baxter saw a man making his escape. We could not chase after him because all hands were needed to douse the fire, but Baxter recognised him.'

'Who was he?' Harry demanded.

'One of Lord Garston's men.'

The language Dexter and Harry used was not fit for anyone's ears.

'So, my warning went unheeded.'

'What was it you said to him, exactly,' Dexter asked.

'I warned him that if anything happened to me . . .' He tailed off.

'You did not include your property.'

'Damn! That was careless of me. I must pay him another visit.'

'We will all go,' Timothy said firmly. 'I will not have someone causing havoc at Sherfields.'

Harry studied Timothy for a moment. He was growing into a fine man, and responsibility for the farm sat well on him. 'That is a good idea, Tim. We will put on a show of force.'

'It's time Garston was made to understand what he is taking on,' Dexter said.

'It is agreed then. We shall ride over first thing in the morning and catch him before he has time to get out of bed.'

'I am very angry, Harry,' Timothy told him. 'There were horses in there and they could have been harmed if the fire had gone undetected.'

'How much damage was done?'

'Very little, fortunately. The stable lad acted with speed and courage. He had the fire almost under control when we reached him, and he has refused to leave the horses in case the villain returns.'

At that moment Carter slipped quietly into the room. He hesitated when he saw Timothy.

'It is all right, Carter,' Dexter assured him. 'Mr Sherfield can be trusted.'

'Is there something else afoot?' Timothy asked, his eyes wide with interest.

'You are already involved in our problems, Tim,' Harry said, motioning Carter to take a seat. 'You may as well hear the rest of it – in fact, we might need your help.'

The boy looked eagerly from one man to the other. 'I would be happy to help in any way.'

Dexter nodded and turned his attention to Carter. 'Did you have any luck?'

'Yes, sir. A couple of the locals were quite tense, and they did not say or drink much, but one of the men was not so reluctant to confide in me. There is a ship due in from France in two days. It will have to land when the tide is coming in, and that will be about four o'clock in the morning.'

'Well done, Carter.' Harry poured the man a large brandy. 'You did not find out what was the purpose of the visit?'

'No, sir. They wouldn't divulge that; but excitement was in the air, I could feel it.'

'No matter, you have done well.'

'It might be dangerous, sir. It would be wise to take a few men with us, then we could spread out and cover all the escape routes.'

'I'll come with you!' Timothy exclaimed.

Carter looked doubtful.

'I will obey orders,' he assured them all. 'I would not do anything to put the operation in jeopardy.'

'Before we recruit you, Tim,' Harry said seriously, 'you had better hear what we are about.'

For the next hour they explained about the traitor and how Dexter had been commissioned to track the informant down.

'If you wish to change your mind, then that is all right. We three,' Dexter encompassed them in a sweep of his hand, 'are skilled in this kind of work – you are not. If the boat is coming to receive a message from the traitor, then things could become very dangerous.'

'I would still like to help. We cannot have our secrets reaching the enemy, for, I fear, the war will soon be upon us again.'

'It will,' Carter exclaimed. 'No doubt that crafty old devil over there is even now gathering his forces.'

Harry stood up and stretched. 'Let us get some rest. We have a busy two days ahead of us.'

The next morning, Harry strode into the breakfast room. Dexter and Timothy were already there, but the rest of the house was still abed.

'Carter is getting the horses ready. Not yours, of course, Harry; he is wise enough to leave that to you.'

'Wish everyone had that much good sense,' he remarked dryly, helping himself to a large plateful of bacon, eggs and mushrooms.

Well-fortified for the morning, they made their way to the stables.

The head groom was examining a saddle and

frowning fiercely, but leapt to his feet when Harry walked in. 'We found the stitching on your saddle was breaking away and it is being repaired. I was preparing your brother's saddle for use today, but there appears to be a small hole in it, Your Grace.'

'Is that so? Was it damaged in the accident?'

'After the accident it was just put in the tack room. We were so upset that we did not examine it carefully, and it hasn't been used since.' The groom started to probe the leather. 'There seems to be something lodged here.'

Harry looked closely. 'It is so deeply embedded you will need to cut the leather away.'

'No, Your Grace,' the groom said in alarm. 'Let me try to remove it without doing too much damage.'

It took him quite a while, but he would not give up. Then he pulled the object out, held it in his hand and gasped.

'What is it?' Harry demanded.

The groom handed it to him and stepped back, a look of horror on his face.

It was a bullet.

Dexter drew in a deep breath. 'You were right to be suspicious about Robert's death.'

Harry's expression was grim as he addressed the groom. 'You were on the scene quite quickly, I believe.'

'Yes, Your Grace. I was in the field next to the woods.'

181

'What alerted you to believe that something was wrong?'

'I thought I heard a horse in distress. I rode into the woods and saw your brother on the ground.'

'Where was the horse?'

'Standing a few yards away, in thick undergrowth, and it was trembling and sweating badly.'

Harry examined the bullet. 'Now we know why. Someone was either trying to kill Robert or frighten the horse.'

'The bullet is from a small pistol,' Dexter remarked, examining it carefully.

'Yes, you are right,' Harry agreed. 'And whether the assailant meant to kill or frighten is of no matter. This is murder.'

'But who would want to do such a thing?' Timothy wanted to know.

'Only one person I can think of but proving it will be a difficult task.' He slipped the bullet into his pocket. 'Not a word of this to anyone for the moment.'

The groom nodded. 'Understood, Your Grace.'

'Now, if you will get me another saddle, we will be on our way. We have a very important call to make.'

Twelve

Harry strode past the protesting butler, flanked on either side by his two friends. They were an unstoppable force and the frightened man did not even try to bar their passage.

'Tell Lord Garston we are here,' he ordered.

'But he is still abed,' he said, obviously not sure if he should be more afraid of waking his master or standing up to these imposing men.

'Then wake him up, man. This is urgent.'

The butler ran up the stairs and pounded on a door. Angry words were heard – then silence. Garston soon appeared, dishevelled and only half-dressed.

'What is the meaning of this intrusion?' He was

trying to ease his bulk into a jacket.

'We have some grave news and I am afraid it could not wait,' Harry informed him curtly.

'News? What news?'

'One of your men tried to set fire to my stables at Sherfields.' He spoke softly now, but the menace in his voice was obvious.

Garston began to bluster. 'I don't see what that has to do with me. I cannot be responsible for everything they do. And anyway, how do you know it was one of my men?'

'He was seen and recognised,' Timothy informed him.

'How could he be recognised in the dark?' he sneered.

'We never said it was dark,' Dexter remarked smoothly.

Garston looked from one man to another. His careless reply had caught him out and he knew it.

'I assumed it was dark – no one would try that in daylight, and I don't believe that someone who works for me would commit such an act.'

'There is no mistake. There was a bright moon and he was seen by someone who knew him.' Harry took a step towards the agitated man. 'What was his name, Tim?'

'Greenwood.'

'Ah, yes, that's right, Henry Greenwood. He is well

known in the district.' Harry shook his head in mock concern. 'How very careless of you to send someone who would be recognised.'

'I did not send him!'

'Did you not? Well, if you would produce the man so that we could question him, this matter can soon be cleared up.'

'I don't know where he is. He left my employ some days ago.'

'That is a shame,' Dexter remarked mildly.

'Indeed, it is.' Timothy joined in. 'Without the man we have no proof that you are telling the truth, Lord Garston.'

'You see our dilemma.' Harry shrugged his impressive shoulders and took another step forward. 'I fear we must hold you responsible. On my last visit I informed you that my safety was of the utmost importance to you. However, in the light of this regrettable incident, I feel it necessary to enlarge upon that to include all my lands, property, animals, staff, relatives and friends.' He turned to Dexter and Timothy. 'Have I forgotten anything?'

'No,' they said. 'That seems to cover it all.'

'Now, about the gambling debts. I must start calling them in at once.'

'But you gave me three months!' The words came out in a high-pitched squeak.

'The situation has changed. I will expect you to

redeem one a week from now on, and if you do not honour that commitment I shall be obliged to relieve you of this very desirable property.'

'You can't do that!' He was sweating profusely now.

'I can. Your debts are considerable and if you cannot pay them, then I shall have no alternative.' He gave a slight bow. 'We bid you good day.'

When they reached the door, Harry turned, took the bullet out of his pocket and held it up for Garston to see. 'Something very unpleasant has come to light. It seems my brother did not have an accident – he was murdered.'

Harry let the words hang in the air for a few heartbeats, then tossed the bullet up, caught it deftly and replaced it into his pocket. 'I shall not rest until my brother's killer has been apprehended.'

They left then, satisfied that they had accomplished what they came for; Garston was a very frightened man.

As soon as they arrived back at Ranliegh, Harry sought out his grandmother. She was still in her chamber, so he knocked on her door, then walked in and sat on her bed. She was propped up against a mountain of pillows with a tray of tea in front of her.

'Harry. What has been going on this morning? So much coming and going, one could not help but be aware of it.'

'I am sorry if we disturbed you. We had some business to attend to.'

She put the cup down and settled herself comfortably. 'You had better tell me about it.'

He explained about the fire and their visit to Lord Garston, then he took hold of her hands. She appeared very frail this morning, he thought worriedly, and the news he had was bound to upset her.

'Get on with it, my boy. I know there is something else.'

He took the bullet out of his pocket and showed it to her. 'We found this embedded in the saddle Robert used on the day he was killed.'

Her eyes closed for a moment and she gripped his hands with surprising force. When she looked at him again, her eyes were blazing with anger.

'Garston?'

'We think so, but we don't have proof. It is possible he thought to get rid of Robert before he could collect any more of his gambling slips. He must have believed that by getting rid of him the gambling slips would be forgotten.'

His grandmother nodded. 'Did you confront that evil man with this suspicion?'

'I showed him the bullet and told him that we knew Robert had been murdered. I could not do more than that without some evidence of his involvement, but he was a very worried man when we left.'

'Do you think he will come after you?' she asked, her face clouded with concern.

'No, I don't think so. He knows I will take everything away from him if there is another hostile act against me.'

'Let us hope you are right, Harry.'

'What do you want to do about this evidence, Grandmother? Do you want the authorities informed?'

'Without proof they will not consider reopening the investigation. I kept insisting it could not have been an accident, but they dismissed my fears; they thought I was a silly old woman who was out of her mind with grief.'

'That was a bad mistake to make.' He smiled at her gently.

'Humph. I told them they were incompetent fools.'

He could imagine the scene, for he knew how uncomfortable it was to be on the receiving end of her censure. 'Leave it with me. If he was involved, then I will see that he is punished.'

She patted his hand. 'I know you will.'

He stood up to take his leave and breathed a sigh of relief. She had taken the news well.

'Do not look so worried, Harry. I am stronger than I look and have no intention of dying until all our business is sorted out.'

'I'm glad to hear that. I don't know what this family would do without you.'

'This family consists of you and I . . . until you get around to increasing its size.'

She looked at him pointedly and he made a hasty exit.

Isabella had been up early, as usual, and had seen the three men leave. Their expressions had been grim so, wisely, she had kept out of the way. Something was going on and she wished she could help, but they would not think of asking her. It was all very frustrating.

In an effort to idle away the time until her sisters had eaten breakfast, she wandered around the kitchen garden. The variety of vegetables growing was huge and the herb garden was a sheer delight. In fact, the whole of Ranliegh was beautiful, but it was more than a country home – it was a working, productive farm. There were fields given over to wheat and barley, pastureland filled with animals and other parts of the estate were wild, untamed. She liked those the best of all, and her early morning rides had been filled with new discoveries each day.

She crushed a piece of lavender in her fingers and took a deep breath. How lovely it was.

There was still no sign of her family, so she wandered into the drawing room to find the Duchess there, staring out of the window. She looked tired and troubled.

'Are you not well?' she asked, hurrying over and

pulling up a stool to sit on. She reached out and took hold of the elderly lady's hands. 'Is there anything I can do?'

'No, dear child, I am well. A little tired perhaps.' She took a deep breath. 'You smell of lavender, Isabella.'

'I have been in the garden, waiting for my family to finish breakfast.'

'You have much vitality, and I hear you leave the house early every morning. Where do you go?'

'Riding. Ranliegh is a beautiful estate and is seen at its best just as the sun is rising.'

'Indeed, it is, and I used to do the same myself.' She pulled a face. 'Past that now, though.'

'I would be pleased to take you in a carriage – I am quite a competent driver,' she assured her confidently. 'My father taught me.'

'Why, I would like that very much.' Then she whispered, 'You must not tell my grandson, though. He will not permit it, I'm afraid.'

'Oh, we cannot do it then, for I have promised to behave myself.' She looked crestfallen.

'And you find that difficult?' Her Grace asked gently.

'Very difficult. You see, I have a questioning nature and like to investigate everything; I cannot help it and I am always getting into trouble. My father was so angry when I returned home, that he has threatened to find me a husband.'

'And you do not wish to be wed?'

Isabella looked thoughtful. 'I would like a husband and a family, but I would like a gentleman to marry me because he loves me, not for my fortune.'

'I understand. I was the same.'

'Were you? And did you marry the man of your choice?'

'Of course. Once I had made my mind up nothing could turn me. Though, I did not have much opposition from my family. My husband was a fine man.'

'Is your grandson like him?'

'The image of him – in looks and temperament.'

Isabella lapsed into silence for a moment. 'I am sorry to have displeased His Grace. I acted without thinking, which is a lamentable habit of mine, and he was very angry. Not that I blame him,' she added hastily, not wishing to malign his character.

'My grandson has much on his mind, Isabella, and he does not mean to be harsh. You must not let him frighten you.'

'He does not frighten me,' she declared with honesty. 'I was upset because I had caused him to be angry. I really must try to change my ways.'

'No, you must not. You have vitality, curiosity and a loving heart. Any man would be fortunate to have you as his wife.'

'That is hard to believe.' She looked wistful. 'Papa says I am a great trial.'

'Nonsense. See, I have brightened up already; your company has been invigorating.'

The door opened and Harry strode in. He kissed his grandmother's cheek. 'You are looking better.'

'Yes, I have been having a most interesting talk with Isabella and it has chased away my worries.'

Isabella stood up as he entered the room, and when he looked at her, she curtsied.

'I have not been tiring her.' He looked so stern that she thought it wise to offer her defence at once.

'I can see that you have not.'

'Oh.' That was a surprise; he had looked ready to shout at her again.

'We are going for a ride and wondered if you would like to join us? Your sisters are at this moment getting ready.'

'I would like that very much,' she exclaimed eagerly.

Isabella sped off to get changed. It did not take her long and she was soon running into the courtyard just as the men were bringing the horses out.

They trotted along at a sedate pace, which she had difficulty maintaining – her mount was fresh and eager for exercise. On her early morning rides she was able to go at her own pace – which was usually at a good gallop – but in a group she had to moderate her enthusiasm. It was not easy.

At one point she found herself riding beside the Duke. 'I see you are not riding Lucifer, Your Grace, and I should have liked to see him at a gallop.'

'You appear uncommonly interested in my horse,' he remarked, looking at her with suspicion.

'I have not been near him again,' she hastened to assure him. 'However, I would have liked to see him.' She sighed sadly. 'From a distance, of course.'

'He has already been exercised.'

'Yes, I know. I saw you all ride out early this morning.' She looked at him enquiringly. 'You were in a great hurry – was there anything amiss?'

'Some business to attend to, that was all.' The tone of his voice warned her not to pursue the subject.

She started to drop back. He was frowning again. Would she ever learn to curb her curiosity, and why had she mentioned the horse? That was enough to send him into a rage. She should have talked about the weather. The trouble was, she always had sensible ideas when it was too late.

'Why does Lucifer interest you so much?' he asked, reaching out to stop her from moving away from his side.

She was surprised he had returned to the subject. 'He is magnificent; so huge, powerful and intelligent.'

'And that does not frighten you?'

'No. Why should it?'

'Does anything frighten you?'

'I do not think so.' She thought for a while. 'Perhaps my impulsive nature . . . now that does cause me moments of concern. However, your grandmother told me not to try and change.'

He tipped his head back and roared with laughter. 'I am sure she did. You are very much alike, I think.'

'I shall take that as a great compliment.' She grinned cheekily at him.

'Hmm.' He surveyed her carefully and appeared to come to a decision. 'When we get back from our ride, I shall take you to see Lucifer again.'

'Oh, will you? I would like that very much.' She beamed in excitement.

He nodded. 'However, you will not go near him unless I am present. Is that understood?'

'I shall do as you say. And thank you.'

She could not resist a gallop then. He had forgiven her. She had quite fallen in love with the animal, and even though he had a fierce reputation, she was positive he would never hurt her – very much like his master.

The ride took her to a part of the estate she had never been to before. At the top of the rise was the most beautiful view: the rolling countryside was green and fertile, and the sea, only a short distance away, was shimmering in the sunlight. They dismounted and sat looking at the scene.

Isabella was pleased to see that Angelina was more relaxed. They were a short distance from the rest of the party and the Duke was pointing something out to her. Her sister was smiling.

'They appear to be getting along better.' The captain sat beside her.

'Yes, indeed.' Why wasn't she happy about that? 'Do you think he will offer for her, Captain?'

'I cannot say. It is what his grandmother would like, but he will have to be sure it is the right thing for your sister and himself.'

'He will do as his grandmother wishes, will he not? He loves her greatly.'

'Yes, he does, and he will avoid upsetting her if he can. However, in the matter of choosing a wife, he will make the final decision, and Her Grace knows that.'

'Yes, of course.'

They made their way back then, and as the groom led the horses away, Isabella looked expectantly at the tall, dark man standing beside her.

'Shall we see Lucifer now, Your Grace?'

He nodded and strode towards the stables.

The horse whinnied as they approached and tossed his head. 'Hello, old boy, I have brought you a visitor.'

She put her hand out to open the door.

'No! You do not go inside.'

'Very well.' She was not going to argue. This was a huge concession on his part, and he was obviously uneasy about her approaching the animal. She rubbed Lucifer's nose and he dropped his massive head towards her pocket.

'Oh, see, he remembers,' she exclaimed. 'May I give him an apple?'

Harry took one out of a barrel, handed it to her and watched the horse's every move. The apple was taken quite gently and munched with appreciation.

'He is so beautiful,' she sighed. 'Have you thought of putting him out to stud? He would have magnificent offspring, and I have noticed several fine quality mares on the paddock.' She continued to pet the horse who had taken on an amazingly docile look.

'I have thought about it, but what if they inherited his temperament?' He studied her, clearly surprised that a young lady should discuss such a topic.

'I doubt they would be as aggressive. I would think Lucifer had been maltreated before you took him over.'

'Quite likely.' He caressed the animal fondly. 'Now, we must go.'

She had difficulty keeping up with his long, impatient stride. 'Thank you for allowing me to see him again. How I would love to ride him.'

He stopped so suddenly that she nearly tripped over him.

'Don't you ever try it! That is something I will never forgive.'

'But if you were there?'

'No!' He glared at her. 'You do know the meaning of that word?'

She nodded and closed her mouth tightly to stop more words spilling out. Oh dear, she had overstepped the bounds again.

For the rest of the day and the next, she tried to hold her tongue and stay out of his way. He took Angelina riding several times, and each time her sister returned she seemed more and more uneasy. Time was getting short, the ball was only days away, and what was going to happen then?

As far as Isabella was concerned, the ball was a blessing. She had taken on much of the arranging, under the Duchess's guidance, of course. It was a splendid outlet for her energy, and she revelled in the challenge.

That night she was restless and could not sleep. It was the early hours of the morning when she heard sounds outside her window. She looked down and saw three men outside. They were all dressed in black, but she knew who they were by their stature, and the two magnificent war horses were unmistakable. A fourth man joined them, and she guessed it was Carter.

They did not mount but led their horses away from the house. She leant out of the window to watch them and was overcome with excitement. Where were they going that it required such secrecy?

She started to dress hurriedly, choosing a dark riding habit and not stopping to consider what she was doing; she had to know what was going on. Whatever was happening, it was too mysterious for her to ignore, and if she was careful they would never know she was there.

She crept down the stairs, trying to avoid the ones she knew creaked. The kitchen was dark and silent as she groped her way to the back door, and after easing the bolts back, she stepped into the yard and hurried to the stables.

She saddled a quiet, steady mare, and like the men, she led her horse away from the house before mounting. Then she urged it into a trot, keeping to the grassy verges in order to muffle the sound of the hooves.

She was lucky – they had not hurried, and she reached the crossroads just in time to see them disappearing.

They were heading for the coast.

Thirteen

Harry crawled towards the edge of the cliff. There was enough light from the moon to be able to see the beach clearly, but the problem was they would also be visible if they were not very careful.

He reached a good vantage point, found a small hollow and laid flat in it. Carter was on the beach somewhere and Dexter and Timothy had taken up positions a little further along. Nothing was happening yet, but if their information was correct, there should be activity at any moment.

The back of his neck prickled. Damn! There was that feeling again; it had plagued him constantly on their way here and Carter had doubled back to check but found nothing. That had not eased his mind, because his instinct told him they were being followed, and it never let him down. When you had become used to being stalked by hostile forces who wanted to kill you, your senses were heightened.

He heard the yap of the fox in the distance and knew it was Dexter alerting him to the incoming boat.

A cloud hid the moon, and as darkness swept across his hiding place, he heard someone walking towards him. The footfall was soft and cautious, hardly audible. He had been right; someone had followed them.

He did not move a muscle; his breathing was quiet and evenly regulated.

He waited.

Then, when he glimpsed a foot close to him, he acted with lightning speed. In a split second the interloper was pinned underneath him with his hands over their mouth. The manoeuvre had been carried out without a sound.

Harry straddled the person, trapping him between his powerful thighs – then he froze. If there had not been a need for silence he would have sworn out loud. There was no mistaking the feel of soft, feminine curves underneath him.

It was a woman.

The moon came from behind the cloud and he was looking into a pair of blue eyes, wide with shock.

With his hand still over her mouth, he lowered his

head until he was level with her ear. 'Keep silent and very still,' he growled.

She tried to nod.

He stayed in that position as he could hear sounds of people coming along the cliff, then they started to clamber down the hidden pathway to his left, and he estimated that there must be about four or five of them. Add them to the men about to come ashore and things could get very dangerous, and now he had this damned, stupid, interfering woman to protect.

He let out a pent-up breath. They had not been seen, which was miraculous. It was going to give him great pleasure to put this infuriating termagant across his knee and give her the hiding she deserved, but as appealing as the idea was, he was reacting to the soft, womanly feel of her. He could not be concerned about that, though, because it was imperative they were not seen or heard.

Isabella moved again and he whispered in her ear, 'If you value your life, keep still and do not utter a sound.'

She pushed his chest, her eyes begging him to move.

He knew he must be crushing her, so he shifted his weight until he was stretched out beside her, but he kept one leg across her body, effectively pinning her to the ground. He did not trust her.

'Get off me!' she gasped.

'Quiet!'

'You are heavy . . .'

That was all she had time to say as his mouth covered hers. He had only meant to shock her into silence, but she felt and tasted so delicious, he could not stop himself, and the kiss went on and on. Quite lost to anything but sensation, the reason for him being here faded into the background.

A sound from the beach brought him back to reality. Good God! What was he doing? To hell with what his grandmother thought – he would have to get himself a mistress.

The sound of men coming up the path made him lift his head. 'Do not move,' he ordered in a growled whisper, then he crawled towards the edge.

On their way up the men were labouring, gasping for breath. He stopped at a place where he could see and not be seen, and the first thing to appear was a barrel, then a man, and after that another four more barrels were rolled onto the cliff top. The men hoisted them onto their shoulders and lumbered off into the darkness.

Smugglers! But had there been a messenger on the beach as well, perhaps using this operation as a cover? He would have to rely on Carter for that information as he had been too occupied to see much. The woman was a menace.

He grimaced as he remembered the way he had kissed her. Hell, he was supposed to be marrying her sister, and now he really was in a mess.

There was a rustling beside him, and Isabella

appeared, on her hands and knees. 'Have they gone?' she whispered.

'I told you not to move.'

'They did not see me; I moved along the ground as you did.' She sounded quite proud of herself.

He stood up and pulled her to her feet. 'What the hell are you doing here?'

'I was awake and saw you leave. I wanted to know what you were being so secretive about.'

'This is none of your business! You could have put us all in jeopardy.'

'But I did not. You gave me no chance – I was down before I had time to draw breath.' She rubbed her hip.

'You were fortunate I only restrained you. If I had been in France you would now be dead.'

She glared at him accusingly. 'Your conduct has not been exemplary.'

'I was under extreme provocation.'

'And that excuses your actions?'

It did not, and he knew it. 'I must apologise for my conduct. However, you didn't protest overmuch.'

'How could I?' she said, scornfully. 'With your great weight across me, I could not move so much as an inch. Anyway,' she looked away from his blazing eyes, 'I found it . . . interesting.'

'Interesting?' He nearly choked. 'I swear you don't have the faintest notion of the danger you were in.'

'You would have caused me no harm,' she told him confidently.

He shook his head in bewilderment. Good grief! He had never come across anyone like her before, and it was no wonder her father had been unable to find her a husband.

'You should not be so trusting.' His harsh expression was back. 'And your reckless nature needs controlling.'

'Miss Isabella! What are you doing here?' Dexter exclaimed as he reached them. He was closely followed by Timothy and Carter, both staring at her in astonishment.

'She followed us,' Harry informed them.

'But I didn't see you when I doubled back to take a look.' Carter could not hide his amazement.

'I saw you coming and hid,' she told him proudly.

'My word, Miss, you would have made a fine soldier.'

Harry put a stop to this exchange. What she needed was a set down, not praise. 'What was going on down there, Carter?'

'Smuggling, sir. Brandy from France by the look of it. Young Percy was there all right, so that proves that the little devil is getting his money illegally. He was the one giving orders, so it appears he is running a very lucrative smuggling operation.'

'No sign of any other activity?'

'No, sir. They unloaded the boat and left. I was

close enough to see if anything else changed hands, but it didn't, I am certain of that.'

'Not what we are looking for, then.' Dexter was disappointed.

Harry turned to Carter. 'Where were they heading with their bounty?'

'Back to the village, would be my guess.'

'Right, let's have a scout around before returning to Ranliegh.'

'Oh, good.' Isabella picked up her skirt and started towards her horse.

Harry caught hold of her. 'Not you! You have caused enough havoc for one night. Carter will take you back. Where is your horse?'

'With yours, of course.'

He glared at her. 'How did you find them?'

'Lucifer told me where they were, he heard me coming.'

Dexter chuckled. 'Betrayed by your own horse, Harry.'

'I must have a word with that animal, he is getting disloyal.' His disgusted comment made the others grin.

'He likes me, and he has enough sense to know that I mean no harm.'

Harry had had enough. 'Take her back, Carter, before I lose my temper again. And you,' he turned to Isabella, 'will do as you are told, and I will see you in the library at half past ten.'

'No harm has been done . . .'

'Enough! For heaven's sake get her back without anyone seeing her. There will be uproar if this escapade is discovered, and not a word about this – is that understood?' Everyone nodded, except Isabella. 'That includes you.'

'Do you think me some silly female who cannot keep a secret?' She sounded highly offended.

He shook his head ruefully. She did not even know the trouble she was in, or the impossible situation she had now placed on him.

They watched her go, protesting all the time, and Dexter murmured, 'I have never encountered such recklessness in a woman. Her father must be in despair of her.'

Harry ground his teeth in frustration. 'She should be locked up.'

Isabella did not want to go back to Ranliegh, but she had no choice, and she still did not know why they had been there. They had been watching smugglers, but she had discerned from their conversation that that had not been what they were after. There was something else going on, and she would dearly love to know what it was. Her curious nature had always brought her trouble, and she was used to it, but she could not regret her impulsive action. It had been the most exciting thing she had ever experienced.

It did not take long to get back to the house, and it was still too early for anyone to be up, much to Isabella's relief.

Carter gave her a gentle push towards the house. 'Now quickly, off you go.'

The kitchens were deserted, and she made it back to her room without incident. She quickly removed her soiled riding habit and set about cleaning the worse of the grass and dirt from it, then she tucked it in her closet, behind her other clothes, hoping it would not be noticed. The mess they were in would be very hard to explain away.

After a quick wash, she brushed her hair thoroughly, removing any loose pieces of grass, put on her nightgown and slipped into bed. And not a moment too soon, there were sounds of the servants starting their morning chores. She smiled to herself. No one would ever know she had left the house.

She was not feeling quite so confident as she knocked on the library door at half past ten. During the short time before dawn, the realisation of what she had done had begun to sink in, and the memory of his kiss would not be erased. That had been her first passionate encounter, and quite honestly, she had found it beautiful. She envied her sister, for he was obviously a man with great emotional depth. He had only acted that way in an effort to keep her quiet, of course, but nevertheless, it had been quite an experience.

Envy was not something she had ever experienced before, so she brushed it ruthlessly aside and entered the room, ready to face his wrath.

He had his back to her, looking out of the window. She waited for him to turn around and when he did, she curtsied gracefully.

'Close the door. We don't wish this conversation to be overheard.'

His angry expression did not bode well for her and she prayed that he was not going to send her away. She looked at his mouth, now set in a grim line, and remembered his kisses again. Then his lips had been soft, coaxing a response from her.

'Sit down, please.'

She sat as gracefully as possible. Trying very hard not to show her agitation. He studied her speculatively for a moment, then turned his head and looked out of the window again. She found the silence unnerving.

'Did you discover anything else, last night?' she blurted out, her curiosity getting the better of her again.

'No.'

The reply was short and curt, so she decided it would not be wise to ask any more questions. Indeed, she should not have asked that one.

'First,' he said suddenly, making her jump. 'I must apologise for my conduct last night.'

'You had every right to be angry, Your Grace. I do not blame you for that.'

She was taken by surprise at his apology – that was not what she had expected at all.

'I am not talking about my justifiable anger,' he snapped.

'Oh,' she coloured slightly. 'You mean . . .' The words tailed off.

'Let us put it into words, shall we? It is quite unnecessary to be coy.'

She looked him straight in the eyes. 'You kissed me.'

'Bravo!' His sarcastic tone cut through her. 'Now we have the matter into the open.'

'We are the only ones who know about it,' she hastened to assure him.

'Be quiet!'

She sighed and shut up.

'I shall approach your father and offer for you.'

She leapt to her feet in alarm. 'No, no, you cannot do that!'

'I cannot do anything else.'

The look of disgust and resignation on his face made her angry. 'Stop trying to act like a gentleman. You were a soldier again last night, and you reacted like one, Major.' She would not be coerced into a marriage just because he felt honour-bound to wed her. Especially when it was a prospect that clearly appalled him.

She was standing in front of him, hands on hips,

head tipped back so she could look him in the eyes. 'I would make you a dreadful wife, and if you approach my father you will have to tell him why you are choosing me instead of my sister.'

'I don't want this any more than you, but I see no other way.'

''But nobody knows!' She felt like stamping her foot in exasperation.

'I compromised you. Don't you understand?' He had raised his voice alarmingly.

'Shush,' she urged. 'Do you want the whole house to hear?'

'Don't you care that your reputation will be lost?' He moderated his tone.

'Don't be silly!' She was exasperated. These men with their stupid code of honour. 'I do not want or need your self-sacrifice. That would plunge us into the kind of marriage I have fought to avoid, and if you proceed with this preposterous idea, I shall refuse.'

'You father will not allow you to do so.'

They were now facing each other like prize fighters. Each one as stubborn as the other.

'Then I shall leave home. I have independent means.'

He backed away, shaken. She loved her family, and yet she would rather leave them than face a marriage she did not want. 'I am only trying to do right by you.'

'I understand that, and I respect your strong sense

of honour, but this is not necessary. I returned to my room undetected, and no harm has been done.'

She gave him an easy smile, sensing victory. He was beginning to waver.

'If that is what you want?' He made a gesture of surrender.

'It is.'

'You can rest assured that none of us will mention your presence last night.'

'I trust you all implicitly.' She turned to leave the room, taking deep breaths of relief. A disaster had been averted. There could not be a worse fate than being married to a man who had offered for you only out of a sense of honour – he would resent her for the rest of his life.

'Just a moment. I hope you did not sustain any injuries.' He looked slightly amused now. 'I thought I was dealing with a man.'

'No. The thick grass cushioned my fall, but for a moment I did think I was going to suffocate.' She gave him an impudent grin. 'You are rather heavy.'

The corners of his mouth twitched, but he did not allow a smile to form. He just nodded and turned back to the window, effectively dismissing her.

As the door closed, Harry's shoulders began to shake in silent laughter. Whether it was relief or amusement, he was not too sure. A mixture of the two, probably.

'Stop trying to act like a gentleman,' she had told

him with force. My God! He didn't think she had even realised the danger she had been in. At that moment she had been in more peril from him than the men on the beach.

'Have you been shouting at Isabella again, Harry?' His grandmother came into the room. 'I heard raised voices.'

'We have been arguing again, Grandmother,' he told her dryly.

'But why?'

He shrugged. 'We cannot seem to have a civilised conversation. She is too outspoken, and I find her constant curiosity irritating.'

She gave him a keen glance. 'You were laughing to yourself when I entered.'

'A touch of hysteria – she has that effect upon me. She should be locked up out of harm's way.'

'Or married with a brood of children to keep her occupied.'

'Her father has that in mind, and he is already casting around for a suitable husband for her. Though where he is going to find such a paragon, I have no notion.'

'Let us hope there is such a man. It is by far the best thing for her, because she would make an admirable wife for the man who can handle her.'

'On the subject of marriage.' He helped his grandmother into a chair. 'Angelina is a charming girl, but she is still uneasy in my presence, and in view of that, I am not at all sure that she will be the right wife for me.'

'Are you not, Harry?'

She had a look of pure innocence on her face. He knew it well and did not trust it. However, now that he had his grandmother's attention, he continued to state his doubts. And after last night, those doubts were increasing.

'If everyone is expecting an announcement at the ball, then I fear I cannot comply. We both need more time.'

'Of course. If you are not sure about a union between you, then you must leave it for a while.'

He could not believe he was hearing this. 'And if I do decide against this proposed marriage?'

'Then you will tell me and her father.' She smiled affectionately at him. 'All I want is for you to be happy. You will make the right choice, and do not feel obliged to rush things.'

He was speechless.

She stood up and walked towards the door, muttering happily to herself. 'It is all proceeding nicely. Yes, just as I expected.'

Harry watched her in astonishment. What the blazes was she talking about? What was proceeding nicely? As far as he could see, everything was an unholy mess.

Fourteen

Harry was on the rise, looking out to sea when Dexter found him. His friend dismounted and sat beside him.

'Thought I would find you here. Tell me to go away if you need solitude.'

'No, I welcome your company. I was just puzzling over grandmother's strange mood.'

'Really? I have just seen her, and she appears to be in good spirit.'

'That's the trouble. When she is being too accommodating, I become uneasy.'

He friend laughed. 'I know she has sneaky ways of achieving her aims, but what is she up to now?'

'She has suddenly declared that I do not have to rush into finding a wife.'

'Oh! That does sound ominous. It is a complete turn-about, and I think you have need to be uneasy, Harry.'

'She will reveal her hand, eventually.' Harry plucked a piece of grass and started to chew on it, gazing into the distance.

'How did your interview go with Miss Isabella this morning?'

Harry made a sound like a strangled laugh. 'It was very enlightening; she does not hold on to her words.'

'She was not contrite then?'

'Contrite?! I don't think she knows the meaning of the word. I was trying to do the gentlemanly thing, and she flays me with her sharp tongue. She is much too forthright in her speech and told me to stop trying to act like a gentleman.' He then gave Dexter an outline of what had happened, including his passionate encounter with her, and by the time he had finished, Dexter was doubled up with mirth.

'Good Lord, Harry. She is quite the most unusual female we have ever encountered. She has given you quite a set-down.'

A grin tugged at the corners of Harry's mouth. He was not at all put-out by her forceful refusal. In fact, he admired her for her stand, and he felt as if a burden had been lifted from his shoulders. Not only had he been let off lightly after the incident with Isabella, but his grandmother had given him a breathing space. And yet . . . there was something nagging away at the back of his mind, but he just couldn't decide what it was.

'I know that frown,' Dexter remarked. 'What is troubling you still?'

'I don't know,' he sighed. 'I'm making a terrible mess of trying to find a wife, am I not?'

'You are being pushed, that is all, Harry. If you had been left to your own choice . . .' Dexter stopped in mid-sentence. 'Who's this coming in such a hurry?'

They watched the horseman coming towards them. It was Carter.

'I have some news, sir. I met one of the men involved in the smuggling; he was telling me about an establishment just along the coast. He said a lot of the nobility go there.'

'A brothel?' Harry asked.

'More than that. There is gambling and quiet rooms for gentlemen to meet in, and he reckons that a lot of underhand business goes on there. I thought I should tell you at once because they wouldn't let me in such a place,' he added dolefully.

'And no doubt they serve the best French brandy?' Dexter asked.

'Undoubtedly, sir.'

'What say we pay this house a visit tonight, Harry?'

He nodded in agreement. 'I could do with a diversion.'

The large, elegant house was set in acres of its own grounds, and the long tree-lined driveway led up to and impressive entrance. The lawns and flower beds were so immaculately tended that it did not look as if a weed dared to take root.

Dexter whistled as they cantered up the driveway. 'Doesn't look like a brothel.'

'No. I have seen this place before, but never thought it was a house of ill repute. It must be very exclusive, for they have kept the secret well.'

The inside was even more impressive. No gaudy decorations or half-clad females. In fact, it had the appearance of a gentleman's club, expect for the presence of expensively dressed women.

'Very exclusive!' Dexter muttered under his breath.

A woman glided towards them. She was past fifty, Harry assessed, but very well presented and wearing a dress of dark blue velvet. She was elegant and still beautiful, until you looked into her eyes. The harshness showing there revealed her as a calculating woman and not one to be trifled with.

'Good evening, gentlemen. You have not graced my house with your presence before.'

'That is our loss.' Harry bowed gracefully and turned to Dexter. 'Do you not agree?'

'Indeed. You have a most impressive establishment.'

'May I ask how you came to hear about us?'

'A friend. You come highly recommended.' Harry bestowed on her a smile of lethal charm.

Dexter wondered why he did not use that on Angelina – she would have fallen at his feet, like all the women. Even this hard-bitten businesswoman was wilting under his amber gaze.

She inclined her head. 'Then you are welcome, sirs. You will find everything you need for your entertainment. My girls are of the highest quality and well looked after, you need have no fears about them.'

She gave Dexter an assessing look. 'I have a young girl, only just arrived, and I believe she would please you, sir.'

'If she comes with your recommendation, then I am sure she would.'

She turned her attention back to Harry. 'Of course, if you would like personal service?'

'That is very generous of you,' he told her, looking impressed.

'I do not often make such an offer.'

He bowed. 'I am flattered, Madam.'

'Now, I am sure you would like to have a look around.' She became the businesswoman again. 'We do not use names here, and I must ask you to be discreet if you encounter anyone you know.'

She bestowed one more, hungry, look on him, then turned and walked away.

'You have made an impression, Harry,' Dexter murmured in his ear.

They walked into the gaming room, but high stakes were not being played for. It was clearly a social occasion where gambling was not taken seriously.

'Let us have a drink,' Harry suggested. 'Then we will separate for the evening.'

Madam was waiting for them when they returned to the main lounge.

'Are you happy with the house?' she asked.

'We are most impressed. An ideal place for a man to relax.' Dexter turned on the charm and he was as expert at it as his friend. 'We see the men are playing for modest stakes. Is that the policy of the house?'

'Yes. When large amounts are wagered the atmosphere becomes tense, and that is not the purpose of an evening here.' She gave him an almost friendly smile. 'I will bring Emma to you. She is a lovely girl.'

He bowed. 'Thank you.'

She looked at Harry. 'And you, sir, what is your pleasure?'

'I have yet to decide.' His gaze swept the room and then came back to rest on her. 'There is a wealth of beauty here.'

She smiled again, only this time it was genuine.

'You take your time. Would you like a drink whilst you decide?'

'Brandy, please, for both of us.'

They settled down in comfortable armchairs and watched her glide away.

'You are playing with her, Harry. You have no intention of taking her up on her offer.'

'Of course not. You know I am fastidious in my choice of women – as you are yourself. A mistress who remains loyal is one thing, but this,' he looked around the room, 'is another matter, and is not for me.'

'I agree. However, we will have to appear interested . . .' He stopped on a gasp. 'Good Lord, Harry, is that her? She looks little more than a child, and quite innocent.'

'Don't be fooled,' he said under his breath as they stood up.

'This is the young lady. Of course, as this is her first night here, she will be more expensive.'

'That is understood.'

'I knew I had chosen the right gentleman. Oh, and my girls only drink champagne.'

'Perhaps you would be kind enough to have a bottle sent over,' Dexter said easily, looking as if he was well pleased with the whole arrangement.

'I hope you have deep pockets, my friend,' Harry murmured as the lady hurried away.

'You know I haven't, but you have, and I am sure

you would deem it a pleasure to dub up for the evening.'

'I had better see if I can win some money then.' He was laughing as he made his way to the card room.

He did win, but purposely lost it again. He had been taught how to handle cards by some of the best card sharps in the army. That was why he never gambled seriously; he could manipulate the cards and had a remarkable memory. Those dubious skills, of course, would not be used in public, but he could spot anyone else's attempts to cheat, and men who risked their fortune on the turn of a card were fools in his eyes. There was no chance of anyone doing that here, though, because there was a limit on the stakes.

After about an hour he left the room and wandered back into the lounge. There was no sign of Dexter so he guessed he had gone upstairs, and he had better do the same, or he would arouse suspicion.

He looked the girls over, dismissing those who met his gaze boldly. Then he noticed a man pulling one of the girls towards the stairs, and the look of distaste on her face caught his attention. She was trying to refuse the man, but he would not listen.

He scrutinised her customer, but there was nothing unusual at first glance. He was dressed in the height of fashion, a little too gaudy, but passably good-looking – then the man turned and Harry saw him full face. No wonder the girl was protesting; there was a strange wild look in his eyes, and he had a cruel mouth. His character was stamped across his face, branding him as a violent man. The girl had reason to be afraid of him.

He watched them disappear and quickly made his choice. He noticed the girl sitting in the corner, looking as if she hoped no one would see her. Perfect. He walked across, bowed politely and ordered the obligatory bottle of champagne. Without wasting any time, he picked up the bottle and two glasses, then he motioned towards the stairs. The girl stood up obediently and led the way to her room, which like everything else in the house, was tastefully furnished and comfortable.

She started to unlace her dress and he held up his hand.

'There's no need for that.'

She looked startled. 'Do you not want me to undress, sir?'

'No.' He turned the full force of his smile on her. 'I would like to talk and enjoy this champagne. Is that not permitted?'

'Yes, sir. If that's what you want. You will have to pay just the same, though,' she added hastily.

'I understand that. Do you get many who only want to talk?'

'A few, sir. The gentlemen who come here might have wealth, but some of them are lonely.' She eyed him thoughtfully. 'You don't look like a man who is lonely, though.'

'I'm not. I came with a friend tonight and thought I had better show some interest, or Madam would not let me in again.'

The girl giggled. 'You look wealthy; she would not refuse you entrance.'

'Oh, I thought she was careful about her clientele.'

'Well, she is, but sometimes she lets men in we would rather not see.'

'Like the unpleasant young man who dragged your friend off?' he asked.

He had the girl in the right mood now; she had relaxed and was drinking freely. She shuddered. 'We all hope he won't choose us.'

'If he is so very unpleasant, why is he allowed in?' He filled her glass again. He wouldn't need to drink the disgusting stuff at this rate.

'We are not sure. Madam knows about him, because she has to tend our bruises afterwards, but waves away our complaints. He spends a lot of money, and we think he must be well connected.'

'Hmm. I have never seen him before. Do you know his name?'

'Well,' she giggled, we are not supposed to know customers' names, but I did hear someone call him Harcourt.'

'Harcourt?'

'Yes, sir. Have you heard of him?'

'Can't say I have. Now, tell me about this house.'

He endured over an hour of her chatter, learnt a great deal about her life, not enough about the woman in charge, and nothing of interest about the clientele. When he went downstairs again, Dexter was there.

'I have had enough of this place,' Harry told him. He paid the exorbitant bill and assured Madam that they would come again.

'What was your girl like?' Harry asked jokingly, as they rode away.

'As you guessed – not so innocent. It's a trick played on newcomers. The girl was a bit surly when I refused her, but after I had plied her with drink, she was happy enough to talk.'

'Anything useful?'

'Nothing we are looking for. Did you find out anything interesting?'

'I did recognise a few faces, but none of them would have access to secret information. There was one rather nasty character there though – Harcourt. Did you see him?'

Dexter shook his head. 'He was mentioned. None of the girls like him, but he appears to have a free run of the place.'

'I wonder why?'

'Bella. I must talk with you.' Angelina hurried into the room. She was bristling with outrage.

Isabella looked at her in stunned amazement. Was this her gentle sister?

'It is the outside of enough! I will not be treated in this manner.'

'What are you talking about, Angel? Who has upset you?'

'Do you need to ask that? His Grace, of course.'

Isabella sighed. 'Do stop pacing about, you are making me feel giddy.'

Her sister sat on the bed and curled her legs underneath her. She looked like a small, angry and frightened child.'

'What has he done now?'

'Nothing! That is the problem. The ball is almost upon us and I still do not know if he is going to offer for me.' Her bottom lip jutted out and trembled. 'I do not think he even likes me.'

'Have you spoken to father?'

'Papa says we must wait.' She jumped up and started to pace the room again. 'I have been waiting on him and I will not wait any longer! I want to know what his intentions are. I do not wish to marry him, but if that is to be my fate, then I must know now.' She stamped her foot. 'Why can't he make his mind up? This uncertainty is distressing.'

'Calm down, Angel. This is not like you.'

'I will not calm down! I cannot bear this. I curtsy, I smile, try to be agreeable, and all the time I want to scream at him – make up your mind. Life with him will be dreadful, for we do not suit, Bella – we do not suit . . .' Tears started to run down her cheeks. 'Do something, Bella.'

She had never seen her sister so distraught and realised, for the first time, what a strain she had been under. And she was right; it was time the infuriating man declared his intentions.

Angelina came and put her arms around her distraught sister. 'He frightens me, Bella. He is so strong and forbidding in his manner. Life with him will be beyond all bearing.'

'Go back to your room, Angel, and I will clear this matter up.' She would not have her sister upset in this manner.

He was difficult to find, but at last she tracked him down to the ballroom, supervising the placement of the chairs. Her anger had been building up by the minute and she stormed up to him. 'I would like to have a word with you.'

He led her into a nearby room, which would be used as the ladies' retiring room, then he closed the door and raised a brow in query.

'You are upsetting my sister.'

'In what way?' he asked blandly.

'You are dithering. The poor girl is being kept on tenterhooks, not knowing what her future will be.'

'Is she so anxious to wed, then?' His eyes began to glow with fury.

'You know very well that she is not, but she an obedient girl and will do whatever father orders. She will wed you, if that is what you want, regardless of her own feelings, so have some pity and make your intentions clear.'

His anger was obvious. 'Why do you think I have held off this long? Your sister is terrified in my presence. She flinches when I help her off her horse, so how can I inflict myself on her in a more intimate way when she does that? This delay has been caused by her attitude. I cannot marry a woman who finds my touch distasteful.'

'That is unfortunate, but it will pass. She will come around . . . eventually.'

'Eventually is not good enough.' His voice was steadily rising in volume. 'As you well know, this family is in desperate need of an heir. How will that be accomplished? Come on, tell me!'

'Control your temper! A gentleman would not keep shouting.'

'Ah, but I am not a gentleman, am I? I am merely a rough soldier – that was your opinion, I believe?'

'I did not call you a rough soldier! I simply implied that you had slipped back into the role of soldier.' She had the grace to blush as she remembered the incident on the cliff top.

He was not placated. 'And what have you to say about your actions, Miss Winslow? You did not appear to be shocked or frightened.'

'I am not frightened of you . . .'

Before she had time to enlarge on her statement, she was dragged into his arms and kissed with ruthless efficiency. Struggle would have been futile against his strength – and much to her shame she did not want to resist.

'No,' he murmured under his breath as he pulled away from her, 'you are not frightened of me, but you should be.'

He turned sharply and walked towards the window. She waited, saying nothing. She needed these few moments to gather together the rags of her composure.

She watched his huge shoulders rise and fall as he took in a deep breath and then let it out again. She knew his emotions must be in turmoil as were hers. Then he faced her, his expression cold, distant.

'I shall be in the rose garden. Ask your sister to join me there.'

Harry stormed out. What on earth was the matter with him? When he was with that girl all reason fled. She was the most infuriating female he had ever encountered, and she had the temerity to stand before him, hands on hips and eyes turning the colour of a stormy sky. Was it any wonder he silenced her in the only effective way. But she had the right of it; he was not acting like a gentleman towards these two sisters.

He strode along the path, heading for the gardens, muttering angrily to himself. He had to calm down before Angelina arrived.

'You sent for me, Your Grace.'

She spoke quietly, which was like music to his ears after the blazing row he had just been involved in. He led her to a seat.

'Your sister has informed me that you are unhappy.'

'I am sorry, Your Grace. I should not have involved her in my silly worries, but we do tend to lean on her, and she must find us quite a burden.'

'I am sure she does not see it like that.'

'I hope you did not shout at her again.' She looked down in embarrassment.

He grimaced. 'We always shout, Miss Angelina. We have a most unfortunate effect upon each other.'

'That is because you are both strong people.'

'No doubt you are right. However, we are not here to discuss your sister. I am aware that you do not like me.'

'Oh, no, that is not so—'

He stopped her with an understanding smile. 'You are afraid of me and view the prospect of marriage to me with some trepidation.'

'We would not suit, Your Grace. You would soon become bored with me.'

He marvelled at the length of the sentence. 'The suggestion of an alliance between us has been hatched by our families. However, I also have grave doubts

229

that we would be a suitable match.'

She nodded vigorously. 'They have made a mistake.'

'Perhaps. You are a beautiful and gentle girl, and any man would be honoured to have you for his wife, but I don't want to make you unhappy. Would you be willing to spend a little more time with me? I am not as fearsome as you believe.' He gave her a winning smile.

'I am sure you are not. Mama says I get silly notions in my head at times.'

'Then do you think we could try to get acquainted without worrying about a betrothal? I promise you that if you are still of the same opinion in two or three weeks', I shall put an end to the matter.'

'Would you?' She gazed at him with relief.

'You have my word on it. You need have no fears.'

'Thank you. That is comforting to know.'

'Then the matter is agreed between us, then. Now, go back and tell your sister that all is well.'

She stood up and curtsied, then almost ran back towards the house.

It was fortunate he was not easily put-down. To have two beautiful sisters who did not consider him the catch of the season, could be unsettling for a man. He tipped his head back and laughed out loud. But not him, he felt light-hearted for the first time since he had returned home.

Fifteen

The whole house was in uproar. Harry stepped aside as another huge basket of flowers walked past him, the servant completely obscured by the foliage.

The place was rapidly filling up, and he was not happy. Why had his grandmother insisted upon such a grand occasion?

'Do move, Your Grace.' Isabella was trying to reach around him to straighten the drapes. 'You are in the way.'

He stepped out of her way and cast an anxious glance at his grandmother.

'You need not be concerned that your grandmother will overtire herself. I shall not allow it.'

'Bossy,' he muttered as she pushed him further out of the way.

'When it is necessary.' She obviously had excellent hearing as well. 'Now, will you please go away. Take Lucifer for a good gallop; I am sure he would relish the exercise.'

'He is getting plenty of exercise,' he told her testily. 'I have put him in with the mares, as you suggested.'

'Oh, well, he is all right then,' she replied in a preoccupied way, still intent on getting the drapes to hang properly.

'He is having more fun than I am,' he growled, thoroughly irritated at being ordered around in his own home.

'I am very pleased to hear that, Your Grace.'

He studied her speculatively – not sure if she was paying attention or not. Then he heard his grandmother chuckle.

'Leave Bella alone, Harry, and do as she says. We will never be ready in time if you keep getting underfoot.'

He was about to protest when Dexter hurried towards him with a look of desperation on his face. 'I hope you don't need me, Harry, because I am getting out of here. I am being pursued by one of the Glanville sisters.'

The Duchess looked at Dexter, a wicked gleam of mirth in her eyes. 'Which sister?'

He lifted his hands in horror. 'They both look alike, and I think the other one is looking for you, Harry.'

'Poor things,' she sighed. 'Here they come. Do try to be nice to them.'

A similar expression of horror appeared on Harry's face. 'I'm coming with you.' Then both men turned smartly on their heels and marched out of the ballroom in true military style.

Isabella could not contain her amusement any longer. 'Oh, ma'am, that was wicked of you – there is no sign of the girls.'

'I know, but it was effective in getting them out of the way, and I did not want Harry at my shoulder all the time telling me to slow down. I swear if he had his way I would never rise from the couch.'

'He is concerned because he loves you.'

'Yes, I know that. Underneath his stern exterior is a kind and forgiving man. Look what he has done for the man who attacked him in London.'

Isabella was immediately attentive. 'Who was that?'

'Why, the one who came down with us. Did you not know?'

'Dobson?'

She nodded. 'Took him out of poverty and crime and has given him and his family a decent place to live and gainful employment. Not many men have a big enough heart to do that.'

'Indeed not,' Isabella breathed in awe.

'I am surprised you did not know. After all, you did visit him the morning after the incident.'

'You know about that!' Isabella was aghast, she had thought that a well-kept secret.

The elderly lady patted her hand. 'There isn't much that I am not aware of.'

'You have a trusted servant who keeps you informed?'

'Something like that, but I also have good eyes and a sharp mind still, thank goodness. I can usually discern what is going on by watching people. The way they stand, move, or their attitude when they are talking to someone can be very revealing.' She gave Isabella a conspiratorial wink. 'You should cultivate the art, my dear, it can be very useful in life.'

'I am sure it must be.' She leaned forward and said quietly, 'You must give me instruction.'

'We will start tonight. I shall point out a few of the more obvious clues.'

'Thank you,' Isabella said enthusiastically.

'Your sister appears to be in a happier frame of mind today,' she remarked, changing the subject suddenly.

'Yes, she is in good spirits.'

'There is no need for her to be fearful.' She gave Isabella a pointed look. 'I think my grandson will soon come to his senses. The signs are promising.'

A frown furrowed her brow as she watched the Duchess walk away. What signs? Angel was absolutely certain they would not suit, and the Duke was as undecided as ever.

An hour or so later the preparations were complete.

The room was filled with flowers, the perfume of many varieties filling the air. The elegant pillars had garlands twined around them and the orchestra stand was surrounded with a profusion of multicoloured blooms. It was a stunning sight.

'Perfect,' the Duchess sighed. 'Now we must rest before the evening festivities.'

Isabella did not sleep. She visited her favourite place, the herb garden, and found a secluded seat in which to relax in the warm sunshine. It had been a busy morning's work, and she had been able to take a lot of the responsibility away from the Duchess. She might still exhibit a good deal of vitality, but she was a great age and needed looking after.

She closed her eyes and let her mind wander. So, Dobson had been his attacker, and Harry had given him a chance of a new life. A truly charitable act.

Her thoughts turned to the ball. If Angel were wise she would hold fast to his side tonight, for every unattached female would be after him. She smiled in glee as she imagined his reaction to being pursued. He would hate it. But it might be just the thing to make him focus his mind upon Angel.

With so much attention it was doubtful if she would even get a dance with him, and perhaps that was for the best, for she found his touch quite disturbing.

However, Captain Atterton would be there, and she could protect him from the Glanville sisters. She had once considered him as a husband, but that idea had melted away. He was charming and enormously likeable, but there was no spark between them, and she wanted the kind of excitement the Duke's kisses had aroused. A marriage of convenience would not be enough for her.

Harry slipped his jacket off, rolled up his sleeve and took a firm grip on the pole.

'When I say now, everybody heave.'

Dexter, Timothy and Dobson nodded.

'Now.'

They all pushed together and heard to roots start to crack.

'Baxter, try and cut through that thick root.' Harry gasped with the effort. 'We might be able to pry it loose then.'

There were groans of relief as the huge tree-stump came away.

'I'm so pleased you arrived,' Timothy panted, wiping his brow. 'We have been trying for days to get the blasted thing out.'

'What are you going to do with the field?' Dexter asked.

'Plant soft fruit. Removing the dead tree has given us a clear space. This section has been left to run wild, but the soil is good, and it's a shame to waste it.' His eyes shone with pleasure as he told them of his plans.

Mrs Baxter arrived with a tray of drinks. Each man

took a glass and emptied it in one gulp.

'Thank you, Mrs Baxter, that was thirsty work.' Harry picked up his coat and started to brush the dirt from it.

'If I may be so bold, Your Grace?' Mrs Baxter had clearly lost her fear of this big man. 'Look at the state you are all in. You will have to clean up before you leave.'

'We will do that when we get back to Ranliegh.'

'But you can't walk in looking like that! What will people say?'

Harry laughed, and winked conspiratorially. 'We will creep in the back way, Mrs Baxter.'

She didn't look convinced and walked away muttering, 'It will never do. A duke looking and behaving like a labourer.'

Dexter wiped his dirty hands on the seat of his trousers. 'I suppose we had better be heading back, Harry.'

He nodded reluctantly, looking at the newly cleared field. He had enjoyed this bout of hard labour; it had been invigorating. He was a bit like Lucifer, in need of constant exercise, and the thought of dressing up and prancing sedately around the dance floor held little appeal.

Timothy chuckled. 'We had better hope no one sees us.'

They were out of luck because Isabella was by the servants' entrance making the final check on the food for the evening.

'Heavens above!' She exclaimed. 'What have you been doing to get so dishevelled?'

'Shush, not so loud,' Dexter pleaded. 'We are trying to sneak in unnoticed.'

'I can understand why.' She looked them up and down and grimaced. 'You are filthy. Have you been rolling in the dirt?'

'No.' Timothy grinned. 'We have been removing a large tree-trunk from the ground.'

'Do you not have labourers to do that work?'

'Of course, but,' he pointed to the two towering men beside him, 'where would you find such strength?'

'That is true.' She was keeping a straight face with difficulty. 'Well, you had better follow me and I shall guide you in the quietest route back to your rooms.'

She checked every corridor before beckoning them on. 'It is fortunate that most of the guests are resting before the nights festivities,' she whispered.

Harry had his door half-open when he leant over and said quietly in her ear, 'You seem to know the best routes in and out of this house.'

'I do. I am in the habit of rising early and I do not wish to disturb anyone. Now, I shall see that baths are prepared for you all.'

In just over an hour, three clean, immaculately dressed men, emerged from their rooms, and Harry took his place beside his grandmother.

He turned his attention to the crush. His grandmother had invited the cream of society, and she had been correct – most of them had accepted her invitation, but he suspected that the majority had come out of curiosity. They knew he had to marry – and quickly. The rumour that he was going to choose Angelina had been circulating since he had arrived back home, and they were expecting an announcement tonight. He smiled grimly. Well, they were going to be disappointed.

Angelina smiled prettily as he led her on to the dance floor. 'You are happier after our talk?'

'Oh, yes, Your Grace. It had eased my mind considerably, for I know now that I shall have a say in the matter, and that is very comforting.'

'Good. There is no reason why we cannot enjoy ourselves tonight.'

'None at all, but of course there is bound to be speculation.'

'I know.' He gave a roguish grin. 'Let us keep them guessing, shall we?'

She laughed out loud and many heads turned in their direction.

He took her back to her parents and had the next dance with Charlotte. She was a lovely girl and although she had a lively disposition, he did not think she was as reckless as her elder sister. He hoped not anyway; one like that in the family was quite enough.

The evening was in full swing and he had just finished dancing with Isabella when he noticed a familiar face in the crowd.

'I have seen Harcourt here,' he murmured to Dexter. 'He is partnering the lady in bright pink.'

'Wonder how he came by the invitation. Was his name on the list?'

He shook his head. 'I didn't see it.'

They watched as he headed for the Duchess. She spoke to him for a few minutes, and when he took his leave, Harry went over to her. 'Who is that?' he asked casually.

'He is Lady Stanton's stepbrother, and he informed me that as they were unable to attend, he took it upon himself to come in their stead. Impudent young devil!'

'Did you not order him out?'

'No. He is here now and may as well stay. Why are you so interested in him?'

'I have seen him somewhere and wondered who he was,' he answered with a casual shrug.

She gave him a keen glance. 'You would not like to tell me where?'

'No, Grandmother, I would not. Now, tell me what you know about him.'

'The present Lady Stanton's father married again – a most unsuitable lady – and she brought her son with her. His stepsister does not care for him, for it is rumoured that his character is doubtful.'

Harry did not need to be told about that, as he had seen for himself the unsavoury nature of the man.

'Since she married Lord Stanton, the boy has taken to spending quite a lot of time with them. She does not welcome him, but he comes anyway.'

'Does he have money of his own?'

'No. He relies on Stanton to provide for him, and I do wonder how he manages to dress in such a fashion, for I believe he only receives a small allowance.'

Dexter and Timothy had joined them and were listening avidly.

'Is that information of any use to you?' she asked shrewdly.

Harry grinned. 'I do believe it might be. We shall keep an eye on him.'

The three of them left the ballroom then, and Harry led them to a small room where they could have a private discussion.

'What do you think, Dexter?'

'Well, I have checked up on Lord Stanton and ruled him out. However, suppose he doesn't know someone else is seeing secret files?'

'Exactly,' Harry exclaimed. 'This might be just what we have been looking for. But before we get too excited, Dexter, is he involved in the smuggling operation? If he is, then that could be the source of his wealth.'

'I don't think so. Will you ask Carter to find out?'

'What can I do?' Timothy asked is suppressed excitement.

'Nothing at this time, Tim, but we shall probably need you later. Now let us see if we can find Carter.'

He was in the kitchen, enjoying a meal with the servants, and as they entered he jumped to his feet.

'A quick word, Carter, please.'

They moved out of earshot of the others and Harry explained what they wanted.

'I'll go tonight, sir. You leave it with me.'

They made their way back to the ballroom, well satisfied. The evening had taken a turn for the better

The Duchess beckoned to Isabella. 'Come and sit beside me, my dear. I was going to give you some instruction in the art of discerning what people are about.'

She sat down, all attentive.

'We shall start with those three, I think.' She nodded towards the door.

Isabella saw the Duke, the Captain and Mr Sherfield enter the room.

'Now, my grandson and Dexter you will find hard to read – they are masters at deception – but take a close look at young Timothy. Tell me what you see.'

Isabella studied him carefully. 'He is excited, I think.'

'Well done! They are up to something.'

'But why should you think that? This is a grand occasion and Mr Sherfield might well find it exciting.'

'No, my dear, the boy would not be overawed by such a gathering. He is from a good family and well used to such things. Something else has stirred him up. Now what about the other two?'

'Hmm. I would surmise that they are a trifle bored?'

'Exactly. That is what they wish you to think. I know those boys well, and they are at their most dangerous when they have that look about them. Never trust it, Isabella.'

'I see,' she said politely.

'Now, let us turn our attention to someone else. Let me see . . . ah, yes. Do you see that young man in the corner? He is talking to a lady in bright pink.'

'Yes, I see him.'

'But do you really see him? Take a closer look, and notice the way he is standing, his expression, the gestures he is making with his hands.'

Isabella felt a shiver run down her back. 'I do not like him.'

'Good, good. You have every right to be repelled by him. You have a keen eye and a sharp mind, Isabella. I don't think it will take you long to perfect the art.'

Their conversation came to an end as Harry approached, bowing before her.

'May I have the pleasure of another dance?' He raised one eyebrow in query.

'Two dances in one evening, Your Grace?' She could not resist the question. 'I declare I am feeling quite spoilt.'

A grin tugged at the corners of his mouth. 'We survived one dance without shouting at each other, and I thought it would be interesting to see if we could do it again.'

'I am sure we could. I am in far too tranquil a mood to want to argue with you tonight, and you are acting the perfect gentleman.'

'I make every effort.'

Her eyes sparkled with devilment. 'You have cleaned up very well.'

He chuckled then. 'Compliments as well. This is indeed a unique experience.'

When the buffet was served, the Ranlieghs and the Winslows all shared a table, and the public display of friendship between them was causing much interest. Isabella had heard many whispers of speculation during the evening, but she knew their curiosity was not going to be satisfied this night.

After everyone had eaten, the orchestra took its place again and Harry led Angelina on to the dance floor to start the dancing off once more.

'I do believe my grandson is enjoying himself,' the Duchess remarked.

'I'm sure he is, ma'am; he appears to be in a most agreeable mood. We have even managed to share two dances without one cross word between us.'

'And about time too,' the Duchess remarked under her breath.

Isabella was not short of partners and hardly sat down all evening. Charlotte had a queue of young hopefuls waiting upon her every smile and laugh. Angelina also had a constant crowd around her; however, they all melted away when the three men approached. No one dared to stand in the Duke's or the captain's way, and even Mr Sherfield, as young as he was had the stature and character that commanded respect.

Before the evening came to an end, the Duchess decided to retire, and Isabella was relieved, for the lady was beginning to look very fatigued.

'I shall escort you, ma'am.'

'Nonsense, Isabella. You stay and enjoy the dancing.'

But she would not be put off. 'It has been a great success. You must be very pleased.'

'Indeed I am.' She sat wearily on the bed and Isabella eased the shoes off her swollen feet.

'You have been overdoing it,' she scolded. 'I do not want to see you until dinner tomorrow.'

'Just as you say, my dear. Now will you summon my maid?'

'Is she all right?' Harry asked as she came back into the ballroom.

'Rather tired, I'm afraid. Her feet were swollen, and I have ordered her to stay in bed tomorrow.'

'And she agreed?' he asked in astonishment.

'Of course she did. She is quite reasonable when handled correctly.'

'Who is?' Dexter asked, coming to join them.

'Grandmother.'

'Is she? Good Lord, Harry, we never discovered how to do that, did we?'

The captain then swept Isabella on to the dance floor, and the rest of the evening went quickly. It had been a most enjoyable time, but she sighed with relief as the last of the guests left or were safely tucked up in their rooms.

Harry was fulsome in his praise for the help the Winslows had given his grandmother, and as Isabella looked at the immaculate gentleman in front of her, she smiled, remembering the state he had arrived in this afternoon, and the way they had crept along the corridors, trying to get to their rooms without being seen.

Harry, obviously guessing her thoughts, gave her an impudent wink and left the room.

Sixteen

Another carriage of departing guests rumbled down the driveway and Isabella did a quick mental check – that was not even half of them. It was nearly noon and some were still abed; others were showing a distinct reluctance to leave.

Harry was pacing restlessly. 'How many more, for heaven's sake?'

'Far too many. Some are still asleep and there are about eight in the blue lounge who are showing no sign of packing up, so would you please go and make it clear that they are expected to leave today. Everyone has been offered a sumptuous hamper for the journey. Her Grace wants the house cleared and back to normal by this evening.'

He grunted and strode off, but soon returned. 'They are packing at this moment.'

'Good. If you would be kind enough to see the others are roused from their beds.'

He went again without a murmur.

'Can we help, Bella?'

'Indeed, you can.' She answered her sisters briskly. 'You can both walk around the house and wish everyone you meet a pleasant journey home.'

'But suppose they do not intend to leave today?' Angelina queried. 'What shall we say then?'

'The same. Tell them it is a pleasant day for travelling.'

Charlotte giggled and hurried away with her sister.

Isabella had seen off another group by the time Harry returned.

He saluted smartly. 'Everyone is awake and moving.'

She ignored his inference that she was acting like a commanding officer.

'Thank you. Now you can go, if you wish, for I feel you are anxious to be elsewhere.'

'I can't leave you with all this chaos.' The protest was half-hearted.

'Nonsense. My sisters are helping. The captain and Mr Sherfield are waiting for you by the stables.'

He considered her for a moment, then did a surprising thing – he stooped down and kissed her fleetingly on the lips. Then he turned and marched away, whistling a cheerful tune.

She watched his retreating back quite nonplussed. He did appear to be exceedingly fond of kissing.

'At last, Harry, we thought you would never get away.'

'I have been given my marching orders, Dexter.'

'By Miss Isabella, I assume?'

Timothy burst out laughing. 'Who else would have the courage to do so?'

'What did Carter find out.' Dexter was anxious for news.

'He is certain Harcourt is not involved in the smuggling. He is quite well known in the village and no one likes or trusts him because they believe he is not right in the head.'

'I tend to agree with that. However, he must be involved in something. His clothes were of top quality and if he frequents Madam's house, then he is not lacking in funds. I think it is time we got Sergeant Drake down here.'

'In the meantime, Dexter, we should pay our respects to Lord Stanton. We would be lax in our duty if we did not call on him.'

Lord Stanton was delighted to see them. 'Good of you to call. I heard you were both home safe, the Lord be praised. I don't know what your poor grandmother would have done had she lost you as well, Harry. She must have been frantic with worry.'

Harry nodded. 'I am sorry I was not here to help her, but it took a while for the message to reach me, and by the time I managed to get passage home, Robert was also dead.'

'Yes, the whole affair was devastating. I was with your father at the time; he just collapsed.' He shook his head. 'Then for Robert to be killed like that.'

'It was a tragedy.' Harry did not mention the bullet.

'We trust your wife is well?' Dexter asked politely.

'Yes. Getting near her time, and she rests in the afternoons, but you must both come and meet her after the child is born.'

Harry smiled. 'Her stepbrother attended grandmother's ball last night. Came in your stead, I believe?'

'Did he?' He looked astonished and rather angry. 'I never gave him permission to do that. Apologise to your grandmother for me. His conduct is quite inexcusable!'

At that moment a servant entered the room carrying a package.

Lord Stanton put his signature to a piece of paper. 'Give this to the messenger and leave the papers in my study.'

The servant bowed and left the room.

'Do you still work for the War Office?' Dexter asked casually, although he already knew the answer.

'Been there ever since I retired from the army. Still like to feel I am doing my bit.'

They made polite conversation for about an hour and then left, promising to call again.

'That package was from the War Office, Harry, I saw the seal.'

'Yes, and if he leaves it around, then someone might well be obtaining information that way. We must have Harcourt watched.'

'I shall return to London tomorrow, and bring Sergeant Drake back with me.'

'That is a sound idea. If Harcourt is the culprit, we need to know who he is handing the information to.'

They enjoyed an invigorating ride back to Ranliegh.

The head groom met them. 'Your Grace, would you take Lucifer out of the field now? I did try approaching him, but he became aggressive.'

'But you know you shouldn't go near him unless I am present.'

'I know that, Your Grace, but as he didn't hurt the young lady, I thought I would try.' The man looked apologetic.

'It is a mystery why he becomes docile when she is around, but he is not to be trusted.'

'He certainly isn't today.' He rubbed his arm.

'Are you hurt?'

'Just bruised, Your Grace.'

'I'll get the devil back into his stall.'

Harry vaulted the fence and walked into the middle of the field. 'Come on you bad-tempered beast,' he taunted.

Lucifer thundered up and stopped a few feet from him. They eyed each other for a while, then the horse dropped his head, acknowledging that Harry was the master.

'That's right, and don't you forget it. Now, it is time for you to go back to your cosy stall, old boy,' Harry murmured affectionately. 'Enjoyed yourself, have you?'

Lucifer tossed his head and showed his teeth.

'He is smiling again,' said a familiar female voice.

He thought for a moment that she was in the field with them and spun round, then, breathed a sigh of relief. She was on the other side of the fence.

Lucifer made no fuss about going back. Harry saw to his needs and was about to leave the stall when he saw Isabella looking over the partition.

'May I give him an apple?'

He tipped his head back and at the roof as if asking for divine intervention. Good Lord, everyone was terrified of this animal. He was massive, black as night and with an unpredictable temper, but she saw no reason to fear him. It was inexplicable.

He looked at Lucifer, who was watching them intently. 'Are you going to behave yourself if I allow this?'

The horse snorted and walked towards Isabella.

She was holding the tempting treat out and her hand looked so tiny. Lucifer took the apple, very gently, and stepped back to enjoy it. Harry let out a pent-up breath. Though why he should be so concerned for her he did not know. She was strong-willed and would do what she wanted, regardless of his misgivings. Look how she had followed them that night of the smugglers.

'How does she do that?' the groom asked, when she had gone back to the house. 'You would think the beast was a gentle lamb when she is near him.'

'I cannot fathom it,' Harry remarked, then turned on his heel and headed for the house. And, indeed he couldn't understand it. They had been in some fierce battles together, and Lucifer was as lethal with his teeth and hooves as he himself had been with a sword.

He walked through the front door and stopped suddenly. After the bedlam of the past few days, all was peace and tranquillity. It was heaven.

His grandmother was up and sitting with Lady Winslow. He went straight over to her. 'How are you feeling?'

'I am well rested, Harry. And isn't it wonderful to have the house back in order again?'

'It certainly is. I didn't think it possible to clear it in one day.'

'Isabella has worked untiringly. She can be very commanding when she has a task to fulfil.'

'So I have observed,' he said dryly. 'Oh, by the way,

Dexter will be leaving for London in the morning.'

'Is he going to stay there?'

'No, he will be away for a few days only.'

Five days had passed, and Harry was becoming impatient. He had spent the time taking Angelina out for rides, trying to avoid Isabella, and seeing to the business of the estate, so he was relieved when a message arrived from Dexter: "Meet me at Lord Stanton's – D."

Harry was soon on his way, eager to see what it was all about. The first person he saw when he arrived was Sergeant Drake, dressed in the Stanton livery.

He bowed. 'The captain will explain, sir. He is in the library with Lord Stanton.'

They were deep in conversation when he was shown in.

'Harry, you have made good time,' Dexter said.

'I came as soon as I received your message.'

'Glad you are here.' Lord Stanton looked a very worried man. 'This is a terrible business. I shall resign from the War Office.'

Dexter shook his head emphatically. 'You must not do that. We don't know if Harcourt is the culprit, so we need your help.'

'I will do anything.'

'Good. I will explain the plan.'

Lord Stanton poured them all a drink, and Harry waited eagerly to hear what Dexter had to say.

'I met my contact and explained our suspicions. It was decided to take Lord Stanton into our confidence, and he has agreed that Drake should work in the house. Harcourt will not take notice of a new servant, and he will be able to watch him when he visits.'

Lord Stanton took a large gulp of brandy. 'If he is caught going through the papers are you going to arrest him?'

'No. We want to find out who his contact is—'

'But wouldn't that be dangerous?' he interrupted. 'If you lost sight of him the secrets could be sent to Bonaparte.'

'We have thought of that. You will be receiving your papers as usual, but from now on the information contained in them will be false.'

'Ah, that is a sound idea, and I can but hope that it is not the boy. Although my dear wife has no love for her stepbrother, I don't wish to have her upset at this time.'

'That is understandable.' Harry leant forward. 'We will be very discreet, and if it does turn out to be him, the news can be kept from her until after your child is born.'

Lord Stanton breathed an audible sigh of relief. 'Thank you.'

'When are you expecting Harcourt again?' Dexter asked.

'He turns up at any time, never stays away for long. Comes in concern for his stepsister, he says. Never could quite believe that though, for she has told me that he has always been quite objectionable to her, but suddenly he claims to be fond of her. Lies, of course.' He shook his head in dismay. 'Should have been more careful when he was around.'

'Please don't distress yourself.' Harry did not want Lord Stanton to give the game away with his worry. 'It is imperative you act as normal.'

'I will not let you down. I shall do everything in my power to catch the devil; whether he is family or not, he must be stopped.'

Harry stood up. 'Our suspicions may prove to be unfounded.'

'Let us hope so, for my wife's sake. She is a gentle person and will be greatly distressed if her stepbrother is engaged in espionage.'

'Please try not to worry, Lord Stanton.' Dexter stood up. 'Do not treat Harcourt any differently.'

On the way back they stopped at an inn for a meal, where they took a private room and could talk freely.

'I have some news for you about Garston, Harry. He is back in town and gambling recklessly.'

'Is he having any success?'

Dexter shook his head. 'Not according to the gossip. They say he is losing heavily and has an air of desperation about him.'

Harry's smile was grim. 'That is because I have started to press him for payment, I expect.'

'Has he bought back any markers yet?'

'No, and that accounts for his frantic gambling, I expect.'

'If he is incurring more debt, we need to be vigilant, Harry, and not drop our guard.'

They were in a determined mood and well fed when they mounted to resume their journey.

'Have you boys had anything to eat?' the Duchess asked, when they walked into the drawing room.

Harry did not miss the brief look of relief which spread across her face when she saw them both. This whole business was a strain on her, although she tried not to show it, and he was suddenly impatient to see an end to the intrigue. He hoped this lead would resolve things.

He smiled and bent to kiss her cheek. 'We have eaten, Grandmother.'

'In one of those terrible hostelries, I suppose?'

'The food was palatable.' Dexter bowed low over her hand.

'Is it nearly over, Dexter?' she asked softly.

'We are closing in, ma'am. Try not to worry – you know I will guard Harry with my life if it becomes necessary.'

She patted his hand. 'I am concerned for the two of you. From young boys the three of you were inseparable, and you are just as dear to me.'

There was a knock on the door and the butler came

in. He bowed. 'There is a messenger to see Captain Atterton. I have shown him into the library, sir.'

Dexter was immediately on his feet.

Harry excused himself and walked out into the garden. It was a beautiful evening and he felt too restless to stay indoors making idle chatter. He was beginning to understand how restricting Isabella must find it. She had an adventurous spirit, and perhaps that was why Lucifer had taken to her. The animal was intelligent, so had he seen something of a kindred spirit in her?

'Harry.' Dexter came and walked beside him. 'It was fortunate we left Lord Stanton's when we did, for Harcourt arrived soon after, and he said in his letter that the boy appears to be in a highly excitable state. Drake will contact us as soon as there is anything to report, but he does not think it will be long. Harcourt is like a powder keg waiting to explode.'

'Capital! Some action at last, I think.'

He nodded. 'I would like to see an end to this business. Your grandmother is worrying, Harry.'

'Yes, I have tried to soothe her fears,' he shrugged expressively, 'but I don't think she will relax until I am safely married.'

'What are you going to do about Miss Angelina?'

'Heaven knows! She would make a perfect wife and mother for my children, but I do not wish to have a wife who is terrified of me.'

'There are plenty who are not.' Dexter chuckled

softly, remembering their time in the army.

'A camp follower would not make a suitable wife. Just imagine what grandmother would have to say about that.' Harry's laugh echoed through the dark garden.

Dexter shuddered. 'That is too terrible to contemplate.'

There was a soft footfall behind them. They turned together.

Carter shook his head and grimaced. 'I keep trying to take you unawares, but your senses are too sharp.'

'Been to the village, Carter?'

'Yes, sir, and I have some news. There is another boat expected in from France in two days, I was told.'

'Smugglers again?' Harry asked.

'Don't know, sir. The locals don't appear to be as excited about this one. Are you going to go to the cove?'

'Yes. This appears to be a break in the usual routine. Thank you, Carter.'

'Sir.' He marched smartly away.

Dexter grinned boyishly. 'Into battle again, my friend?'

Seventeen

Harry paced restlessly. He didn't dare leave the house because Dexter had gone to meet his contact and he was anxious for news about the ship arriving from France.

'You will wear a hole in the carpet if you parade up and down much more.'

He spun round and glared at Isabella, disconcerted that he had not heard her approach. 'It is my damned carpet!'

'Oh dear,' she remarked mildly. 'Why don't you take Lucifer for a good gallop? That should ease both your tempers.'

Fortunately, he didn't have time to reply, as Dexter burst into the room. 'What did he have to say?' he demanded, not giving his friend time to draw breath.

The captain looked at Isabella.

'You do not need to be concerned.' She looked expectantly from one gentleman to the other. 'I shall not betray any secrets and I am aware that you are involved in something dangerous. There is speculation that the treaty with Napoleon will soon be broken and we shall be at war again. I feel it is something to do with that.'

Both men looked at her in astonishment.

'You have a very sharp mind, Miss Isabella,' Dexter told her, 'and you seem remarkably well informed.'

'I take a great interest in what is going on.'

'You might as well speak freely, Dexter. I am sure Isabella can be trusted.'

She beamed again. 'I do believe that was a compliment!'

Harry ignored her sarcasm and didn't take his eyes off Dexter.

'They have caught another messenger, but this time before he reached the French coast. The boat he was on was damaged in rough weather, but unfortunately for him, it was a naval ship which came to his rescue. They had been alerted to look for anything unusual, and this man was unduly nervous, so they searched him.'

Harry noticed that Isabella's eyes were wide with excitement.

'Were they able to get him to talk?'

'Unfortunately, no. As soon as they found the papers on him, he threw himself overboard.'

Harry whistled through his teeth. 'That was a desperate measure. The man must be terrified of his masters.'

Dexter agreed. 'The interesting news is that the information was the same as the last papers sent to Lord Stanton – word for word. There is no doubt that the leak is from that source.'

'It could be Harcourt, Percy or any member of the Stanton staff.' Harry ran a hand distractedly through his hair. 'More papers have been delivered this very day to Stanton, and Drake will keep a close watch on them. The boat is due in again any time now.'

'Unfortunately, I will not be able to help you, Harry. I have been called to London for an urgent meeting and must leave at once. You will need to get closer, and the cave might be a good place to hide.'

'I had come to the same conclusion.'

'You must not go to the cove on your own, for your grandmother would never forgive me if you came to harm.'

'I won't take any chances and Carter will be close by.'

'Make sure he is. Now I must be on my way. May I take one of your animals, Harry? London is no place for a war horse.'

'Of course.' He watched Dexter hurry out of the room.

'Thank you for allowing me to stay.' Isabella clasped her hands excitedly.

'You must not speak a word of this to anyone. Do you understand that? Lives could be at risk if you do.'

'I understand,' she told him earnestly.

He nodded and started to walk away from her.

'Are you still attached to the army?' she asked rather breathlessly as she tried to keep up with his long stride.

'No, but Dexter is.'

She did a little run to catch up with him.

He stopped suddenly, just before they reached the staircase. 'Are you following me?'

'Yes, Your Grace – with difficulty.' Her answer was matter of fact.

'Is there not something else you would rather be doing?'

She looked thoughtful for a moment. 'I do not think so, and I have more questions to ask you.'

'Isabella,' he sighed in exasperation. 'I have things to attend to. I understand your curiosity, but I am somewhat preoccupied today.' He gave a distracted smile. 'You must excuse me if I dash away.'

Carter was coming up the stairs to meet him. 'Sir, I have just received news. A boat is expected tonight.'

'What time?'

'Same time, same place.'

'Well done, Carter. Your friends are beginning to trust you, it seems.'

'Yes, sir. Didn't take long.'

'See if you can persuade them to let you go along. This

boat is arriving sooner than expected. We need to find out who is involved, and if it is purely a smuggling operation.'

When they reached the library, Harry told him that Dexter would be away.

'He'll be mad about being called away at this time. Who are you going to take with you tonight?'

'I'll go on my own. I intend to hide in the cave; there is a good view of the beach from there.'

Carter pursed his lips. 'You will have to be careful or you will be trapped and at their mercy if they see you.'

'I shall be in place long before they arrive, and I am relying on you to be with the smugglers – if that is what they are up to this time.'

'I'll be there, sir. You can count on it.'

There was a moon shining, Harry noticed with satisfaction, and he should be able to see the beach clearly. He closed the door quietly, made his way to the stables and Lucifer greeted him with a silent toss of the head. It was amazing how this horse knew when to be quiet.

He led him across the yard on to the grass, then he stopped in utter disbelief. Dexter's horse was there.

The moon had slipped behind a cloud for the moment, and Harry thought Dexter had changed his mind about going to London – but it was not his friend on top of the huge animal. The stirrups had been shortened and contained small feet. He looked up just as the moon shone again and met a blue gaze.

'How did you get up there?' he growled.

'I used bales of hay to stand on.' She gave a satisfied smile.

'And what the blazes are you wearing?' He was ready to explode. He had been making a great effort to be kind to her – but this was too much.

'Breeches.' She wiggled in the saddle. 'Very comfortable.'

'Oh, my God!' He didn't know whether to laugh or rage.

'I have spent all afternoon making them fit,' she told him with pride. 'I am not a seamstress, but I believe they have turned out rather well.'

'Just what do you think you are doing here?' It was a stupid question; he already knew the answer.

'I am coming with you. I overheard Carter telling you about the smugglers.'

'You are not coming with me!'

'Careful - do not raise your voice or you will awaken the household.'

'You cannot be seen dressed in such a way,' he said through gritted teeth.

'I doubt anyone will see me this time of night, and if they do they will take me for a boy. I have secured my hair under this cap.' She patted one of the stable lad's hats.

He looked her over and shook his head. 'Impossible. You don't look anything like a boy.'

She glanced down at her ample bosom and grimaced. 'Well, they will think we are indulging in an illicit assignation. I can be a very good actress,' she told him earnestly.

He buried his face in Lucifer's neck and groaned. What was the use? There was no reasoning with her, and time was short. He swung into the saddle, but he tried one more thing to make her return to the house. 'It will be a very uncomfortable few hours, and I cannot risk you being an encumbrance.'

'I am not some silly female who will have a fit of the vapours in an emergency,' she told him haughtily. 'And you cannot go alone.'

He gave a snort of disgust. 'And you think you could protect me?'

'If I have to.' She patted her pocket. 'I have brought a knife with me. It is only a small one, but I could inflict some damage with it.'

'Don't you dare use it,' he snapped. 'I have no desire to see you go to the gallows for murder.'

She smiled sweetly, a look of innocence on her face. 'Of course not, it is merely a precaution.'

He had to admit defeat. There was no more time to waste, and it should be safe enough. 'You will follow my instructions without question.' He used his most commanding voice, but it was a waste of effort, for she was not intimidated by his tone.

She grinned and nodded excitedly.

'One more thing. You are placing yourself in a compromising situation and I shall not offer you marriage again.'

'I should hope not!' With a toss of her head she urged her horse forward.

When they were well away from the house they broke into a gentle trot, keeping to the grass verges. He was relieved to see she was handling the large horse competently.

Leaving the animals well hidden, they made their way down the cliff path. Harry went first and held out his hand to help her.

'I can manage,' she whispered.

A recent shower had made the path greasy and they slithered down the steepest part but reached the beach without injury.

'The tide is still in. Do we have to wade through the water?'

'I have chosen this time as we don't want to leave footprints in the sand.'

'Oh, I never thought of that.' She looked at him admiringly. 'How very clever of you.' Then she glanced at the water with distaste.

'It is no use you baulking at the first hurdle, Isabella. You insisted on coming.'

He stepped onto the beach. The water came over his boots to the depth of about six inches. 'You are hardly going to drown in this, are you?'

'There is no need for sarcasm,' she remarked with a toss of her head.

'Come along, we are wasting time.' He relented. 'Do you want me to carry you?'

'No, I do not!' She stepped into the water and looked at him defiantly. 'Lead the way then.'

The cave was damp, cold and very dark, and he cursed his stupidity in allowing her to come – not that she had given him much choice. They were well hidden and would not be in any danger from the smugglers, but the cold and wet was something he had not considered. He estimated that it would be another half an hour before the tide had receded enough for the men to use the beach.

Water dripped from the roof of the cave down his neck. Damn! He could not allow her to endure such conditions. He took hold of her hand and pulled her back on to the beach.

'What are doing?'

'I am taking you back to the horses. This is not a fit place for you.'

She pulled free and sloshed back into the cave. 'There is not time for that – the smugglers could arrive at any moment. See, the tide is going out rapidly. You will leave footprints if you try to come back.'

She was right, it was too late to change his mind.

'You do not need to be concerned for I am well wrapped-up.'

Nevertheless, he felt her shiver. He undid his coat and pulled her against him, then slid his arms around her and leant against the side of the cave. 'We shall have to keep each other warm.'

All he got was a muffled response.

It was with a surge of relief when he heard the sound of men approaching and he could let go of Isabella. He blessed his iron self-control, for only that had kept him from forgetting his mission and letting his desire take over. To have had this warm, infuriating woman pressed close to him had been torture. He could not understand it – he did not even like her.

They watched the boat arrive and the men rush forward to unload it. Harry saw, with satisfaction, that Carter was with them.

The moon was shining brightly, and the activity could clearly be seen. Harry saw nothing untoward and was convinced the men were involved in smuggling only, but Carter would be able to verify that.

When the men had disappeared and the boat was well out to sea again, Harry went to move out of the cave, but Isabella stopped him.

'There's still someone on the beach,' she whispered.

'Where?' He had not noticed anything.

'Over there.' She pointed to their left. 'There is someone standing in the shadow of the cliff. I saw him move a moment ago.'

'You have very sharp eyes. I cannot see anything.'

'He has moved back into the shadows, but he is there. Your whole attention had been focused on the boat and the men, but I have been looking elsewhere and I saw him slide into the cove just as the boat arrived.'

Harry put his arm around her shoulders and gave a gentle hug. 'Thank you, Isabella. He is obviously spying on them.'

At that moment the figure moved out and started to walk away from them. Harry caught his breath. He knew that walk; he had seen it once before.

'Do you know him?'

'Perhaps. If only he would turn around I would dearly love to see his face.'

As if in answer to his request, the man turned towards the cave and looked up. Probably checking that the smugglers were well away.

'You have your wish. Do you recognise him now?'

'Oh, yes. I know him.'

'Who is he, pray tell me?'

'It is best you don't know his name. He is a very dangerous man.' Harry watched until he was out of sight. The man on the beach had been the same one he had seen hurrying away from the fair, and he now knew who he was.

But what had he been doing here?

Eighteen

'Why are you still in bed, Bella? Are you unwell?'

Isabella sat up and pushed the hair out of her eyes. It did not seem as if she had been asleep for more than a few minutes.

'No, I am quite well. Am I not allowed a little indulgence, Lotte?'

'Of course you are, but it is most unusual for you not to be up at dawn. I was concerned to see you still asleep.'

She threw the covers back. 'Then I must be up at once,' she joked. 'I would not wish to cause you worry.'

Charlotte laughed. 'There is no need to hurry.

Mama has gone home to assist father; they are making plans for renovations to the house.'

'Oh, yes, she did tell me.' Isabella stretched. Her adventures of the night did not appear to have had any adverse effect upon her.

'Now, shall you get up, Bella? It is a fine day and I would enjoy a ride.'

'I shall be with you directly, Lotte.'

Isabella watched her sister bounce from the room and hugged her knees. By the time she had reached her bed this morning, she had been overcome with fatigue, and she had fallen into a deep sleep, but it had been a sleep full of dreams – uneasy dreams. That man hiding on the beach had figured largely in them. He troubled her, but she did not know why.

Her thoughts drifted back to the cave. How exciting it had been. She blushed as she remembered how Harry had held her in his arms; it had been so comfortable and cosy. Of course, it had only been to keep each other warm, for it had been exceedingly cold in there, and he had been the perfect gentleman – this time. However, the memory of his strong arms holding her was causing her some unease. It was her reaction to his closeness which was worrying. She had liked it. How was she ever going to look her sister in the eyes, or him, for that matter, if he became her brother-in-law?

She jumped out of bed. An energetic ride was

272

needed this morning – that would clear her head of any silly notions. She was fussing about nothing. No one else had known they had been alone together in a cave, and she was certain that the Duke, with his strong sense of honour, was not going to spread the news abroad. How the ladies would love a piece of gossip like this!

Harry had not been to bed, but it did not worry him; he was used to staying awake for long periods. Indeed, his life had often depended upon him doing just that.

Carter had arrived back an hour after him, and he had told him about the hidden spectator. They had agreed that Carter should drop a word of warning to his new friends as they could still be useful and might feel in Carter's debt.

Harry watched Charlotte and Isabella ride off, and he wondered what she had done with the breeches. He chuckled. What an uproar her mode of dress would have caused had she been seen in them, and an even bigger scandal if anyone knew of his reaction. She had a most unsettling effect upon him, and he would be wise to keep away from her, but the blasted girl kept turning up at the most unexpected moments.

He ran a hand through his thick hair. He could not marry Angelina now, even if she were willing – especially as he was having such lascivious thoughts about her sister. But why he was reacting in this way was a mystery. He spent his time either wanting to rage at her or ravish her, and it would not do.

'Sir,' Carter entered the room. 'There is a messenger from Lord Stanton. His Lordship begs you to come at once.'

Harry was on his way immediately.

Lord Stanton was in his study with his son, Percy. The boy was deathly pale and shaking.

'Harry,' Stanton exclaimed in relief. 'Good of you to come so promptly.'

'What has happened?'

'This.' Lord Stanton thrust a letter into his hands. 'I am being blackmailed.'

Harry read it carefully. So that was what the man had been doing on the beach. He was obviously desperate for money to go to these lengths. It was no light matter to try and blackmail someone of Lord Stanton's eminence.

'How can I help?'

'You know the man, so I thought you might be able to advise us. I did not know who else to turn to. I will not submit to threats. He has to be stopped, but I am at my wits end to know how to go about it.'

'Are these allegations true?' He already knew the answer, but he looked directly at Percy, who was unable to meet his gaze.

'That does not matter.' Lord Stanton put his arm around his son's shoulders in a protective manner. 'He has made me a solemn promise that he will cease gambling and will not meet these men again.'

Harry was pleased to see father and son reconciled, and it was heartening to see Stanton jump to his son's defence. Perhaps it would instil some good sense in the boy. 'You have been playing a very dangerous game, Percy.'

'I know that, Your Grace.' The boy was trembling with fear. 'I don't want to go to prison. I will stay and help my father run the estate.'

'Will you also give me your promise on that?'

'I promise, I promise. Please, can you help us?' There was a note of hysteria in Percy's voice.

Harry's smile was lethal. 'I do believe I can. Let him think you are going to pay – reply to the letter and explain that it will take you several days to meet his demand.'

'What then?'

'I will be back in two days, and by then I should have the means to make him drop his blackmail demand.'

He left behind two very relieved men.

When he got back to Ranliegh, his grandmother was alone in the garden room. He stooped down in front of her. 'I am going to London and shall be away for two days.'

'Is it on Dexter's business?' she asked.

'No, Grandmother. Our business.'

'Garston,' she sighed. 'What has happened?'

He gave her a brief outline of events.

'Is there no end to that man's infamous crimes?'

'We shall deal with him, have no fear.'

She shook her head. 'It is useless telling me that, for I shall not rest until he has been locked behind bars.'

'That time is not far off.'

She did not look convinced. 'You will not go alone, Harry? Promise me.'

'Carter will accompany me everywhere.'

Harry settled into a deep leather chair at his club and waited. Carter had spread the word and was sitting close by, appearing to be asleep like many of the members.

He did not have long to wait. The business was soon concluded, and by the end of the afternoon he had purchased four more of Garston's gambling notes.

It was difficult to understand why these men were foolish enough to sit down with the man. He had a bad reputation, so they must be aware that he could not cover his losses. However, that was not his concern. He had profited by the transactions – the gentlemen had been grateful enough to take only a percentage of the debts.

* * *

They started back at dawn the next morning.

'What are your plans, sir?' Carter asked as they broke their journey at an inn.

'I shall visit Garston as soon as we arrive back. I intend to place him in such a perilous financial position that he will have to do as I say.'

'You are sure he was the man at the fair?'

'Positive. His walk is unmistakable.'

'And we still don't know what he was doing at the fair.'

'No. The more I look back on the incident, the more puzzled I become. However, we must deal with one problem at a time.'

'Like putting an end to his blackmail attempt.'

'Exactly. He will have to develop a very bad memory if he wishes to keep his estate.'

'I don't think we should ride into the enemy's camp alone, sir. It's a pity the captain is away. The two of you together are enough to frighten a whole regiment.'

Harry laughed. 'Are we that formidable?'

'Yes, sir. The only person you have not been able to quell with a glance is Miss Isabella Winslow. Perhaps we should take her with us.' Carter grinned at his joke.

Harry raised his hands in horror. 'Whatever you do, Carter, don't mention a word of this to her. She will be mounted up and waiting for us if you do.'

'Oh, dear me, no, sir. The lady is far too adventurous.'

And wasn't that the truth.

Once back at Ranliegh, Harry dismounted. 'We will change horses and have something to eat first.'

Much to his surprise, Dexter was waiting for him. 'Harry, what on earth is going on?'

He explained about Garston and his attempt to blackmail Lord Stanton.

His friend listened and whistled softly. 'You have the means to ruin him. Best have someone watch your back.'

'I have Carter.'

'I must come as well,' Dexter told him.

In less than half an hour they were on their way.

'Hope he will be at home,' Dexter remarked, as they cantered through the gate.

'He will be. He is expecting a messenger from Lord Stanton with the blackmail money.'

Carter gave a gleeful grin. 'Instead he will be getting us.'

'And that certainly is not what Garston has been expecting.'

'I know the first payment is due.' Garston jumped to his defence. 'If you will give me a few more days I shall be able to redeem the debts.'

Harry did not speak for several seconds but subjected the man to an appraisal which would have unnerved anyone. His gaze was cool and menacing. 'If you intend the money to come from the blackmail attempt on Lord Stanton, then I will find that unacceptable.'

'How . . . how did you know about that?' Garston stammered, the colour leaching from his face.

'He is an old family friend. Something I think you overlooked.'

'His son is engaged in smuggling.'

Harry raised one eyebrow. 'Really? I suggest you are mistaken.'

'If I tell the authorities then the boy will end up in prison.'

'And who will they believe? A family of high standing like the Stantons or you, a man of doubtful reputation with, I suspect, far worse crimes at his feet.'

'That is slanderous!'

'I think not. I have learned some very interesting things about you of late.'

Garston managed a sneer. 'Whatever your suspicions, you have no proof.'

Harry gave a grim smile of satisfaction. The man was becoming careless. He would not list the crimes he believed he had carried out; he would rather let Garston worry and wonder just how much he did know. In truth it was very little, but he was not going to reveal that fact. Time to come to the point of the visit.

'This is a list of the gambling markers now in my possession.' He handed it to Garston. 'As you will see, it amounts to a great deal of money.'

The list shook in Garston's sweaty fingers.

'I could claim your estate right now.'

The paper rattled.

'However, I am inclined to be generous. I will give you one month from this day to raise the money – by legal means. You will withdraw your blackmail demand from Lord Stanton and his son. If you do not, I shall arrive on your doorstep with the bailiffs.'

The man looked ready to expire. 'I don't have any choice, do I?'

'None at all,' Harry said simply.

'How am I to raise this much in one month?' he wailed all composure gone.

There were many empty places on the walls where family pictures had once hung. 'That could prove difficult but raise it you must. I have been lenient with you thus far, and it is time for you to face the consequences of your actions. Gambling is a fool's game and you would do well to learn that lesson.'

'You are too high and mighty to gamble, I suppose?' Sweat was running down his pasty face.

'I only indulge when I am sure of winning.' The threat was obvious. Lord Garston could not be in doubt about his intentions – one wrong move and he would lose everything.

'You are the Devil incarnate, sir.'

'As I have been told.' He gave a perfunctory bow and walked towards the door. 'Oh, and don't think to thwart me by gambling away your estate, for it is already mine.'

He strode from the house, mounted his horse and they rode away.

'All go well?' Dexter asked, as they left the estate far behind them.

'Yes. We shall hear no more of blackmail, I think. However, I have pushed him to the brink and a trapped, wounded animal is doubly dangerous.'

'We shall stay alert, sir,' Carter assured him.

'That would be wise. And thank you; your presence here today was a great help. Garston looked out of the window at you more than once, and he did not dare to call for assistance from his staff.'

It was late afternoon when they arrived back at Ranliegh.

'What are your plans now?' Dexter asked, as they dismounted.

'I shall send word to Lord Stanton. He should hear no more of this matter now and let us hope that Percy has learnt his lesson.

'Young fool. He is lucky his father rallied round to help him.'

'Lord Stanton would do well to buy Percy a commission in the army. That might help to straighten him out.'

Dexter gave a strangled laugh. 'He does not look like officer material.'

'No, perhaps you are right.' Harry slapped Lucifer on the rump. 'Back to your stall, old boy. I will come and see you in a moment.'

The horse trotted away with a toss of his head, defying anyone to stop him reaching his cosy stable.

Harry went into the library, wrote the letter to Lord Stanton and sent one of his trusted servants to deliver it, then he saw to his horse who was waiting impatiently to be unsaddled.

'It is no good you making a fuss, old boy,' he scolded. 'If you would let someone else do this you would have been comfortable long ago.' The horse turned back his lip in a familiar gesture, and his expression said – just let them try.

Nineteen

The next morning, Harry met Angelina coming out of her room, and decided that he could delay no longer. 'Will you walk with me?'

'Yes, Your Grace. I shall just fetch my wrap.'

He watched her hurry away. What if Angelina had changed her mind and decided to wed him after all? He would be honour-bound to go ahead with the betrothal, it would be a disaster for both of them and he had grave doubts that it would be a fruitful marriage.

She was soon back, clutching her wrap. He eased it out of her grip, placed it around her shoulders, and she shivered at his touch. No, he thought, as she moved away from him, this would not do, but he must find out if she still viewed a marriage between them as undesirable.

He found a secluded seat in a section of the garden which was surrounded by a high hedge. It afforded protection from the wind, which was blowing today, and the watery sun felt pleasantly warm. 'Have you had enough time to come to a decision about us?'

She nodded and looked at him imploringly. 'I have not changed my mind.'

He felt a surge of relief, but pursued the subject, needing to know how she really felt. 'You do not think you could care for me?'

She gave him a startled glance. 'You do not need caring for, Your Grace.'

What the blazes was she talking about? Of course he wanted someone to care for him. He drew in a deep breath as that realisation hit him with the force of a blow.

'Why do you say that? Do I appear so cold-hearted to you?'

'Oh, no! I didn't mean to imply that. I know you to be a very kind and considerate man, but you are also strong and self-sufficient.'

He gazed into space, still shaken by the revelation that he was not impervious to the usual needs of a man – the need to have a wife and family of his own. Someone he could love and care for.

'Do you think you might get used to me?'

She shook her head emphatically. 'No, no. I have heard you shouting at Bella, and I would live in fear of displeasing you. And I would.' She gave him another beseeching look. 'You would have little patience with me.'

He knew she was right, for she would drive him to distraction in a very short time. He needed someone who would not tiptoe anxiously around him. He could be volatile at times, and this timid, beautiful butterfly would soon be crushed. He could not do that to her – or himself.

'Very well, Angelina. We will put an end to this now.'

'Oh, Your Grace,' she cried in relief. 'But my father will be very angry. He was set on our betrothal.'

'You may leave your father to me. When is he to join us?'

'Today, I believe.'

'Then I shall approach him as soon as he arrives.' He stood up.

'Shall I be with you when you see my father?'

'There is no need for you to be.'

The look she gave him was one of utter gratitude.

He smiled encouragingly at her. 'There is nothing to fear; your father is a reasonable man.'

They walked back to the house together, and as she ran up the stairs Harry sighed and went in search of his grandmother. He found her in the drawing room, relaxing in a beam of sunlight coming through the window.

'Hello, my dear, would you like tea?'

'No thank you, Grandmother. I need to talk to you.' He pulled up a chair close to her.

She waited for him to settle, saying nothing.

'I have just seen Angelina, and I am sorry to tell you that marriage between us is out of the question.'

She still said nothing, so he continued. 'I know you were of the opinion she would make a good wife – and so she will, but not for me.'

'She is too timid for you.'

'Exactly.' He grimaced. 'She claims my personality overwhelms her.'

'I expect it does.'

He gave her a startled glance.

'I must say, Harry, it has taken you long enough to find this out.'

He was almost speechless. 'I was trying to please you. After all you chose her,' he protested.

'I did put her forward for your consideration; they are a good family, and one we could be proud of an alliance with. However, the choice has always been in your hands – and the girl's, of course.'

Now he was devoid of speech. Why hadn't she told him all this at the beginning?

'You must see Sir George as soon as he returns. He

will be disappointed, but not surprised, I think. You have made the right decision.'

He shook his head vigorously. There must be something wrong with his hearing.

'The Winslows will be back today, in time for dinner. I have invited them to stay while the renovations to their house are taking place. That does not present a problem for you?'

'None,' he managed to say.

'Good. Now, the need for you to wed is still paramount. What are you going to do about it?'

Ha! That sounded more like his grandmother. 'Find someone else.'

'Be quick about it, Harry. You are not getting any younger.'

Sir George could not hide his disappointment, but as Harry's grandmother had predicted, he did not appear to be surprised.

'She could come to care for you,' he suggested hopefully.

'That is doubtful. She is afraid of me and I don't want an unwilling wife. It would be purgatory for both of us.'

'I do understand. A suitable match can be a blessing, as I have discovered with my dear wife. However, I must admit to being disappointed, as of our three daughters, Angelina is the one who causes us the most concern.'

'I would have thought it was the other way around,' Harry remarked dryly.

Sir George smiled. 'No. The other two are well able to take care of themselves. Angelina, on the other hand, needs someone strong to look after her, and I had hoped it would be you.'

'I am sorry. I have spoken with Angelina and we are both of the opinion that a marriage between us would not be a happy one. You must not attach any blame to her for she has tried to be obedient to your wishes.'

'She shall not be chastised over this decision.' He gave Harry an assessing look. 'I would have welcomed you as a son-in-law.'

Harry inclined his head at the compliment.

'What will you do now?'

'I shall have to look elsewhere for a wife. My grandmother has reminded me that I am advancing in years.'

Sir George roared with laughter. 'Nonsense! You are in your prime, just the right age to take on the responsibilities of a wife and family. The Duchess is pushing you; she is a formidable lady.'

'She is, indeed, but I have a great affection for her, and that is why I have tried to please her in this matter.'

'Of course, quite understandable. Is she disappointed?'

Harry shrugged. 'To tell the truth, I am not sure. Her reaction was puzzling.'

'Hmmm, she is not one to show her feelings.'

It was Harry's turn to laugh. 'Only when it is to her advantage.'

'You wouldn't consider one of the other girls?' he asked hesitantly, obviously reluctant to give up hope.

'Charlotte is too young for me and the other one . . .' He hesitated not wishing to offend. 'One would never know what she was going to do next.'

The father looked crestfallen. 'You have noticed that, of course, for I know you have had occasion to reprimand her.'

'Once or twice.' Heavens, if her father only knew the whole of it.'

'Headstrong. Always has been, and far too inquisitive.'

Harry nodded his head in agreement. 'Must be a trial to you.'

'Should have been firmer with her, but she has beguiling ways and we all love her.' He sighed gustily. 'I am quite outnumbered with four females in the house – I do not stand a chance.'

'Difficult,' Harry remarked, trying to keep a straight face. He knew Sir George ruled his family with a strong, but loving hand.

The dinner gong sounded, and the two men walked into the dining room talking amicably.

Harry saw Angelina give them an anxious look. He nodded and when she saw her father smiling, she relaxed.

There was a light-hearted atmosphere at the dinner table that evening. His grandmother was in especially good spirits, and he was highly suspicious.

'Bella, are you asleep?' Angelina put her head around the door.

'No, Angel. Come in.'

She sat on the bed and bounced up and down. 'I couldn't wait until morning to tell you, for I am so happy. Papa sent for me – the Duke has been to see him.'

It felt as if Isabella's heart sank to the lower regions of her body. 'And you are to be wed?'

'No,' she exclaimed excitedly. 'If that were the case I should not be so joyous. Papa said His Grace had explained, that in his opinion, we would not make a good match.'

'Was father angry?'

'No! That is the wonderful thing.'

'Angel do stop jiggling. I shall be bounced out of bed in a moment.' Isabella smiled as she watched her excited sister make a supreme effort to keep still.

'So, it is settled. Papa said we are to return to London soon and look for suitable husbands.'

The idea did not appeal to Isabella. While she had been listening to her sister, it seemed as if the blinds had opened. She was in love with the Duke. She felt like crying.

'Oh, Bella, do not look so downcast. We shall enjoy ourselves – you love to dance, don't you?'

'Of course.' She pushed away her unhappy thoughts for the sake of her sister. 'We shall dance the night away at many balls. Now, off you go to bed. I am so pleased you are happy, Angel.'

When her sister had returned to her own room, Isabella buried her head in the pillow and tried not to let her heart shatter into a million pieces. What a very foolish thing to do. All was clear now. This was why she found him so exciting – she had fallen in love with him.

It was a blessing her sister was not going to be his wife. The thought of them being together . . .

She gave a groan of despair. He would have to marry – and it would not be to her. He considered her a nuisance. All was lost. Isabella knew she would never hold her own child in her arms, because even if her father found her a husband, she could never marry him. She would never love anyone but Major Harry Sterling.

She slept fitfully and awoke just as dawn was creeping over the horizon. A good hard gallop was what she needed to shake her out of the dismals.

Within half an hour she was heading for the rise, and when she reached there she jumped off the horse and threw herself down on the damp grass to watch the sun rise in a cloudless sky.

She sighed at the beauty and felt her inner torment ease. It was foolish to feel so sad – she must accept her fate. There was much to look forward to and she was surrounded by a loving family; that was more than many women had. And no doubt, in time, her sisters would wed and have children, so she would be able to love and help care for those.

Standing up she dusted herself down and smiled. There were still many exciting things to do.

Twenty

'Sirs!' Carter burst into the room. 'Word from Sergeant Drake; it looks as if our suspicions were correct. Drake saw Harcourt in His Lordship's study going through his papers. He left a short time ago and has taken off along the coast road. The sergeant is following.'

'Get the captain's horse ready, Carter. Dexter, you find grandmother and tell her where we are going, while I saddle Lucifer.'

They were soon on their way, making for the coastal road.

'He has a good start on us. Hope Drake doesn't lose him.' Dexter muttered.

After about an hour they stopped.

'Damn,' Harry cursed. 'We are not even sure if we are heading in the right direction. He could have turned off anywhere.'

'The instructions I received clearly said this way,' Carter informed him. 'Drake could not have been more specific.'

'He will get a message to us somehow, Harry. He knows we will be following and he's a good man.'

'Well, until we do hear from him there is little we can do. There is a town not far ahead, so we might as well rest the horses for a while and get some refreshments. There's little point riding aimlessly around the countryside, and there is bound to be an inn we can rest at.'

'That's a sound idea. The horses need a drink and so do we.' Carter was always thirsty.

Two young boys ran towards them as they clattered into the yard. One stepped towards Lucifer and Harry waved him away. The boy eyed the animal with suspicion.

'Isn't he safe, mister?'

'No, I'll see to him.'

He loosened the girth and was about to turn away when he felt a tug at his breeches. A small, dirty hand was clutching on to him.

'Psst, mister?'

He hunkered down and look into an equally grubby face.

'You the Major?' the urchin whispered.

'Why do you want to know?'

'This man said he would be riding a big black 'orse.' He gave Lucifer a look of awe. An' that's the biggest, blackest 'orse I've ever seen. What you call him?'

'Lucifer.'

'That's a funny word. What's it mean?'

'Devil.'

The boy giggled. 'That's about right, mister.'

They were straying from the point, so Harry brought the conversation back to this mysterious man. 'What did this man ask you to do.'

'Eh? Oh, I got a message for the Major. That you?'

Harry nodded. 'What was the message?'

A crafty look appeared in his eyes. ''E said you'd give me . . . a . . . penny.'

The corners of Harry's mouth twitched. The rascal was obviously trying to decide how much he could prise out of him. 'Agreed.'

'He said you was to turn back.'

Harry frowned.

'That's all he said, 'onest.' He held out his hand. 'Come on, mister, you got your message.'

He pulled some coins out of his pocket and placed three pennies into the eager little hand. 'This is our secret.' He gave the boy a wink.

The pennies disappeared with great speed into the tattered trousers. 'You bet, sir.'

Ah, he'd been elevated to 'sir' after that bountiful payment. But the respect didn't last long, because as he walked towards the inn, the boy bellowed at the top of his voice, 'Hey, mister.'

Harry turned.

'You fight in the war?'

He nodded.

'Cor, bet that scared 'em. You're nearly as big as your 'orse.'

Harry ducked his head to enter the inn and was greeted with roars of laughter from his companions and wide grins from the other customers.

'Cheeky young devil,' he said with good humour as he sat down.

'Don't pay him no mind, sir.' A tray of drinks was plonked on the table. 'Had a big mouth from the minute he was born.'

The woman walked away muttering that it was time the kid learned not to be saucy to men of quality.

'What was that all about?' Carter asked, after nearly draining his glass in one gulp.

'Drake has been here and left a message with that impudent urchin.'

'Good. Knew he wouldn't let us down.' Dexter took a swig of his ale. 'What did he say? Are we heading in the right direction?'

'No. He said we are to turn around and go back.'

'Why, sir? That doesn't make sense.'

Harry shrugged. 'I am assured that that was what he said.'

'In that case we had better do as he says,' Carter replied.

They finished their drinks and left the inn. Drake met them when they were no more than four miles from Ranliegh.

'Ah, thank goodness. You got my message.'

'We did,' Dexter told him, 'but I'm damned if we understand it. Where is Harcourt?'

'I lost him somewhere around here.'

'You had better explain,' Dexter urged. 'Start from the beginning.'

'Well, Harcourt had been going through Lord Stanton's papers. I spied him myself, and when he left the house, I followed him. He went straight to that town and met up with a young girl. She lives in a hovel on the edge of the woods, and he was with her for about an hour. After that he headed straight back the way he had come. I thought I'd been wrong about him going to pass the information on, so I rushed to the inn and left a message, just in case you came that way. The boy promised to keep a watch for you.'

'He carried out his commission,' Harry informed him with a grin.

'I didn't have time to be fussy about the person I recruited, Your Grace, but I knew if you hadn't sighted me, you would probably stop and try to decide what to do next. The inn was the most likely place.'

'That was good thinking, Sergeant,' Dexter told him. 'What happened after that?'

'Well, like I said, I thought I'd been wrong. Harcourt was obviously paying a social call because he never made contact with anyone else.'

'There might have been someone with the girl.'

'No, Captain. I peeked through the window. They were alone and he wasn't interested in anything but the girl, if you know what I mean? Not a soul went in or came out; there was only one door and I never took my eyes off it.'

'It looks as if this was a waste of time.' Carter looked gloomy.

'That's what I thought, but I'm not sure now.'

'What has made you change your mind?' Harry wanted to know.

'Well, it looked as if he was going straight back to Lord Stanton's. I was tracking him, keeping well out of sight and he hadn't seen me, I was sure, but then he disappeared.'

Harry dismounted. 'Around here, you say?'

'Yes, he did not come much past this point. I'm good at tracking,' he stated proudly. 'I'd stake my life on the fact that he has gone to ground somewhere within a mile of where we are standing.'

They all scanned the area, looking for anything that might give them a clue.

'Where the devil could he have gone, Harry? There isn't much here.' Dexter turned to Drake. 'Could he have met a boat?' The sea is but a short distance away.'

'No, sir. I would have seen signs along the beach area if he had done so. As you can see, the ground gets increasingly rough and stony and it's not easy to pick up the trail.' He looked ashamed. 'I'm sorry, sir, I've let you down.'

'Nonsense, man. You have done a good job,' Dexter assured him. 'At least we know that he is probably operating out of this area, and that means his contact is someone local. It has narrowed the area of search.'

'We will have him next time, Sergeant, have no fear.' Harry remounted. 'If I remember correctly there is a coaching inn just over that rise.'

'You're right, there is, Harry, and I had forgotten that. It could be a likely meeting place. We must prod him into making another trip. I'll get the War Office to send another batch of papers to Lord Stanton with information he will not be able to resist.' Dexter smiled in satisfaction. 'Go back now, Drake, and keep your eyes open. Let us know the moment he makes a move again.'

'I'll not lose him a second time, sir, you can count on it.' He rode away with a look of grim determination on his face.

* * *

The next morning His Grace was in a fury.

'Harry! Will you please stop crashing around the place,' the Duchess told him. 'All I can hear are doors opening and closing. Who are you looking for?'

He strode into the garden room looking thoroughly out of sorts. 'Where is she?'

'Who, dear?'

'Isabella, of course.'

'Is it important?' she looked puzzled.

'Important? Of course it's important. She went out for an early morning ride – unaccompanied, of course. The stable lad found her horse in the yard and that is why I have been searching for her. No one has seen her, not even her maid.'

'Are you certain she is not in the house?'

'Positive.' He prowled agitatedly around the room. 'I cannot let her out of my sight, for she constantly gets into mischief of some kind.'

'Is she in the garden?' his grandmother said, ignoring the outburst.

'That is being searched at this moment.'

There was a knock on the door and Carter entered. 'There is no sign of her. Everywhere has been searched and she is nowhere to be found.'

'Get the horses ready and as many men as you can muster.' He was already striding out of the room.

'Let us split up and we can search more ground that

way. Does anyone know where she likes to ride in the morning?'

Everyone shook their heads.

'She likes to explore,' the head groom informed him. 'She could be anywhere on the estate.'

Instinct took Harry at a fast gallop to the rise overlooking the sea. She had loved it up there, and he hoped to God that she was there and unhurt. His insides clenched when he thought about Garston. Had he pushed him too far? Would he be vindictive enough to harm one of his guests? He had warned him not to, but he had the feeling that Lord Garston was unstable and not far from madness. He urged Lucifer faster. He would see the man hung if he had hurt her. However, if this was one of her silly escapades, he would be furious.

He was almost at the top of the rise when he saw a small figure. She was sitting up and looking out to sea. He thundered up and was kneeling beside her in an instant. 'Are you hurt?'

'No, Your Grace.' She smiled sweetly at him. 'Is this not the most exquisite view? I watched the sun rise and it was truly dramatic.'

He could not believe it. She was sitting here admiring the view when he had all the available men on the estate out looking for her. 'Your horse came back without you,' he told her through clenched teeth. Hell fire, but he was furious.

'I expect he did. I left him to enjoy the dew-covered

301

grass and something must have spooked him.'

'And how, pray, were you intending to get back?'

'I would have had to walk.'

'That would have taken you hours.'

'Oh, it's no more than an hour from here.'

'Did it not occur to you that we might be concerned for your safety?'

'Yes, it did, but there was little I could do about it. I'm sorry.'

He took hold of her arms and stood her up. 'An apology will not suffice this time.'

After remounting he bent down, took hold of her under the arms and hauled her up to sit in front of him. She gasped at the speed of her ascent.

As they started back, two of the men met them.

'Oh, thank goodness you have found her, Your Grace.' His steward looked relieved. 'Are you all right, Miss?'

'She is unhurt,' Harry snapped. 'She did not tether her horse and he ran away.' His voice was dripping with sarcasm. 'Call off the search, and let the men get back to their work.'

The journey was accomplished in grim silence, for he did not dare speak. Of all the stupid, careless . . .

When they arrived back, willing hands were reaching up to help her down, exclaiming their relief at seeing her unhurt. He dismounted and spun her round to face him.

'You will go and let my grandmother know you are all right, and apologise for causing her worry, then you will wait for me in the library.' Only a fool would disobey him in this mood.

Lucifer received a very rough rub down, which he seemed to relish, and after his horse's needs were taken care of, Harry stormed into the house. He had hoped his temper would have cooled down by the time he had finished with Lucifer, but it hadn't.

She was waiting, looking a little apprehensive, but not unduly worried. He closed the door firmly behind him and glared at her.

'You will not go riding again without an escort.' He spoke softly, determined not to raise his voice. She looked small and fragile, but he recognised the determined tilt of her head. Suddenly he did not want to argue with her. She could have been out there somewhere, injured or even worse.

'But I always take my morning ride alone. I like it that way.'

Oh Lord, why did she always have to defy him? 'Then you will change the habit while you are my guest.'

'I like to go out at dawn. Who can I ask to accompany me at that time?'

'If there is no one available then you must come to me,'

'I cannot do that. You exercise Lucifer, and I could

not possibly keep up – you would find it tiresome to moderate your pace.'

He was trying – he really was. He took a deep breath and stepped towards her. 'I find it tiresome searching for you.'

She did not back away. Her head tilted to a more acute angle. 'You have no need for concern; I was still on your land and in no danger.'

'My brother was still on his land when he was killed.' He could not hide the pain in his voice.

'Oh, I am sorry.' She stopped arguing at once, a look of compassion on her face. 'How thoughtless of me not to remember that. After such an experience you would naturally be worried. I should have started back at once, but the sunrise was breath taking. I must beg your forgiveness.'

He looked at her expressive face and remembered what it had felt like to hold her in his arms. It was only physical attraction, but it was unwanted and a nuisance. 'If you understand my concern, then you will do as I ask and not ride without an escort.' He spoke sharply.

'I will do as you say.' She left the room with dignity.

He swore roundly. His rejection of her sympathy and understanding had been curt. But surely she could see that he had had enough of her thoughtless actions. Why did she persist. What was the matter with her. More to the point – what was the matter with him. His reaction to her presence was beyond all understanding.

Twenty-One

Harry shuffled papers around his desk with a distracted air.

'You are restless, Harry, and that is not like you.' Dexter came and sat down. 'You have always been the master at the waiting game.'

He shrugged. 'I can't seem to settle at anything.'

'It will not be long, and everything is in place. The false papers are with Lord Stanton, Harcourt is in residence, and we have six well trained soldiers camping in your barn. Timothy and Dobson are also here, and we are ready to move at a moment's notice.'

'I know, and I am confident we shall catch them this time.'

Dexter frowned at his friend. 'Miss Isabella has been avoiding you.'

'Yes.'

'Was it because you had to go searching for her a few days ago?'

'Yes.'

'You are very uncommunicative, Harry. I take it you don't want to talk about it.'

'That is correct.'

'Have you asked yourself why you react in such a forceful way to her?' his friend asked.

'What sort of damned fool question is that? I know why: she drives me to distraction, and I am afraid to take my eyes off her in case she gets into more trouble. She has a talent for doing that. Haven't you noticed?'

They were saved from a discussion about the meddling recklessness of the said lady, by Carter.

'Harcourt is on the move, and everyone is mounting up at this moment.'

Harry was off and running, his booted heels ringing on the yard cobbles. The head groom had the saddle ready and it did not take him long to join the others in the yard. They took off at a gallop.

'What is going on, Bella?' Angelina ran into her sister's room.

Isabella was already hanging out of the window.

'I don't know, but it must be something very urgent; they are in a great hurry.'

'Why have they got so many soldiers with them? Napoleon hasn't landed along the coast, has he?'

'No, Angel. Don't get yourself worked up, for we are at peace, remember?'

'Of course.' She giggled. 'How very foolish of me – but all the noise and shouting frightened me for a moment.'

'I do not think it is anything we need be concerned about.' She bit her lip anxiously. 'I expect they have some private business to attend to.'

'And for that they need an escort?' Angelina remarked.

'Perhaps they have been asked to pass on their skills to those soldiers. They used to go behind enemy lines to gather information, I believe.' Charlotte leaned precariously out of the window.

'Yes, indeed. I think Lotte has the most likely explanation,' Bella said brightly. 'It must take special training to carry out those missions.'

She knew that His Grace and the captain were engaged in a dangerous game – and for the first time in her life she was truly frightened. She wanted to run to the stables, saddle a horse and take off after them, but she couldn't do that. This time she really must keep out of it. Her heart was hammering away, but there was no need to be fearful, she told herself. They had plenty of trained men with them, so all she could do was wait and pray for their safety.

'Bella.' Charlotte interrupted her troubled thoughts. 'May I go into the village? I have need to visit the shops.'

'Do you want to go, Angel?'

'No, thank you, Bella. I would rather stay here.'

'Very well, Lotte, but you must take Agnes with you.'

'Why don't you both come? Mother and father are at our house, the Duchess has gone to visit a friend, and all the men have left.'

'Then we shall have a peaceful couple of hours, will we not, Bella?'

'Yes, we shall.'

The time seemed to pass slowly to Isabella. Every moment held an agony of worry for the men, particularly the Duke, for she loved him with all her being. There was no use denying it, and she did not attempt to do so anymore. The fact that he did not – and never would – love her, was of no consequence. The fear that he might be in danger . . .

'Lotte should have returned by now,' Angelina remarked, looking up from her needlework.

She glanced at the clock. 'I expect she has been distracted by something. She will be here shortly.'

'I don't know, Bella. She should have been back long since.'

No sooner had the concern been expressed when

they heard someone running. Agnes burst into the room in floods of tears and on the point of hysteria.

'Oh, Miss,' she wailed, 'there was nothing I could do.'

The sisters helped her into a chair, and Angelina mopped the wet face.

'Tell us what has happened,' Isabella ordered.

'It was all so quick, Miss.' She dissolved into another bout of weeping.

Anxiety rushed through Isabella, but she had to keep calm. 'Agnes, where is Charlotte?'

'She's been . . .' she hiccupped, 'kidnapped.'

'Kidnapped? By whom?' Both sisters spoke at the same time.

'I don't know,' the girl wailed. 'We were walking along the street when this big carriage slows down beside us, and the next thing I knew Miss Charlotte was being dragged into it and they raced away.' She hugged her sides, rocking back and forth. 'I could hear her shouting.'

'What are we going to do, Bella?' There was a note of desperation in her sister's voice.

Ever practical, she tried to calm Agnes down. 'Which direction did they head?'

'Straight through the village and on to the main London Road. I ran after them as long as I could,' she sobbed loudly.

'Calm yourself, Agnes. There is no blame attached

to you, but you must answer my questions. We shall accomplish nothing if we panic.'

The distressed girl quietened down at the voice of authority.

'You mentioned the carriage was large. Describe it.'

'It was a travelling carriage – black.'

'Anything we might recognise it by?'

'It had something on the side, but it was covered up.'

'Were they heading towards London or away from it?'

'Away from it.'

'Well done, Agnes. Now, do you feel strong enough to run to the stables and get two horses ready?'

Agnes gaped at her. 'You are not going after them yourself, are you, Miss?'

'We are the only ones here, and we cannot leave our sister at the mercy of some fiend. Now go!'

The maid ran out of the room.

'When is Papa due back, Angel?'

'Today. I do not know the exact time. They are calling on friends on their way here, so they are probably not at home.'

Isabella hastily scribbled a note and placed it on the mantelshelf in front of the clock, where it would not be missed.

'Shall I see if I can find some workers to come with us?'

'We don't have time to seek assistance. Every moment lost takes Lotte away from us and reduces our chances of catching up with her.' She looked at her sister's white face. 'You do not have to come, Angel; you can stay here and direct father when he arrives.'

'I will not let you go alone, Bella.' A rare look of stubbornness crossed her face.

Isabella saw it, nodded and hurried into the yard.

A young lad was holding the horses.

'I want you to watch for Sir George. When he returns tell him there is an urgent message for him on the mantelshelf in the blue room.'

'Yes, Miss.'

They rode through the village as fast as possible and Isabella wished she had her breeches on so she could ride astride the horse.

'I pray we don't miss them,' Angelina gasped.

'They are in a large, cumbersome carriage, so they will have to keep to the main road. There will also be a need to stop and change horses, and that is when we will have a chance of catching up with them.'

What they were going to do then, Isabella had no idea.

Dexter held up his hand to bring the riders to a halt. 'This is close enough we don't want to scare them off. The major and myself will ride in first. Tim, you follow with Carter and Dobson.' He turned to the soldiers. 'I want you to skirt around the inn and approach it from the other side, but don't come in until I give the order.'

Harry did not speak. This was Dexter's operation and he was quite happy to follow his instructions, for his friend was a first-class tactician. He felt a tingle of excitement run through him. It was the same feeling he had always experienced before a mission.

They rode in like two weary travellers in need of sustenance and rest, taking care of their own mounts, which was not commented upon because of the size and fractious natures of the war horses, thus enabling the others to take up their positions. When everyone was in place, they walked into the hostelry.

Harcourt was standing by a door which led to the upstairs rooms. Harry gave Carter a slight nod and watched him walk towards the door and take up a casual stance beside it. That was one avenue of retreat cut off.

Harcourt handed something to the person he was standing with. The accomplice had their back to him, but he recognised the person immediately. Harry could have laughed. Of course, he should have guessed.

He moved forward and spoke in fluent French. 'This is an unexpected place to meet you again, Madam.'

She spun round, then realised her mistake. 'Why, sir, that is a strange tongue you were talking in.'

'It is your own language – did you not recognise it?' He looked suitably crestfallen. 'I was always told I had an excellent grasp of the language.'

Harcourt, sensing danger, had started to back away, only to come up against Dobson. With Harry and Dexter in front of him and Carter blocking the stairs, there was no escape. He knew the game was up.

'It's all her fault!' He pointed a trembling hand. 'She made me do it.'

She gave him a look of loathing and pushed the papers down her bosom.

'I'll take those from you.' Harry held out his hand.

'You will not. They are my private letters.' Her usually faultless English accent began to slip. 'They are in a place out of reach of any gentleman.'

'Ah,' Harry sighed, 'whatever made you think I was a gentleman?'

He dipped his hand into her dress and pulled the papers out, then he handed them to Dexter. These are yours I believe?'

He looked them over and smiled. 'Indeed. This is all the proof we need.'

'I am puzzled, Madam,' Harry said. 'Why chance a meeting here when Harcourt could have brought them to your establishment? He is often there, I understand.'

'Gentlemen are not allowed past the doors in daylight hours. It is a firm rule of the house and everyone knows it, so it would have looked suspicious.'

'But he could have handed them to you tonight.'

She knew her lucrative spying operation had been

discovered, so she did not bother to deny anything. 'I have a messenger waiting.'

'And where would that be?' Dexter stepped into the conversation.

She tossed her head and laughed. 'That is something I will not tell you. When I do not arrive on time he will go back to France. I will not betray him.'

He gave a slight bow of his head in acknowledgement. 'You will be handed over to the military. Perhaps then you will change your mind?'

He barked an order and the soldiers came in immediately. 'Take these two away. You have your instructions.'

Carter followed them out and was gone for only a few minutes. He returned, frowning deeply. 'Sir, there are two of your horses in the stables.'

He didn't have time to comment because at that moment the air was rent with the sound of a struggle and a stifled scream. He was up the stairs in two strides. It was easy to determine which room the noise was coming from, but the door was locked, so he put his shoulder to it, and it burst open.

The sight that met him turned his blood to ice. Angelina was gagged and trussed up on the bed, kicking the wall behind her to attract attention to their plight. Charlotte had her hands tied behind her and was trying to get out of the clutches of a man – a man Harry knew well. With a muttered oath he wrenched him away from the girl who was still fighting.

'Charlotte, stop that, you are safe now. Tim,' he shouted, 'take care of her.'

Out of the corner of his eye he could see that Dexter and Carter had released Angelina, who was sobbing out a story, but the poor girl was thoroughly frightened and talking in incoherent bursts.

Seeing that everything was being taken care of, Harry turned his attention to the cursing man, struggling to get out of an iron grip.

'Garston, you will hang for this,' he snarled. Holding on to him with one hand, he reached out for a piece of rope, which had previously been used to bind Angelina, and wound it securely around Garston's hands. Then he spun him round to face him. 'What is this all about?' he demanded.

Charlotte came up to Garston and slapped him across the face. 'That is for the abuse we have suffered from you.'

'It's all your fault, Ranliegh. If you hadn't started pushing for the money, I would not have had to resort to this.'

Garston was a very unhealthy colour and shaking with fear.

'I know what his plan was, Your Grace. He thought to compromise me, thinking I would have to wed him.' Charlotte cast him a look of utter disgust. 'That way he would have had control of my fortune.'

Suddenly Harry was aware that something was missing – or to be precise, someone. He had been cold with fury before, but now the blood was rushing around his body in alarm. 'Where is Isabella?'

'We don't know, Your Grace,' Isabella cried. 'That odious man had her taken away just before you arrived. We caught up with them as they pulled into the inn, but Lord Garston and his men overpowered us and dragged us up here. Isabella was fighting fiercely, threatening that you would soon overtake us and stop his evil game. He became angry at the mention of your name and gave his men some instructions we could not hear.'

He lifted Garston off his feet and propped him against the wall. 'Where is she?'

The man began to laugh hysterically. He was now completely out of control, as if something inside him had snapped. 'You'll never find her, and if you do, it will be too late.'

'What do you mean by that?' Harry spoke softly, but if Garston had been in control of his faculties, he would have realised he was only a moment away from death.

'I should have ignored your threats,' the man blubbered, 'and dealt with you the same way I did your brother.'

'I know you murdered him, and now we have the proof. This room is full of witnesses to your statement.'

'I don't care, I shall deny everything.' He made a choking sound and Harry loosened his grip. He had to find out where Isabella was, and he did not want Garston to expire before he had the information. 'Where is she?'

'Too late – too late – too late,' he chanted.

'Oh, Lord, she was in peril, and this beast was insane. He had to get to her. Harry threw Garston at Dexter as if the man weighed no more than a feather. 'Don't let him out of your sight.'

Then he was off and running. As he tumbled down the stairs, he could hear Garston chanting: 'Too late… too late…'

Twenty-Two

Harry crouched low over Lucifer's head and urged him on towards the sea, hoping he had guessed correctly. He was oblivious to the driving rain as Garston's demented chant rang in his ears. He must not be too late. He loved her.

Why had he not recognised this before? His desire for her had not been a mere physical attraction; he loved her to a point of desperation.

What was it his grandmother had said? 'The answer is in front of you', or something like that. He had blindly refused to look, and it had taken a disaster like this to open his eyes. Too late . . . too late . . .

'Come on, old boy,' he urged his horse on. The

animal lengthened his stride and his massive hooves thundered over the ground.

They came upon them suddenly. There were two horses and one of the men had Isabella clasped in front of him.

Harry gave a low battle-cry to Lucifer. The animal pricked up his ears, tossed his head, and lunged into the fray, sinking his teeth into the leg of one rider. The man gave a howl of pain and spurred his horse into a gallop, leaving his companion behind. Then Lucifer spun broadside in front of the other horse and barred his way, giving Harry the chance to leap from the saddle and pull Isabella from the man's grasp.

He left everything else to the not-so-tender mercies of Lucifer and ignored the sounds of terror as he laid Isabella down. She was unconscious with a nasty bruise on her temple and a cut lip. He pushed her dripping wet hair out of her eyes and cradled her in his arms. 'Bella! Answer me,' he pleaded.

Then he heard a snort and a jet-black head came down and muzzled her gently, pushing as if urging her to open her eyes. Much to Harry's relief, she did.

Suddenly she was holding on to him and crying. 'My sisters are in danger.'

'Shush, my darling. They are safe and so are you.'

When the flood of tears had ceased, she looked up at him with troubled eyes. 'Are my sisters truly safe?'

'Yes – Dexter and Timothy are with them. They are quite unharmed. Come, I'll take you to them.' He placed his cloak around her shoulders – not that it would do much good, they were both drenched right through.

Harry swung Isabella up until she was sitting astride Lucifer, then he sat behind her, pulled her close to his chest and the big horse turned towards the inn at Harry's command.

The violent events had obviously shaken Isabella and she lost consciousness again in his arms. He cursed the rain, which was still falling in a steady downpour. The journey seemed interminable.

He burst into the inn carrying Isabella and leaving a trail of water in their wake. 'I want a room,' he roared, without breaking his stride as he headed up the stairs. He kicked open the first door he came to. 'Light the fire.'

Isabella had regained her senses and was shivering with shock, her eyes drooping with fatigue.

'Stay awake!' He shook her and let out a pent-up breath when she opened her eyes.

'Bully,' he thought she muttered, but he didn't care what she called him. She was safe and that was all that mattered to him.

'Your Grace.' Angelina moved towards her sister. 'Bella's clothes are in a disgusting state and must be removed.'

'I'll do it.' He stood Isabella on her feet, holding on tightly with one hand in case she collapsed, and pushed her sister away. It would take the girl too long to undress her.

With one tug at the neck, the tattered gown dropped on to the floor. The rest of her clothes followed in the same way. Someone thrust a large towel into his hands, and he wrapped it around her, rubbing in an effort to get some warmth into her frozen body.

She moaned and looked at him accusingly. 'That hurts.'

'I'm sorry, but you are chilled to the bone and need to get warm.'

A quick glance around the room showed him that it contained everything he would need. There was a large armchair in front of a blazing fire and bowls of steaming broth standing on the table. He continued trying to get her circulation going.

Angelina caught hold of his arm. 'Enough, Your Grace.'

He stopped abruptly, willing himself to calm down. His hand smoothed away the hair from her face and he kissed her gently on the cheek. 'Forgive me for my rough treatment,' he murmured.

She gave a weak smile of understanding.

'Let me put this around her.' Angelina had pulled a blanked off the bed.

When this was done, he put her into the chair, tucking the blanket securely around her until only her head was visible.

There was the sound of heavy footsteps on the stairs and Sir George erupted into the room. He went straight to Isabella's side. 'What has happened?'

Charlotte put her arm around her distressed father. 'It is a long and terrible story, Father. I was kidnapped by Lord Garston, and Isabella and Angelina came after me. That evil man tried to harm Bella, and if it had not been for His Grace . . .'

He looked at Harry, who was standing motionless, looking at Isabella. 'I am in your debt.'

He dismissed it with a wave of his hand. Angelina was coaxing her sister to eat the broth, and he did not take his eyes off her until the bowl was empty, then he sighed with relief.

Dexter and Carter came into the room carrying a bottle of brandy and some glasses.

'Thought you might need this, sir.'

He took the bottle and poured out a generous amount, then he hunkered down in front of Isabella. 'Try and drink some of this. It will warm you inside.'

No one in the room could miss the tenderness he was showing her, and certainly not Isabella, who looked at him in wide-eyes astonishment. She obediently took a few sips, then shook her head and pulled a face. He put the glass on the table and went to stand up.

With a struggle, she released a hand from the blanket and caught hold of his sleeve. 'I am forever in your debt.'

'The only thing I want from you is your love,' he told her, not caring who heard him.

She smiled for the first time. 'You already have that.'

'And you have mine, Bella.' He kissed her fleetingly on the lips. 'It is time you called me Harry.'

'Whatever you say, Harry.' She favoured him with an impish grin. 'You will see that I can be obedient at times.'

He sat back on his heels with a look of mock relief. 'I am glad to hear it, for I would not like us to spend the rest of our lives fighting.'

He rose smoothly to his feet. 'A word with you, Sir George.'

Striding from the room he closed the door behind them and did not waste any time. 'I would like to marry Isabella. May I have your permission?'

'Of course.' He beamed with pleasure, then he frowned. 'But will she accept you? She has turned everyone else down.'

'I will not allow her to refuse,' he stated simply.

'Ah.' Sir George nodded wisely. 'I think this will be a most suitable match.'

Harry grimaced and looked at his clothes; they had suffered badly from the frantic gallop and the rain. 'I apologise for approaching you in this condition.'

'No need to apologise. The Winslow family have much to thank you for. If it had not been for your prompt action, we might have lost one or more of our daughters this day.'

'Sir,' Carter came up to them. 'I have found you some dry clothes. They are rough but will suffice until yours are dry.

Harry peeled off his wet clothing right there, and with relief slipped into the others, not caring that they were too small.

'Do you know why Charlotte was kidnapped?' Sir George asked.

'It is clear now. You told me that Garston had once offered for Charlotte and been refused. I think he meant to compromise her so that she would have had to wed him.'

'Then he was mistaken! I would never have allowed my daughter to marry such a fiend.' Sir George looked at Harry and frowned. 'This is not the first time he has tried, is it?'

'No. It was Charlotte who was the target at the fair.'

'And you foiled him there as well. How can I ever repay you?'

'To have Bella as my wife is all I could ever ask.' He turned towards the door. 'Now let us go and see how the girls are recovering.'

After checking that all was well with them, Harry approached his friend. 'I'll kill Garston for this, Dexter,' he growled.

'You don't need to – he's already dead.'

'What? Did he try to escape?'

'He did while I was tending the girls, but Carter

caught him just as he reached the stairs.'

'And killed him?'

'Well . . . Carter insisted that he had tripped in his haste to get away and had fallen down the stairs and broken his neck . . .'

'Ah, but you think it more likely that Carter broke his neck and then threw him down the stairs?'

Dexter shrugged. 'Everyone believed it to be an accident and I thought it prudent to leave it at that.'

'Quite right.'

So, it was over.

When Harry looked towards Isabella again, he saw that Angelina was asleep with her head on her sister's lap. He picked her up and laid her on the bed. Charlotte looked exhausted as well.

'Sir George, your daughters have had a very traumatic time. It would be best if you took them back to Ranliegh.'

'I agree, but they cannot sit a horse.'

'Sir,' Carter stepped forward. 'Lord Garston's carriage is in the yard, and he will not be needing it again.'

'See that it is made ready, Carter.' He addressed Sir George again. 'The captain, Timothy and Dobson will accompany you. I don't think it would be wise to move Isabella at the moment. She will need her maid and some clothes.'

He nodded. 'I'll come back with them myself.' He

took another look at his eldest daughter, now sleeping soundly in front of the fire. 'Suppose she needs assistance? It will be some time before her maid can get here.'

'The landlady will help, she is a sensible soul,' Carter said, as he came back into the room. 'The carriage is waiting.'

'Come, Father.' Charlotte took hold of his arm. 'Isabella will be well cared for, and Angelina is on the point of exhaustion. I will tell you the whole story on the way home.'

He smiled affectionately at his youngest daughter. 'You are right. Captain, will you help Angelina to the carriage?'

'Of course.' She was awake and only needed a supporting arm, but he helped her gently.

Harry watched them leave and noticed how Dexter was tenderly looking after Angelina. Charlotte was also gazing gratefully at Timothy, who was showing her the utmost solicitude. With a deep sigh he realised that he had been blind to the growing affection between them, and he hoped Sir George would be understanding towards Dexter and Timothy. But that was in the future. His sole concern was for the lovely girl sleeping in front of the fire. He put another log on the fire, swept Isabella up and sat in the chair with her in his arms.

She dragged her eyes open and obviously realised she was in a compromising situation with him again.

'You do not have to wed me because of this unfortunate incident.'

'You are going to be my wife because I love you.'

'I have not been asked,' she told him with a little of her old spirit.

'I shall not allow you to refuse, and I don't think you will.'

'Oh, and why is that?'

'Because you love me.'

'How do you know that?'

'You told me.'

She snuggled closer. 'Did I?' Her eyes started to close again and so did his.

Harry woke suddenly. Carter was tapping him on the shoulder. 'Would you like something to eat, sir?'

'No, thank you, Carter. We need rest and quiet first; we will eat later.'

'Very well, sir. I will see you are not disturbed.' He marched smartly out of the room.

'Are you still cold?' Harry asked in alarm as he felt Isabella shiver.

'A little, but I can feel your warmth seeping into me. If you could just hold me a little closer.'

Bella, if I come any closer we shall have to wed immediately.'

'That sounds like a good idea to me. I am not in the first flush of youth, you know.'

'Really? I would say you are in perfect condition.'

'Why, thank you, Harry.'

This light-hearted teasing was tearing his control to shreds, and she knew it.

'I suspect you are trying to behave like a gentleman again, my love. Where has the soldier gone?'

He laughed, remembering the last time she had accused him of trying to act like a gentleman. 'The soldier is having a battle of his life, but in this instance I am going to be a gentleman, for you need rest and sleep after the rough treatment you have endured.'

'I am not teasing. After the way you fought for me today, my only wish is to show my love and make you happy. We could have lost our lives today, and I was so frightened. The thought of dying without ever letting you know how much I loved you, was agony. Today has shown me how precious life is, and we must not waste it.'

'We will be married as soon as possible, and I am sure that between us we can speed things up considerably.'

'I have no doubt about that.' She snuggled closer and was asleep again, utterly exhausted from her ordeal. Harry looked down at her lovely face and smiled. It had been a difficult mission to find a suitable wife, but now the soldier could relax from battle and delight in his victory.

Epilogue

Kent, 1803

It had been a year full of blessings. Harry ceased his pacing and gazed out of the window, deep in thought. Within one month of rescuing Isabella, they had been married, for he had refused to wait longer. Their love for each other was deep and enduring, and he had never thought it possible he would have a marriage which was a love match. In his opinion, that happened to only a fortunate few, and to find himself as one of those favoured men was beyond his wildest dreams.

Their days were not always tranquil, of course. They still argued and occasionally shouted at each other, but he would not have it any other way. She was a spirited, unique lady.

He smiled when he remembered his grandmother's reaction to the news of their betrothal. 'Took you long enough, Harry. I knew she was the right one for you.'

When he had asked why she had not suggested Isabella in the first place, she had replied with a wicked grin. 'I did believe Angelina was the right one, but I realised my mistake as soon as I saw you together. However, I said nothing, knowing you had to make your own decision. You came to your senses eventually.'

Thank goodness he had. And there was more reason for being joyous. He had given Garston's estate to Dexter, and he and Angelina were to be wed next month. Then there was Timothy and Charlotte. Sir George was making them wait for another year but had given his consent to the betrothal. Harry had also given Sherfields to Timothy and it would be his family home. He had been pleased to be able to help his friends in this way, for he had no need of the extra land; he already had treasures beyond measure.

The cause for concern was that they were once again at war with Napoleon, but he would not take part in this next skirmish. His family came first now.

Harry cursed impatiently, spun on his heel and ran

up the stairs. Taking them three at a time. Enough. He was not going to take any more of this. An officious looking lady barred his way.

'You cannot go in there, Your Grace.'

Without a word, he lifted her off her feet, placed her to one side and entered the room. In an instant he was beside the bed, taking hold of Isabella's hand and kissing it gently. 'I could not stay downstairs any longer, I must be here with you. It is taking a very long time.'

She smiled bravely. 'It does appear to be so, but I am assured that things are progressing at a satisfactory pace.'

He looked at the woman in attendance. 'Is that so?'

'Yes, Your Grace. The first one usually takes a time to arrive, but the Duchess is strong and in good health. She will sail through this, you will see.'

Harry grimaced and held on to his wife as another contraction came. The midwife had a strange idea about the ease of the birth process, and he would have borne the pain himself gladly, if that had been possible.

'You must leave, Your Grace,' the lady demanded again. 'This is no place for a gentleman.'

He smoothed his wife's hair away from her face as she began to relax again. His hand was shaking. 'Shall we tell her I am no gentleman?' he whispered.

They both grinned at the remembered joke.

'Don't ask me to leave, my love.'

'My husband will stay,' she said in a voice that rang with authority, then gripped his hand as another spasm caught her.

'How much longer is this going on?' he demanded.

'Quite soon now. The Duchess is almost ready to give birth.' She gave him a disapproving look. It was unthinkable to have a man present at such a time.

For the next hour he talked to her, held her hand and encouraged her through the contractions.

Then everything started to happen, and he watched in awe as their child rushed into this life. As he gazed in wonder at the baby exercising its lungs, Isabella pulled on his hand.

'What do we have, Harry?'

He was devoid of speech at that moment.

'You have a fine son,' the midwife informed them. 'Quite perfect.'

She reached up and toucher her husband's face. 'Just like his father.'

The baby was cleaned, wrapped in a shawl and placed in her arms, and Harry was overcome with pride for his beautiful wife. His vision became cloudy as he gazed at mother and child. They had a son!

'Harry, take our son to see his great grandmother,' Isabella urged.

He lifted the babe from her arms, then walked

carefully down the stairs and into the garden room where his grandmother was waiting.

He placed the child into her outstretched arms and pulled the shawl aside.

'A boy, Grandmother,' he whispered.

He was amazed when she looked up and her eyes were swimming with tears. He had never seen her cry before.

'It was not such an onerous duty, was it, Harry?'

'No, Grandmother.' He reached out and gently touched the child's delicate hand, watching in wonder as his son grasped his finger. 'Not a duty at all.'

BERYL MATTHEWS was born in London but now lives in a small village in Hampshire. As a young girl her ambition was to become a professional singer, but the need to earn a wage drove her into an office, where she worked her way up from tea girl to credit controller. After retiring she joined a Writers' Circle in the hope of fulfilling her dream of becoming a published author. With her first book published at the age of seventy-one, she has since written over twenty novels.